# CRIMINALPARADISE

# CRIMINALPARADISE

*a novel*

## STEVEN M. THOMAS

Ballantine Books
New York

This is a work of fiction. Names, characters, places, and incidents are the products of the author's imagination or are used fictitiously. Any resemblance to actual events, locales, or persons, living or dead, is entirely coincidental.

Copyright © 2008 by Steven M. Thomas

All rights reserved.

Published in the United States by Ballantine Books, an imprint of The Random House Publishing Group, a division of Random House, Inc., New York.

BALLANTINE and colophon are registered trademarks of Random House, Inc.

LIBRARY OF CONGRESS CATALOGING-IN-PUBLICATION DATA
Thomas, Steven M.
Criminal paradise: a novel/Steven M. Thomas.
    p.   cm.
ISBN 978-0-345-49781-9
1. Thieves—Fiction.   2. Orange County (Calif.)—Fiction.   I. Title.
PS3620.H6428C75   2008        813'.6—dc22        2007030723

Printed in the United States of America on acid-free paper

www.ballantinebooks.com

9 8 7 6 5 4 3 2 1

FIRST EDITION

Book design by Casey Hampton

*For Susan Parker,*
*Ken Smith, David Carkeet*
*and all my other writing teachers*

# CRIMINALPARADISE

# CHAPTER ONE

**We were robbing** the Cow Town on Harbor Boulevard. It's a big, barn-shaped steak house with a split-rail fence in front that does a land-office business on Father's Day, the third-richest day of the year for most restaurants. All evening, circus acts of like-faced families had crowded in the entrance making the silly jokes that have no meaning to outsiders, young and middle-aged adults taking their fathers and grandfathers out for a meal that showed appreciation, but proved independence. The restaurant had closed at midnight and the last back-slapping, toothpick-chewing customers were gone by twelve-thirty. Most of the employees were gone, too. There were five people inside: the manager, the cashier, two dishwashers and a busboy.

The restaurant had an L-shaped parking lot that lay in front and along the left side of the building. Two junkers and two modest sedans were parked in the side lot. The dishwashers rode together. A chain-link fence overgrown with flowering honeysuckle vines ran along the back of the parking lot and building, continuing across the rear of an overgrown field on the far side. The blacktop alley between the fence and the back of the restaurant was just wide enough for a garbage or delivery truck to squeeze in. Beyond the fence were the backyards of little stucco houses where lower-middle-class citizens were sleeping in their sagging, lower-middle-class beds, oblivious to life's infinite possibilities.

Crouched against the back wall of the restaurant in the shadow of a wooden partition that screened the Dumpster, I took a deep breath, inhaling the vomit smell of restaurant garbage along with the perfume of the white and yellow flowers cascading down the fence. It was ten after one, very early in the morning on Monday, June 21, 1995. One of the Mexican dishwashers would be wheeling the last load of half-eaten baked potatoes and gnawed bones out into the dark alley any minute now. The locked back door he would come out of was on the other side of the partition, which extended at a right angle from the building.

The alley was dark because Switch had swung by two nights before, on his way back from selling a guitar in Laguna Beach, and clipped an inconspicuous wire, deactivating the light above the service door. The first night a back light is out, it makes them nervous. They are a little bit careful, slightly on guard. By the third night they are used to it—people fall into ruts that quickly. At the same time, there is no way they'll get an electrician out to find the problem in just two days. Even if the day manager sees the night manager's note and feels like reporting the problem to the maintenance contractor, the electrician will be busy or lazy or drunk and won't be able to get there until the following week.

Reaching under the Dumpster, I pulled out a paper bag containing a polyester ski mask, a pair of brown jersey gloves and a heavy .38-caliber revolver. When I pulled the mask over my head, the adrenaline meter dilated, sending a flush of exhilaration through my branching nerves and blood, filling me with the happiness of the crime. Exhilaration solidified into confidence as I weighed the gun in my hand. It was a Smith & Wesson model 10, blued carbon steel with the four-inch barrel, the same basic double-action six-shooter used by thousands of highway patrolmen and beat cops around the country in the years before they were seduced by the glamour and superior firepower of semiautomatics. At nine and a half inches and thirty-two ounces, it wasn't the easiest gun to conceal, but it was reliable, accurate and big enough to scare the shit out of people—

which is what you want. If they are scared, you don't have to hurt them. And it could be concealed. I'd carried it in and out of many interesting places, tucked in my belt beneath an aloha shirt or sport coat, walked past security guards and cops with a nod and a smile.

It wasn't a fancy pistol, but it had become a talisman for me. I had carried it on every job we'd done in California and gotten away clean every time—no shots fired, no harm done. I was sure this job would go smooth, too. We'd be in and out in ten minutes with seven or eight thousand dollars for our trouble.

The bolt on the inside of the door snapped back and I moved forward to the end of the partition. The alley glowed. The big trash can clunked across the threshold and squeaked over the asphalt. As the dishwasher came around the end of the six-foot-high barrier, I pointed the gun at him and held my finger to my lips. He froze, that look of wonder they get illuminating his face. They wonder if it is really happening to them. They wonder why they ever left the place they came from. I think they wonder, briefly, if they are on TV. I motioned with my hand and the dishwasher moved out of the light from the propped open door, into the darkness of the enclosure.

"*Habla inglés?*"

He shook his head.

"That's okay," I said. "*No hay problema. No hay peligro si hace que yo digo. Comprende?*"

"*Sí,*" he said softly.

You have to know some Spanish to do stickups in Southern California. I couldn't think of the word for trash can so I motioned with the gun and he pulled the gray rubber container into the Dumpster enclosure.

"*Adalante, por favor,*" I said, motioning with the gun again. "*Silencio.*"

Across the alley, my partner came out of a niche where the flower-covered fence jogged around a telephone pole. He'd covered me from the shadows on the off chance of a cop checking the back of the restaurant at closing time. The cop was rated an off chance because I knew from a few minutes research in a newspaper database at a nearby library that the restaurant had not been robbed in several years, and cops get lazy like everyone else.

Beneath his ski mask, Switch had a mobile Irish face that could change from tough to sly to jolly and back again in the time it took him to shake hands with a potential customer. At six feet and 240 pounds, he was two inches shorter than me and about fifty pounds heavier. Half the extra weight was fat, but he was solid underneath the padding. I wouldn't have entered him in a long-distance race, but he could pivot in a flash and slam an opponent with a punch like a mule's kick. He grew up in a city neighborhood around the corner from a gym with a boxing ring. While most of the would-be fighters I knew were practicing strip-mall karate, Switch was wearing out heavy bags, developing his body shots. He still sparred at a gym in Long Beach. Boxing was one of the few things other than guitar playing and Mexican women that I'd seen him stick with for more than a year or two at a time.

His first father-in-law called him the "notorious job-jumper" and didn't mean it in a nice way. He'd had something like a hundred jobs in his twenties and early thirties, everything from Fuller Brush salesman to cable sports announcer. His long economic adolescence had been hard on his marriages and credit report, but it came in handy for us now. He'd moved west fourteen years before, in the early 1980s, and his knowledge of the cash flows and operational details of Southland businesses was a valuable resource.

Switch glanced back and forth as he transported his bulk across the alley on the balls of his feet, a sawed-off shotgun held inconspicuously along his right thigh. There was no traffic on the side street, no activity on the lot, and the three of us entered the back door of the restaurant in conga line formation. Switch closed and locked the door behind us.

# CHAPTER **TWO**

**We were in** a corridor twenty feet long and five feet wide with two closed doors on each side. Quarry-tile floor, yellow walls with ketchup smears. A slice of the kitchen was visible at the end of the hall, stoves and fryers along the far wall of a large room with a stainless steel prep table in the middle. The dishwasher was cycling somewhere out of sight to the right. The roaring sound was comfortable as a blanket, providing perfect auditory camouflage.

"*Donde está el jefe?*" I whispered. The Mexican, a tiny old man with a head the size of a cantaloupe, pointed to the second door on the right. His brown hand shook. "*Y otro mexicano?*" He pointed to the right again, and jerked his thumb, indicating around the corner.

"Watch mi amigo," I said to Switch. "I'll grab the manager."

"*Sí, señor,*" Switch said, mocking me a little. After all the señoritas, his Spanish was better than mine.

I needed to get everybody in the restaurant together quickly and without incident. The manager was the key. As long as he cooperated, everyone else would, too. Taking another deep breath, I gave the office doorknob a quick turn and stepped into the room. A skinny white guy, about forty-five, dressed in black pants and a white shirt with the sleeves rolled up to his elbows, sat at a desk in the far corner of the room. He looked up from the paperwork in front of him with a hangdog expression on his narrow face. At first glance, I thought he was an albino. He was that pale. His washed-out blond hair wasn't quite white, however, and his worried eyes were brown. He was a victim of too much white bread and fluorescent light, not genetics.

"This is a robbery," I said, and before I could say anything else, he dove out of his chair, toward me, with surprising energy, landing full length on the floor. I thought he was going for a weapon or an alarm and I sprang forward, stepping on one of his outstretched hands. When his other hand jumped up to cover the back of his head and he began babbling into the tile, I realized it was just an enthusiastic surrender. I took my foot off his hand.

"Easy," I said. "Do what I tell you and no one will get hurt. All we want is the money."

"I'll cooperate," he said, twisting his head to look up at me. "I'll do whatever you say. You want me to open the safe now? I'll do whatever you tell me. It's not my money. Just tell me what you want me to do."

"I want you to take it easy, like I said. Relax." I looked at the black iron cube sitting next to the desk. "How much is in there?"

"Fifty-six ninety-four plus three hundred to open up tomorrow."

"There should be more," I said, my heart shrinking.

"The rest is still out in the register."

My heart reinflated. "Who's out there?"

"Carla and Tim."

"Cashier and busboy?"

"Yes." He twisted his head a little further to get a clearer look up at my ski mask.

"Let's go get them."

"Okay, whatever you say. I just want to cooperate."

"You mentioned that."

Switch's masked face turned toward us as we came out into the hall. The little dishwasher was sitting against the wall, his wrinkled face more curious than frightened. We'd been in the restaurant for about ninety seconds.

"What's your name?" I asked the manager.

"Donald Parker."

"This way, Don." We walked to the end of the hallway. "Call the other dishwasher over here." I gave him a poke with the barrel of my gun, pushing him out into the kitchen.

"Hey, Carlos," he shouted, "come here a minute. Carlos!"

Carlos was younger and larger than the other dishwasher, spoke English. His Aztec face stiffened when he came around the corner and saw two guys in ski masks holding guns. I put him with his compatriot, then walked Don over to the swinging door that led to the dining room. Peeking out the pass-through, I saw the busboy mopping the floor with his back to the kitchen. The cashier's station was out of sight, around a corner to the right. The blinds on the big windows facing Harbor Boulevard were still open. If they had been closed, I would have hustled the manager out into the dining room and grabbed the other two employees. As it was, I stepped back against the wall on the hinge side of the door.

"Call him."

"Tim!" the manager called, pushing the door half open and leaning into the dining room. "Can you come here for a minute, please?"

"What do you want?" the busboy said, still mopping.

"I need to ask you something."

"So ask me."

"I need you to come back here."

"I'm trying to finish up out here, goddamn it," he said, and muttered something under his breath that sounded like "faggot."

"It'll only take a sec," Don said, giving me a nervous glance. His cheap polyester pants were nothing but a sag where his ass should have been. His sandy hair, tousled from squirming on the floor, was thin as a wheat field in a drought. I imagined him driving home late at night worrying about bad beef and stopped-up toilets, trying to figure out how to have a life on $30,000 a year.

I heard the mop bucket clatter and motioned Don back out of the doorway, a few steps into the kitchen.

"What do you want?" the busboy demanded, banging through the door. Seeing him from behind, I took an instant dislike to his narrow-hipped swagger. His legs were exceptionally short, half the length of his upper body, and they minced as he walked. His arms dangled down past his knees.

"This is a stickup," I said softly. He whirled, animal quick, ape arms swinging out loose and wide. Our eyes locked and I could see every muscle in his five-foot-eight frame tense for a leap. His crouched stance reminded me of a chimpanzee's, and he looked like he would be strong as a chimp. Lunging toward him, extending my arm, I cocked the .38 in his face. It was a handsome, stupid face topped by wavy brown hair, a matinee idol face marred only by half-dollar-size ears that stuck straight out from his head. It looked to me like the face of a permanent busboy.

He was half Don's age, and he had probably been clearing dirty dishes off plank tables since he dropped out of junior high school. He would keep on clearing them until his spotter dropped a barbell on his throat or they made a pedophilia charge stick. The brown discs of his irises glittered with fury and his long-fingered hands twitched. He wanted to jump so bad he could taste it. "Back up," I snarled. My gun hand was steady. I had replaced the original walnut stock with a checkered rubber grip with finger grooves that gave me a very secure hold. The half-inch hole where the bullet would come out was six inches from the bridge of the busboy's nose. He quivered on the verge for a moment longer and then slumped, stepping back.

"You prick," he said, shooting a vicious look over his shoulder at the manager, who was standing with his mouth open and his hands clenched together in front of him, singing a soundless hymn.

"Shut up," I said. "Walk back to the office."

I caught a whiff of his body odor as he turned. He had slathered himself with cologne in lieu of bathing, but his scent penetrated the chemical astringency. He smelled like a neglected cage. My legs were watery with the nearness of disaster, and the smell turned my stomach. It was everything I could do to keep from smashing my gun against the back of his head as he strutted into the hallway.

"Facedown on the floor, hands behind your head." He took his time but did as he was told.

"Watch him," I warned Switch.

I was in a hurry to grab the cashier. She could have come around the corner in the dining room while my back was to the pass-through, seen us, and run back to the front to call the cops.

"Let's go," I said to Don.

When he called the cashier from the doorway, she didn't answer.

"Walk out where she can see you."

I watched him through the crack between the rubber-edged door and its frame. He stopped at the corner, staring over toward the entry, took another step forward and looked back and forth around the restaurant.

"Call her," I hissed.

"Carla!" There was no answer.

When he turned around, his face was twisted with fear.

"She's not out here."

"Get over here."

In the kitchen, I grabbed him by the front of his shirt with my free hand and slammed him against the wall.

"Where is she?"

"I don't know. Please." He was cringing like it was an Olympic event.

"Is there a gun out there?"

"No."

"Don't lie to me, Don."

"I swear to God."

"Shit," I said. "Lie down on the floor and don't move. Don't look at me." He flopped onto the greasy tile, covering his head with his hands. I jerked my mask off and dropped it on the spun-metal counter by the door. Holding the gun behind my back, shifting it to my right side as I went around the corner, keeping my body between it and the windows, I walked out toward the cashier's station. I saw from a distance that the register drawer was open and empty, the tray removed. The girl *and* the money were gone.

## CHAPTER THREE

**The front door** was locked. She could have gone out and locked it behind her, hands trembling as she turned the key, running away into the night with a fragrant bundle of bills. There was a beige phone on the counter between the bowl of mints and the wall with its faux posters of Western bad men. She might have called the cops before she ran, or she might be running toward a phone. She might be in her car driving to a 7-Eleven or all-night gas station. That would give us a little time. In my mind, I could see the slumped dispatcher snapping back to life when she got the call, slack face stiffening. I imagined her barking into the radio, saw mental images of patrol cars making squealing circles in dark intersections, racing toward the spot where I stood.

Criminals are outcasts before they commit their first crime. If they fit snugly into society's embrace like the businessmen driving back and forth across the city from statistical families to incremental jobs and approved pastimes, they would never have turned to crime in the first place. Robbery and violence just make the criminal more of an outcast than he was before. Ironically, crime also links him intimately to society for the first time. Mere outcasts are easy to ignore, but crime commands attention. When alarms go off and panicked calls come in, society is forced to interact with the criminal on his terms. Its agents rush to find him and hold him close. They want to touch him and talk to him and ask him questions.

I fought back an urge to flee the scene, to run for it while precious seconds lasted. The girl might be hiding in the restaurant. When I turned around I was looking into an alcove. The restrooms. Hope stirred. As I headed that way, I heard a toilet flush. Fear lava-lamped into relief. She was still in the stall when I went into the gleaming ladies' room. The tray with a plump, brown bank bag on top of it was sitting on a white counter between two porcelain sinks.

"Who ease it?" a young female voice asked sharply.

"The restaurant is being robbed," I said.

"You geet the hell out of here, Snuff," she said.

"It's not Snuff. It's a robber. Come on out."

I heard a whisking sound, polyester across nylon, saw her square-toed black shoes below the door. She was peeking out the crack.

"The mowney is on the counter," she said, sounding strangely relieved, as if she was glad I was a robber instead of the person she'd mistaken me for. She spoke a beautiful version of English, clear and precise with a lovely Spanish lilt.

"I know where the money is," I said, holding my hand across the lower part of my face. "You are coming in the back with me."

"What for?" She sounded scared again.

"Come out, or I'm coming in after you."

When she emerged, I saw why the owner of the restaurant had put her up front. She was a plump beauty in her early twenties, with cherub cheeks and full lips. The top edge of her upper lip curved up from both sides and swept down into a sharp V in the middle, looking like the top of a valentine heart. The dark red color was tattooed on. Some of the blood that warmed her brown skin flowed from ancient civilizations that preceded and in some ways surpassed the Spanish and their civilization. Everything about her was sensual and exotic. A white blouse of thin, stretchy material showed off the shape of her breasts. Her short black skirt clung like a high priest's desire to the curves of her ass.

I told her not to look at me, and she kept her eyes down as we walked to the back, her going ahead with the cash drawer. In the kitchen, I put the ski mask on, got Don up and marched the two of them into the rear hallway. Switch was sitting on a plastic chair finishing off a piece of cherry pie, his gun on his lap. His mask was rolled up to uncover his mouth and after he set his empty plate on the floor he smiled and shrugged. Gut sticking out, thick lips rimmed with cherry sauce, he looked like a harmless fat guy. I knew better. He could cover anyone in the hallway in a split second.

"He's been at your pie pantry," I said.

"That's okay, that's all right," Don jabbered. "Take whatever you want."

The dishwashers were laying on the floor next to the busboy. I took the cash drawer from the girl.

"Lie down on the floor," I said.

"They're not going to hurt us," Don said.

"Yes, sir." Her voice and body language were submissive. She would do whatever she was told. Her skirt rode up on her hips as she knelt down and stretched out on her stomach on the red tile. The busboy turned his head to look. I thought I caught Don sneaking a peek, too, but he may have been rolling his eyes in despair.

While I was watching the girl tug her skirt down to cover the backs of her thighs, a cockroach shot out from under one of the storeroom doors. Its robotic skitter carried it halfway to the pie plate before it realized something was up. Stopping abruptly in the middle of the floor, it did a push-up and began to wave its sinister antennas. It was an inch and a half long, jet black.

"Where did *that* come from?" the paste-colored manager whined.

"Out of your ass," the busboy said, smashing the bug with his hand. He picked the ruptured roach up between his index finger and opposable digit. For a second I thought he was going to pop it in his mouth with its antennas still wiggling. But he flicked it at his boss instead. Switch wiped his mouth with a handkerchief and pulled his mask back down over the lower half of his face.

"Odd far him if I was you, pard," he said to Don, disguising his voice with an accent from some deeply inbred part of the Southwest.

Back in the office, it took Don's trembling fingers three tries to get the combination right. When he finally swung the door open, I slapped him on the shoulder.

"Good job."

"Thanks," he said, giving me a sickly smile. Starved for approval, he took a crook's compliment to heart.

On the top shelf of the safe there was another bank bag, larger, blue vinyl, full of money, a bundle of mixed bills with a rubber band doubled around it and a bunch of coin rolls. On the floor of the safe was a folder full of papers and a metal lockbox. The papers were invoices.

"What's in the box?"

"I don't know. He put it there yesterday afternoon and told me not to touch it." A bitter note came into his voice. "Everyone has to do *exactly* what he says."

"Who?"

"The owner."

"Is there a key in there?"

"No."

"Already looked, huh?" He gave me another feeble smile. Something interesting bounced back and forth when I shook the box. I thought about trying to smash it open on the corner of the safe but decided to take it along and open it later. We had to get out, and I liked the idea of a surprise package.

I put the cash from the register, a couple rolls of quarters and the packet of mixed bills in the blue zipper bag.

"Which of those cars on the lot is yours?" I asked.

"The blue Cavalier."

"I'm taking it, but you'll get it back. Give me the keys." Rooting in his pocket, he came up with an asylum master's bunch of keys and held it out to me.

"Just the car keys." He fumbled two Chevy keys off the ring.

Leaving the pouch and the metal box on his desk, I took him back into the hall. We'd been in the restaurant for eleven minutes, a minute longer than I had planned.

"Everybody up," I said. We marched them into the walk-in cooler. The chill atmosphere that flowed out of the room-size refrigerator reminded me of the first stickup I did when I was seventeen years old and still living with my parents in St. Louis. My partner in that crime, a biker from my neighborhood who was eight years older than me, robbed the employees after we put them in the cooler. When the manager was slow giving up his wallet, Reggie smacked him in the face with his gun and broke his nose. He had wanted to take the young waitress into one of the storerooms, but I talked him out of it, told him we didn't have enough time.

Don and the others were looking at me, waiting to see what was going to happen. The busboy's eyes were still bright with malice. I couldn't figure out why he was taking it so personal. Carla was shivering with her arms wrapped around her chest. The little dishwasher had the same fascinated expression he'd had since I surprised him by the Dumpster. The Aztec's face was blank as the stone face of a statue. While Switch covered them, I stuck my gun in my belt and hunted around the kitchen until I found a big screwdriver in a drawer. Using it as a pry bar, I snapped a pin on the inside handle so that the heavy steel door could only be opened from the outside.

"That's it," I said, turning to face our victims. "Thanks for being smart."

One of Carla's hands moved up to her throat, and I saw terror come on like a lightbulb in her eyes.

"You won't suffocate," I said. "This thing is ventilated—right, Don?"

"Y-yes." His voice was shaky with relief.

The girl still looked frightened.

"What is it?" I said.

She shook her head.

"Less go, Billy Boy," Switch said, slipping the name in nicely. "We gotta git!"

"You'll be all right," I told the girl.

As I started to swing the door shut, the manager raised his hand halfway, hesitantly, like a timid kid in a class with a mean teacher.

"Thanks for being—so nice," he said.

I shut them in and jammed the screwdriver through the padlock hole on the handle.

"Billy Boy?" I said.

"You don't like it?"

"It doesn't quite seem like me."

My real name is Robert Rivers. My friends call me Rob, which has become ironic. Women usually call me Robby. The fake name was a tactic we used to misdirect the police. Briefly, I imagined two cops searching through the rap sheets of low-IQ criminals called Billy, looking for one who wore a ski mask and carried a .38, excited to have a clue. It wasn't a bad phony name but in front of the delectable cashier I would have preferred something a little classier—Beauregard, maybe.

"What's that busboy's problem?" Switch said.

"I'm not sure."

I retrieved the loot from Don's office. Just inside the service door, we put the pouch full of money, the lockbox, our ski masks and the sawed-off shotgun in a black pillowcase Switch pulled from his back pocket. As we went down the alley, I plucked a tuft of honeysuckle flowers from the fence and popped them in my mouth. They had a sweet perfumey taste at first but as I ground the silky pulp between my molars, bitterness emerged from the center of the sweetness like the sting of a bee hidden in a blossom. In some ways I liked the bitterness better than the sweetness. It seemed to contain the essence of the flower.

## CHAPTER FOUR

Switch waited in the shadows at the corner of the building while I walked across the lot to Don's car. At one-thirty in the morning the streets were nearly deserted, a single pickup truck winding out its gears, gunning down Harbor toward the Pacific Ocean. I wheeled the Cavalier around and picked up my partner. We turned inland on Harbor, driving past the lighted windows of the restaurant.

Three blocks down, I turned right into the main entrance of the subdivision that lay behind Cow Town, turned right again on a dim side street and parked behind my Cadillac. Both of us scanned the area as we switched cars. The golden globes of porch lights shone by the front doors of several houses but not a soul was stirring. An onshore breeze, still stiff several miles inland, sifted through our private world, rattling the fronds of three willowy palm trees rooted close together in the yard beside the Cadillac. Looking up at their black silhouettes eighty feet above us, I saw they were California fan palms, the only species of palm native to these coasts, the only kind that grew here before the Southern California desert was irrigated with Colorado River water and gasoline, causing landscaped cities to bloom in broad, flat blossoms. After four years in California, palm trees were still mystic to me, apertures through which I glimpsed an archetypal place, part Hollywood movie about Hollywood in its heyday, part Tahiti the way it was before Cook arrived, part Florida in the winter of 1970 when I escaped from my life for the first time, hitchhiking a thousand miles south from the snow-muffled Midwest to walk with fourteen-year-old feet on the dazzling sand of Miami Beach.

"Billy Boy?" Switch interrupted my botanical reverie. "You want to make a getaway sometime this evening?"

"Let's go," I said.

We put our gloves and my pistol in the pillowcase and dropped it in the trunk among my siding and window sample cases. If the cops stopped us on the way back to Long Beach we were just two white guys headed home at closing time, too answered-up and sober to trigger a search of the car. Circling back to Harbor, I paused at a stop sign, put my signal on and turned right, continuing inland, away from the restaurant. As we cruised toward I-405, I touched a silver button on the armrest of my door and the front windows glided down, letting soft sea air flow into the leather-upholstered interior. Switch reached over and turned on the Symphony Sound stereo system, activating an invisible reggae band that filled the car with the thump of a bass guitar cradling a melody dreamed up beneath the swaying palms of Jamaica, along a coast where English privateers hunted Spanish treasure ships, pirates sanctioned by their government and God.

Gradually, we were leaving the world of the crime. It was a letdown and a relief, same as always. A relief because we weren't handcuffed in the back of a cop car with bloody noses and knots on our heads. A letdown because the world of the crime was the place I felt most alive.

A majority of people who win the Medal of Honor are neurotics. They do exceptionally well in combat because they are used to being under intense psychological pressure. Battlefield conditions—chaos, confusion, danger—which unnerve the well-adjusted, seem normal to them. They find themselves, finally, in a world where their inner tensions make sense. While their solid, steady companions crumble, they relax and go about the business of taking out machine-gun nests and rescuing the wounded. It was like that for me when I committed crimes. I wasn't doing anything heroic, but the intensity relaxed me. I'd been angry and out of place in normal society for as long as I could remember. But I was at ease in the world of the crime. So a vein of depression ran through my happiness as we rolled along the deserted boulevard.

"How's the Caddie running?" Switch asked.

I'd had the car for only two months and was still rubbing my thumb against imaginary scratches and playing with the four-way electric seats.

"It's a Cadillac," I said.

"That says it all," he laughed.

Above us, pale city stars glittered honeysuckle white and yellow. The air swirling through the car was a mild sixty-five degrees. It was another gorgeous night along the California coast, the place where the age of exploration ended and people turned inward to explore the world of dreams. We had a Christmas of uncounted loot in the trunk and what might turn out to be happy lives before us.

Just before the 405, I stopped at a pay phone in the parking lot of a fast-food restaurant and called the local cops.

"Hello, this is Swartz."

"Are you a cop?" I asked.

"Well, okay, let's start with that. I'm a cop." I enjoyed the note of surprise in his congenial voice. It was a fifty-year-old voice with a forty-inch waist, but it wasn't stupid. Swartzie knew it was not a run-of-the-mill call.

"Well, I'm a robber," I said. "We just knocked off Cow Town on Harbor Boulevard and there are some people locked in the cooler who'd probably appreciate it if you went over and let them out." I paused for a second, while he tried desperately to think up a clever, TV-cop rejoinder, then hung up. The police would have noticed the cars in the lot and the dining room lights on the next time they went by, investigated, and eventually let the people out, but it might have been five or six o'clock in the morning by then. I didn't want the girl locked up with the busboy that long.

# CHAPTER FIVE

We bounced over the curb into Switch's driveway at 2 A.M. He lived three blocks from the ocean in Belmont Heights, in one of those 1920s bungalows that are an architectural mainstay in the older parts of Long Beach: low-sloped roof with asphalt shingles and wide eaves, a veranda in front, pastel paint on clapboard walls. The pale blue house nestled snugly between two similar bungalows on a lot that maximized the value of land made precious by proximity to the Pacific. There was a handsome, non-native palm tree in the middle of the postage stamp front yard. A sustained orgasm of flowers filled the narrow strip between the driveway and the right side of the house—dahlias with heavy scarlet blooms, yellow begonias, hollyhocks and day lilies in several shades of orange.

A raucous party was spilling out of a house down the block as we got out of the car, heavy metal music rattling bright windows. Two men were arguing in the front yard.

"That's that asshole Melonhead," Switch said.

Belmont Heights is cosmopolitan in a modest way. There are no movie stars but Cher's daughter owns a restaurant on Broadway, which is some consolation, and there is a lively mix of races and economic classes. Along with whites, blacks and Mexicans, people from a dozen other Hispanic and Asian countries wander around in the permanent sunlight, searching alleys and azalea bushes for the American dream. The Paris Market, a kind of urban general store around the corner from Switch's house, is run by a Vietnamese family that fled Saigon during the last chaotic moments of our ugly intervention in their country. The neighborhood gas station is operated by two Iranian brothers with permanent, Richard Nixon–type five o'clock shadows. It is the kind of neighborhood where Jesse Jackson could really let his hair down.

Residents know one another's names and speak when they meet on the wide, concrete sidewalks, which are embossed at each street corner with the name of the contractor who poured them in 1921. Plenty of strangers pass through the neighborhood—people going to or coming from the beach or the bars and coffeehouses on Broadway—but they are known as strangers. I was in an intermediate category, not a member of the community but not a stranger, either. People knew me as a friend of Switch's who came around a lot. A few of them knew my name.

"Turn that music down!" Switch bellowed in the direction of the party house.

"Whud you say?" came the answering yell. The bigger of the two men lurched toward us. He had long hair pulled back in a ponytail, a biker's bushy beard.

"Turn the goddamn music down. People are trying to sleep," Switch shouted.

The man stopped thirty feet away when he saw who Switch was.

"We ain't bothering no one," he said in a drunken voice.

"Just turn it down, Melonhead."

The big biker was shirtless and shoeless, wearing a pair of blue bib overalls.

"Maybe I will, and maybe I won't," he said, staying on his side of the buffer zone.

"Maybe you will," Switch said, starting in his direction.

I grabbed his arm and jerked him back.

"We don't want cops."

"He needs his ass kicked."

"Do it tomorrow."

"You ain't gun do shit," Melonhead slurred, starting back toward the loud house, splay feet smacking warm concrete, big head bobbing.

"I thought you taught him a lesson last fall."

"Looks like he needs a refresher course."

An Arabian sliver of moon glinted among the pinnate fronds of the palm tree as we crossed the lawn to the veranda, and I caught a whiff of complex perfume rising from the summer flowers along the driveway. Going in through the front door we entered a large rectangular room with walnut-colored hardwood floors and white walls, sparsely furnished with contemporary furniture.

On one of the innumerable days that constitute the sleepy, backward drift of the past, someone had removed the wall between a small living room and cramped dining room. When money came back like a long-lost relative at the beginning of the Second World War, or during the early, optimistic days of the Kennedy administration, some big-bellied cigar smoker in overalls had gone to work with a sledgehammer and shovel while an excited housewife hovered in the kitchen. There had been a carpenter who drank little bottles of Coke, a plasterer who sent around the corner for buckets of beer. Between them, the workmen, who were old now, or dead, had created a spacious interior that still surprised me each time I entered the bungalow.

A matching couch and chair upholstered in black leather watched over by a chrome floor lamp, a glass-top coffee table and a thirty-inch TV occupied the front end of the enlarged space. At the far end, a larger glass-top table with six chrome chairs and a black laminate china cabinet made up the dining room suite. There were two doors in the end wall, one on either side of the china cabinet. The one on the left opened into a plant-filled kitchen, the one on the right into the spare bedroom where I slept for the first four months after I arrived in California at the nadir of the post–Cold War recession. The back door opened off that room onto a side porch at the rear of the driveway. The archway that led to the hall was two-thirds of the way back along the left wall. On the kitchen side of the arch, an expensive stereo and several hundred CDs were arranged on built-in shelves. The right wall was a row of casement windows with a view of the neighboring house, fifteen feet away on the other side of the flower-lined driveway. Scattered around the room—one on the couch, two on stands, another leaning in a corner—were a variety of guitars, electric and acoustic. Switch had stuck to guitar playing but he constantly changed types of music, from rock to folk to country to blues and back again.

While I unpacked the pillowcase on the dining room table, Switch turned on a seventies rock station, buttoning the volume down to a whisper. Melanie had found out she was pregnant two months before, and since then he'd been very solicitous. But when I pried the metal box open, the whoop I gave woke her up.

The box wasn't easy to get into. It was heavy-gauge steel with a lock that took a real key, not just a blank with an ear. The latching mechanism was held in place by industrial-strength rivets. The hinge side was just as sturdy. I tried to work the blade of a screwdriver in between the box and lid but couldn't get it in far enough to pry. Then I tried to twist the protruding lock with a pair of vise grips, but they kept slipping off the rounded edges of the steel. Finally, I took it out to the side porch and jumped on it, coming down with one heel and all my weight on the middle of the lid. That sprung the lock halfway. When I took it back to the table, I was able to pop it open with the screwdriver. It contained a bulky manila envelope full of hundred dollar bills and a six-by-eight, black-and-white photograph of a Vietnamese girl. The word *Balboa* and some numbers—62195—were written on the back of the photograph in red ink.

"Something good?" Switch said, looking up from the money he was counting. I tossed him the envelope. When he saw the contents, he shrugged his shoulders up around his ears and scrunched his face into a pucker of illicit delight, like a man watching something lewd through a keyhole. Melanie came through the archway wearing a T-shirt long enough to keep the color of her panties a mystery, flimsy enough to show the shape of her nipples. She was fifteen years younger than Switch and cute as a centerfold.

"Hi, Robby," she said. Giving Switch a kiss on the cheek, she leaned on his shoulder with her eyes half closed. "How'd you guys do?"

Switch emptied the manila envelope beside the other money, spreading the packets of hundreds out with his hand like a deck of cards.

"Wow!" Melanie said, wide awake. "That's so much money. How much is it?"

"Let's find out, Mommy." Switch patted his lap and she sat down, giving him a friendly wiggle of her ass. He was playing it cool in front of his girl, but I knew his heart was pounding as hard as mine. There were a lot of hundreds.

"Either of you want coffee?" I asked, also cool.

"I'll take a cup," Melanie said, giving me her warmest, most approving smile. Sometimes she resented my relationship with her old man, but not tonight.

"Bring it on," Switch said. "And don't make any of that weak, watery shit you usually make. I want to get fired up!"

"Your ass," I said. "Mel—who makes better coffee, me or that piece of pork you're sitting on?"

"It's true," she said, laughing indulgently, giving Switch another kiss. "You make it too strong, honey."

"Great," Switch said, holding his arms out wide with his palms up while Melanie clung to his neck. "I don't get no respect. In my own house, I don't get no respect."

Melanie was half Spanish, half Native American, the same type as the cashier in the restaurant but even prettier, with flawless olive skin and apple cheeks that made her look younger than she was. She had appeared on the scene two years before and quickly established herself as something special. She'd come out of a rough background mysteriously well adjusted and self-reliant. Her mother was an old-school junkie who'd done every cruel thing imaginable to her, intentional and unintentional. Her Mexican gangster father took a full clip in his torso when she was twelve, leaving her in the care of a grandmother who practiced chicken-gut voodoo for all the wrong reasons and dispensed discipline with a four-foot length of broomstick. In spite of all that, she finished high school in East L.A., playing sports and getting good grades. She made decent money as an office manager for a small insurance company and had surprisingly normal values. She went to church, was kind to children, didn't like lying.

I actually dated her first. We met at the art museum and had coffee a couple of times. I took her out to dinner and a movie once and got as far as kissing in the car and rubbing her breasts. But when she laid eyes on Switch, I was history.

It could have been awkward, but I let it slide. Switch and I went back to junior high school and he was the closest thing I had to family in California. The warm feeling I had for Melanie didn't go away when she picked my partner. She was intelligent and easy to talk to and we got along fine as long as I didn't seem to be monopolizing her old man. She usually wasn't unreasonable about that, either. After six months or so, we let her in on our secret lives. She didn't participate, but she accepted what we did.

Having grown up around professional criminals, she knew planning and carrying out profitable crimes required a lot of time and effort. It was only if we stayed out too late, too often, without what she considered good reason, that she turned cold toward me. When that happened, coming in the front door of the bungalow was like walking into the cooler where we left our Cow Town victims.

Since the pregnancy, it had been happening more often. She was still friendly, but I sensed her maneuvering behind the scenes to get Switch to go straight. He'd stuck to the same restaurant equipment sales job since she moved in and he was making good money. He had a shoe box full of cash and jewelry in a floor safe in his office. If he wanted to quit crime, he was in position to do it without losing his lifestyle. I wasn't too worried, though. He came from a hardscrabble clan of country people who had fled the Depression-era Ozarks, skinny as African refugees, and clawed their way into the lower middle class by working overtime in automobile plants and munitions factories in St. Louis. That grim-faced group had raised him with the belief that poverty was the greatest moral and practical evil. His own hard times, up to and including a six-month period of unemployment during the early days of the recession, had reinforced that belief with firsthand experience of the humiliations that go with a lack of cash in a consumer society. The crime money we risked our freedom for was an economic and psychological cushion between him and the specter of his starved grandparents, and I didn't think he would give it up. There certainly was no thought of quitting that night. They had finished counting the cash and Melanie was happy to be a crook's girlfriend.

There was exactly twenty grand in new hundred dollar bills. The serial numbers were sequential in three series of nine thousand, nine thousand, and two thousand. Whoever took the money out of the bank avoided triggering a report to the Internal Revenue Service by keeping the individual cash transactions below ten thousand dollars. Combined with the seventy-eight hundred from the safe and register, it was our third biggest score.

"We'll save this extra money for the baby," Switch said expansively.

"What do you mean?" Melanie asked.

"You know, for a college fund or something. Put it in the bank."

"Whatever you think, babe," Melanie purred.

# CHAPTER SIX

**The photograph wasn't** pornography. It was more like an exhibit at a trial than a page in a men's magazine, a record of a victim entered in evidence against the world that victimized her. It's hard to judge the age of Asian girls. They tend to look younger than they actually are, with small bodies and childish faces. A skillful photographer can make a twenty-year-old Japanese woman look like a sixth-grader. Judging by her smooth vulva and the almost nonexistent shadows beneath her breasts, this girl actually was young, no more than fourteen or fifteen. Her thick, blue-black hair was pulled to one side, hanging down in front of her right shoulder. Her upper lip and left cheek were swollen.

Whoever took the photograph captured more than just the details of the girl's slender body. Staring at the picture, I had a clear sense of the living person whose image was cradled in chemicals on the bed of thick paper. Looking into her eyes, I knew what she was feeling at the moment the flash exploded.

Pornographers usually coax their models to act out one of two sets of fake emotions: excited and lustful or submissive and fearful. When they photograph young models, they encourage the second complex, probing the sadism of jaded voyeurs to create excitement, letting insecure, middle-aged men imagine themselves sexually dominant. The girl in the picture had a glimmer of erotic fear in her dark eyes, waving like the thin, white arm of a drowning person. But the main emotion was sadness.

The expression on her face stirred up the anger about Vietnam that preoccupied me in my late teens and early twenties. I missed going by a couple of years. By the time I signed up for the draft, Nixon, that undertaker of a president hunched with Quaker humility over Uriah Heep hands, had brought most of our soldiers home behind the macabre smoke screen of Vietnamization.

In our grade-school years we believed hand-over-the-heart in the Land of the Free, pledging a nation of ripe fields and prosperous cities stretching from sea to sand-castle sea beneath a Nazarene sun. Then, in high school, when our moral constitutions were at their most vulnerable, we found out our leaders were gangsters, our land as full of corruption as a dead dog is of maggots. Most people got over it after a while, but it still stuck in my craw. Whenever I felt the need to excuse my criminal lifestyle—which wasn't often anymore—I leaned heavily on that disenchantment: Corruption makes sense in a corrupt world. It wasn't my only excuse, or the only reason my heart went out to the girl, but it was what I thought of while I looked at the picture. Some things were too painful to think about.

The girl in the picture was an image of alienation—hurt and alone. At the same time, she looked brave, in a way that only abused children can be brave, and fierce—the offspring of Vietnamese fighters who drove out three great imperial powers in succession, triumphing, finally, over the most powerful nation the world has ever known. It was there in the way she held her shoulders, looking into the lens of an evil eye. She had been fucked in more ways than one. She had been beaten into submission. But it didn't look like she was broken.

"What do you think?" Switch said, looking over my shoulder. We were having a second cup of coffee after splitting the money. Melanie had gone back to bed, telling Switch sweetly not to be too long.

"Who knows?"

"The flesh trade?"

"Could be."

"Oriental girls are hot property on the black market," Switch said. "Some of the reps at work have been going to a house over by the airport that's stocked with Thai girls. They say the girls are young and beautiful and do anything you tell them to. The owner is cleaning up."

"Child prostitution?"

"No—least not as far as I know—the girls are more like sixteen, eighteen, in their early twenties."

"You sound pretty familiar with the place," I said.

"Not me!" Switch held his hands up with his palms toward me like someone surrendering. "I got all the young pussy I need right in there."

"I know. You think the guy who owns the restaurant was planning to buy this girl?"

"Either that, or he just sold her."

"Seems like he would have given the picture to the customer."

"Maybe he was keeping it for his memory book. Either way, it's not our problem. Best thing to do is ditch the picture along with the bank bags and the rest of the gear."

I stayed in my old room that night. Lying in bed before going to sleep, I thought about how far I'd come in financial and practical terms since I came clattering down the 605 in a 1980 Ford pickup with a smashed right fender. The truck had 190,000 miles on the odometer. I had thirty dollars in my pocket. Like the girl in the picture, I was an alien, poor, disoriented and alone. Now I was driving a late-model Sedan DeVille, had $120,000 in a safe deposit box in San Diego and an apartment in Corona del Mar. Plus fourteen thousand dollars. The new money made a warm glow inside me as I drifted off listening to the salt air sigh through the neighborhood, swirling in and out of the open window beside me. I knew the glow wouldn't last, but I went to sleep happy.

# CHAPTER**SEVEN**

**I got up** at six-thirty, showered, and put on some clean clothes I kept in the dresser in the spare room, Levi's and a gray silk aloha shirt. The trash truck showed up right on time at a quarter after seven. I walked down the driveway to meet it with a heavy-duty garbage bag tied up tight. Inside, wrapped individually in grocery bags and mixed with kitchen garbage, were the bank bags and lockbox along with the masks, shoes and gloves we'd worn. We weren't the kind of robbers who get busted for driving around with ski masks stuffed in among beer cans and fast-food wrappers under the front seats of our cars. We never wore the same disguise twice in a row, varied our look with each job to keep the cops from seeing a pattern that would arouse their lethargic interest. A new pair of Reeboks after a stickup was a reasonable business expense. I had no intention of going to prison because of a footprint on a greasy kitchen floor.

Back inside, I heard Switch and Melanie arguing in the bedroom, him verbally waving his arms around above his head, her quiet and reasonable, gradually giving way but trying to salvage a vanity point. Sometime during the night, Switch had decided our windfall was a good excuse for an excursion to Las Vegas. They were arguing about how much gambling money to take with them. Sensible, she wanted to take a thousand. He was pushing for five.

"It's found money, baby," I heard him say through the door. "We can afford it."

"Well, the rest of it should go straight in the bank for the baby."

"I'm taking off," I said to the door.

"What?"

"I'm going now," I yelled.

Switch burst out of the door in a pair of black boxer shorts with a half-eaten banana in his hand. "You taking off?"

"Yeah. You two have a good trip."

"Absolutely. See you in a few days. Stay out of trouble while we're gone."

"I don't think it's me we have to worry about," I said. Through the open doorway behind Switch, I could see the end of their tangled bed, his clothes scattered on the floor. He had kept the place neat enough when he lived by himself, but if he had a woman in the house it never occurred to him to pick anything up. He was very 1950s in that way. Melanie leaned around the corner, holding a towel in front of her.

"Bye, Robby."

"Have fun, Mel. Keep him on a short leash."

"I'll try."

Switch walked to the front door with me. We shook hands.

"Good job," he said.

"You too, man."

It was a green and gold morning, palm fronds glittering in magnifying-glass air. The June gloom had blown off early, leaving the seaside sparkling in a fresh breeze. Making a left on Ocean, I rolled south along the strip of park that overlooks the beach. Across San Pedro Bay, the *Queen Mary* rode at permanent anchor next to the huge dome where Howard Hughes stored the *Spruce Goose* after its one and only flight. Beyond the toy luxury liner, the humpback of the Rancho Palos Verdes peninsula was still dusted with spring green. Farther out at sea, container ships sat below the fan of the horizon. Risking a fender bender, I kept my eyes on the water as I drove, trying to absorb the bright beauty into my psyche. I glanced back at the road in time to see a sky blue DeVille coming toward me in the opposite lane. It was the same year and model as mine. The elegant lady behind the wheel acknowledged me as a fellow Cadillac driver with a nod of her platinum head.

I don't know if five years old is technically late model, but the car I was power steering was in superb condition. It made every trip a pleasure. I bought it from a retired aerospace worker whose lifelong dream of owning a new Caddie was finally fulfilled when he was too old to enjoy it. I don't think it had been out of the garage in a month when I answered the ad a few minutes after the newspapers hit the stands. Some Cadillacs look like big Chevrolets, boring, but this was a top-of-the-line luxury car, maroon with silver wainscoting and a Rolls-Royce-looking grill. It had a maroon leather interior and every electronic trick in the book. The digital odometer showed 38,000 miles when I started it up the first time, and for some reason, ignorance or confusion, the septuagenarian was asking less than half the Blue Book value. Three-quarters of Blue Book is normal for a used car in excellent condition, so the deal was as deluxe as the car.

Besides looking like something the president of France would be chauffeured in to the Follies and being as comfortable as the living room, the car handled great. It cornered on a monorail, holding tight to the inside at high speeds with minimal squeal. A 4.5-liter V8 fuel-injected engine filled the expansive area beneath the hood. Floored, it jumped like a huge jackrabbit from zero to sixty. Even at cruising speed, already going sixty or seventy on the highway, the big engine had the power to snap my head back when I squashed the pedal.

Nineteen-ninety was a miracle year for Sedan DeVilles. When I first thought of getting one, I checked *Consumer Reports'* annual auto issue and found the car rated excellent in every category of reliability, and singled out as the best used car of any type from that model year. The one I was driving was a lucky gem off the 1990 production line, every bolt torqued down an extra quarter turn, each surface triple polished.

When business was good in St. Louis, I drove new trucks and never thought anything about it. When people made envious comments, I didn't know what they were talking about. So I had a new F-250. So what? It was just a truck. New vehicles were good because they didn't break down as often as old ones. Even as a teenager, I was pretty much numb to cars, saw them as a way of getting to and from, not an extension of myself. It wasn't until things went sour in the late eighties and I ended up driving rattletraps and smokers that I realized the psychological impact of automobiles. I found myself becoming self-conscious and defensive, parking around corners from appointments, wondering why everyone but me seemed to be driving something shiny and new. Once, when I was clanking downtown at rush hour to pay my electric bill half an hour before the power was due to be shut off, my muffler came loose on a steep hill and bounced sparking beneath the car as I passed a crowded bus stop. I saw looks of pity on some faces, anger on others; half a dozen people hooted and jeered.

Those memories sharpened the pleasure of owning and operating the Cadillac. I wasn't linking my self-esteem to it, but it was nice to know I had a getaway car that gave me a realistic chance of actually getting away, and that, if I didn't get away, if the cop caravan and TV crews caught up with me, I would at least be emblazoned in public memory behind the wheel of *the* classic American success car.

The boulevards of Los Angeles and Orange County are jammed, nowadays, with German and Japanese luxury cars that cost twice as much as Cadillacs and hold their value better, but the American car retains an aura of happiness and well-being that mere economics can't dispel. I have yet to hear a salesman say, "Yes, indeed, my friend! This is the Lexus of retirement plans," or "That is absolutely the BMW of big-screen TVs!"

# CHAPTER EIGHT

I took Ocean to Second Street, Second to the Coast Highway. South of the San Gabriel River, I stopped at the McDonald's in Seal Beach. One side of the restaurant was packed with early-morning old people, chattering away as if their talk could stop time, trying to one-up one another with observations and jokes as old and worn down as pebbles on the beach three blocks away—"You working hard or hardly working, Mac?" "Oh no, dear, after you. Age before beauty, as they say!"—each remark followed by a burst of mindless cackles. They were a good advertisement for crime, or, at least, for defying society's expectations of normalcy. Whatever else happened to me, I wouldn't end my days huddled in a group in a fast-food restaurant trying to avoid thinking about reality.

There were two cashiers working behind the Formica, a tough-looking Chicano with india-ink tattoos on his shaved head and a petite Asian girl. I opted for the Asian girl's queue. She was cuter than the Mexican. Neither cashier spoke good English and the lines moved slowly. Looking around the restaurant, I started estimating the number of customers and the cash flow.

You never see an empty McDonald's. It's as if the corporation creates a new batch of fast-food zombies for each hamburger heaven they open. A lot of money moves through each franchise. Idly, I thought about the roads around the restaurant, trying to visualize an escape route. It would depend on the time of day. There would be more money and more traffic after the lunch rush. The problem with robbing a busy restaurant at lunchtime is all the people. You never know if there is an off-duty cop in the crowd or someone with a heart condition or a hero complex.

I was jarred from my felonious daydream when a man several places ahead of me in line slammed his hands down on the counter. There was a fat black lady in a lemon yellow sweat suit between me and him. Looking over her shoulder, I saw that he was huge, the size and build of an NBA center. His hands, splayed aggressively on the counter, were huge, too. He would make a good strangler. His hot dog–size fingers were decorated with sparkly rings heavy as brass knuckles. A square-cut diamond glinting on his left hand made my heart skip a beat. It was at least three carats.

"I said I wanted a sausage egg biscuit, not a sausage biscuit," he said in a voice full of compressed fury.

"I sorry, sir! I sorry!" The girl was so intimidated by the man's manner that she bowed as she apologized, bobbing forward from the waist. "Sorry, sir!"

The man wore a dark blue silk suit worth more than the girl would earn all summer. Even from behind, he radiated dangerous authority. Everybody in both lines stared at him. He looked like someone who should be eating breakfast at the Balboa Club, not McDonald's.

"Get me a sausage *egg* biscuit," he said to the girl and then turned the big block of his head toward the Chicano, who was giving him a hostile look. "You got a problem, Paco?" The menace in his voice hit the boy like a fist. His black eyes dropped and his body seemed to shrink.

"Is there a *problem*, sir?" A portly, middle-aged white lady in a manager's uniform came over from the drive-through window. She sounded cocky, ready to handle trouble.

"Yes. Your employees don't know how to fill orders. Who owns this store?"

"I'm sorry, sir." The cockiness was gone. "What do you need that you don't have?"

"For the fourth time, I want a sausage egg biscuit."

Relief reshaped her face when she looked over and saw a sausage egg biscuit beneath the heat lamp.

"Here you are, sir," she said. Her try at a light, friendly tone failed miserably when her voice quavered on the last word.

"Who owns this store?"

"That's really not necessary, sir." She had begun to whine. "You have your sandwich. It's complimentary. No charge."

The man didn't move. He projected weight and solidity above and beyond his size, as if his flesh had the density of iron.

"Spectrum Corporation owns it," the lady said, "but—"

"Give me the number and the name of your boss." His voice was deep and harsh.

Defeated, the manager wrote something on the back of a business card and held it out to him. As he reached out to snatch it from her hand, a watch that looked like a gold Rolex peaked from beneath the fine white fabric of his shirt cuff.

"I can assure you it won't happen again, sir," she said.

"Maybe not. If you hire someone besides gooks and wetbacks."

As he brushed heavily past her, the black lady turned to follow him with sad brown eyes. "That man must have a nail drove in him somewheres," she said softly, looking at me and shaking her head. Her dime-size ceramic earrings were the same yellow as her sweat suit.

"What an asshole," a woman in the other line added, keeping her voice low.

When I paid for my breakfast, the little Asian girl took my money with a trembling hand.

I took my corporate pancakes into the corner of the restaurant farthest from the bedlam coffee klatch and scanned the *Orange County Register* for leads. Originality was another thing—besides research and varying our MO—that made us successful. We robbed places that weren't expecting it. Much of the time that simply meant hitting normal targets but in low-crime neighborhoods, where people weren't on guard.

An inner-city bank is a fortress, physically and psychologically. It has been robbed before and is expecting to be robbed again. Armed guards, Plexiglas, constant patrols by the police. A little branch bank in Irvine, on the other hand, has never been robbed and so is not expecting to be robbed. Technically, in terms of their training, the employees there are expecting it, but psychologically, in human terms, they are not. The same with grocery stores, restaurants and jewelry stores. It's one of the essential ironies of materialism: Where money and goods are scarce, where there isn't much worth stealing, people have a baseball bat ready to swing; where wealth is abundant, precautions often are lax, the pickings easier.

I read a translation of *Les Misérables* when I was in prison in Florida. The main character's life is ruined when he gets caught stealing a loaf of bread. In post-revolutionary France, they frowned on people who stole food, and the authorities hounded the guy like a murderer. I thought of the story a few months earlier when I drove back behind a shopping center in Irvine to look at the rear entrance of a jewelry store. There is a Ralph's grocery store in the same plaza and a bread guy was making his delivery. He disappeared into the store wheeling a rack of bread as I came rolling slowly down the alley, leaving his truck wide open. It was early in the morning and the sun shone on hundreds of golden loaves. Finches twittered in the bougainvillea draped over the adobe wall by the truck. There was no one in sight. I could have filled my trunk with fragrant bread and driven away unmolested. There were no precautions and there would have been no consequences. It would have been a shrug and a curse word to the deliveryman. No one else would have cared, including the cops. In South Central L.A., the same truck would have been locked up tight, the driver careful and dangerous.

Another way around people's expectations is to hit businesses that other robbers haven't thought of. That's where the paper came in handy. From the classified ads to the business section, it was full of information about commercial activity. It stirred up my creativity, gave me new ideas. I found out about new companies and learned operational, cash-flow and personnel details about existing businesses.

A small headline on the second page of the metro section caught my eye: COOL ROBBERS CALL COPS TO AID VICTIMS. Beneath it was a typically garbled account of the robbery. According to the article, the manager was injured during the holdup. The robbers locked the employees in the freezer, not the cooler, and called the police from a car phone in the manager's car, which was still missing. I was trying to think what might have happened to Don, if he had hurt himself trying to break out of the cooler, when I glanced up from the paper and saw the busboy from Cow Town stalk in the door.

I looked away instinctively, shrinking down behind the newspaper. I couldn't believe it was the same guy. Peeking around the edge of the *Register*, I took another look. It was. No mistaking the ape arms and miniature legs, the fifty-cent pieces of flesh sticking straight out below his wavy brown hair. He was better dressed than I would have expected, wearing pressed khaki pants and a red polo shirt. It occurred to me he must buy his shirts in the men's department, his pants in the boy's section. When he turned his wide shoulders sideways, looking around the restaurant, I noticed again how thin his chest was from front to back, as if he'd been sliced off the end of a human extrusion. It was a tough extrusion, thin like the blade of a knife. As he swiveled his handsome face toward me, I felt an icicle of fear plunge into my gut, not fear of the busboy himself, but of what every robber dreads in some corner of his mind, to some degree, all the time: fear of sudden and unexpected detection, of the hand on the shoulder from behind. I knew he couldn't recognize me. He'd only seen me standing, wearing a mask. But I felt totally exposed anyway, as if I were naked with a spotlight shining on me. His eyes were dull, lacking the malicious glitter of the previous night. They passed over me unseeing and locked on to the man in the blue suit.

The busboy's aggressive posture evaporated as he walked over, his strut shriveling into a shuffle. He sat down obediently when the older man nodded at a chair. I was glad to see he was a coward.

There was something disturbing about the big man's face. His coarse features were slightly out of alignment, the left eye and ear higher than the right. His racial composition was blurred, too, an ugly blend of northern European and Asian genetics. He looked Mongolian, but more insidious, like an experiment escaped from an Orwellian nightmare. Leaning forward, his coffee-can-size fists on the table, he talked intensely into the busboy's face, his own meaty face roiling above the wide shoulders of his elegant suit coat. The busboy nodded his smashable head steadily and subserviently. I watched them while I ate my pancakes. On my way out, I walked by their table, trying to eavesdrop.

"You catch that shark-bait motherfucker . . . tell him . . . don't care . . . make sure his ass . . . fucker . . ." was as much as I could hear in the loud restaurant.

I didn't like seeing the busboy while I was having my morning coffee. The shock I felt when he walked in the door left an aura of anxiety as it subsided. But the uneasiness dissipated as I stepped outside. The warm June morning was full of whizzing cars and kids on bikes, old ladies walking old dogs and birds hopping in bushes. No one was paying any attention to me. Looking back from the car, I saw the busboy and the gangster absorbed in each other, faces six inches apart, oblivious to my leaving. There was no way the busboy could recognize me and it wasn't so strange seeing him here. We were only five or six miles from Cow Town. He probably lived in the area. It was just a spooky coincidence.

Very spooky.

## CHAPTER NINE

I drove south through Sunset Beach and came out onto the long, open stretch of the Coast Highway that shoots along the Bolsa Chica and Huntington beaches, wetlands on the left, whitecaps on the right. The parking lots by the snack bars and changing rooms were mostly empty, but cars were beginning to file in. By noon, the beige sand would be packed with people, a carnival of small children and bright umbrellas, pairs of nearly naked young girls prancing past surfers in wet suits, music blaring from portable stereos, Coca-Cola being guzzled by the bucketful, much of it by people who would see the ocean for the first time that day, some by people who would never see it again. Now, at eight-thirty in the morning on the day after Father's Day, the vast playground was as empty as it had been in the forties and fifties, when there was nothing inland but orange groves and cattle ranches; the way it was before the Beach Boys made Huntington famous as Surf City, USA, before Los Angeles swelled after

World War II from two million to ten million people, overflowing onto the unspoiled coastal plain of Orange County.

I crossed the Santa Ana River into Newport Beach, cruising with a heavy stream of morning traffic past the boatyards and crab restaurants of Mariner's Mile. It was a few minutes after nine when I turned off the Coast Highway in Corona del Mar.

During the early decades of the twentieth century, Corona del Mar was a separate city. It merged with Newport in the 1940s to gain access to the larger city's municipal water supply but it still has its own identity, less beachy than Newport and Huntington, more like a well-to-do town from upstate New York set down beside the ocean. The residential area where I live slopes up from the Coast Highway to the edge of a cliff that overlooks the city's secluded beach, a half-mile crescent framed by steep cliffs and decorated with groves of royal palm trees.

When I pulled up in front of the hulking, shingle-style house where I rent an attic apartment, I found Reggie England asleep on the front porch, a forty-seven-year-old biker in worn-out leathers curled up like a baby on the porch swing, resting his shaggy head on his folded hands, snoring loudly. As I came up the steps, the front door popped open and Mrs. Pilly stuck her nose out.

"He said he knows you, Mr. Rivers. I was going to call the police first thing I saw him, but he said he knows you. Wanted to wait inside but I wouldn't let him. He's just too rough-looking. I wouldn't let him in the house. Do you know him? Shall I call the police?"

"No, don't call the police, Mrs. Pilly," I said. She was my landlady, which meant she was nosy, but she liked me. I drank tea with her sometimes and talked about the sad state of the country and we got along fine. Somehow, through some extrasensory landlady perception, she knew I was not the remodeling salesman I claimed to be, despite the business cards in my wallet and sample cases in my trunk. But I paid my rent on time and she let it slide.

Claiming to be a remodeling salesman was good cover. I knew enough about construction to be plausible in the role, and it gave me an excuse to explore rich neighborhoods at night. I'd been given a pass by more than one cop under suspicious circumstances when I showed him my card and said I was looking for the Jacksons at 1540 Ocean, or the Petersons at 1450 Palm, who wanted to add a room to their house because the wife's mother was moving in. The expensive cards were embossed with the phrase *Resi-*

*dential and Commercial Remodeling and Construction,* so I had an excuse to case office buildings and shopping centers, too. The address on the card was a fake suite number in a labyrinthine Costa Mesa office complex so confusing that people who worked there got lost on their way back from lunch. The phone number went to an answering service that didn't sound like an answering service. Mrs. Pilly called the number to check on me when I first moved in, heard the girl say, "Coast Construction. No, Mr. Rivers is out giving a bid. Who shall I say called?" But she still harbored suspicions.

A spry sixty-two, my landlady looked like a woman half that age when seen from a distance, carrying her 130 pounds lightly on a five-and-a-half-foot frame. She gardened and did housework competitively, outcleaning her friends and tending a huge vegetable patch in the backyard, maintaining the large-scale canning skills she learned growing up on a truck farm in Garden Grove. I'd seen pictures of the two-story farmhouse with ornate scrollwork under the eaves that her family had just barely managed to hold on to during the Great Depression. Tough and frugal like most people born in the 1930s, she was also good-hearted and generous, a mainstay of her Methodist church's charities. The blandness of her moon face was relieved by sharp, observant eyes, her soft facial flesh stiffened by pride rooted in the fact that they didn't lose the farm.

"*Is he* a friend of yours?" she asked, wrinkling her nose.

"We grew up together in St. Louis."

"Well, I didn't know. He didn't look to me like a friend of yours."

"Oh, yeah. We're old friends."

"I can't have him sleeping on the porch," she said. She was hungry for information and sensed she wasn't going to get any. In an unguarded moment she had confessed to me that she felt left out of life since her husband's death nine years before. The husband, a stocky marine who made captain near the end of the Korean conflict, colonel at the beginning of the Vietnam War and brigadier in an office building in the midseventies, had been driven into an early grave by the small-arms fire of unfiltered Camel cigarettes and shots of officers' club bourbon. They didn't have children and most of Mrs. Pilly's own family had died or moved away. Her only remaining blood relative in the area was an elderly female cousin who lived up in Orange, and they weren't on speaking terms because of a quarrel of some kind that had taken place thirty years before.

"Of course not," I said. "I'll take care of it."

Reluctantly, she popped back into her cuckoo clock, clicking the door shut behind her.

To paraphrase Voltaire, if Reggie had not existed, it would have been impossible to invent him. The contradictions in his character were too extreme. The exceptional degree of amoral deviousness that inhabited him like a demon, and should have made him repugnant to everyone who knew him very long or well, failed for some reason to diminish his insidious likeability. Among our common acquaintances in St. Louis, I didn't know anyone he hadn't scammed or double-crossed at some point. I knew many people who were repeat victims of his wheedling, jack-in-the-box chicanery. And yet, with few exceptions, those people still maintained relationships with him. If he dropped by uninvited at a backyard barbecue, they would set out a plate of ribs and a can of beer for him. If they needed some product or service in his line, they'd stop by his house.

Everyone likes to number a rascal among their friends, someone who gets away with all the things they would like to get away with, and Reggie played to that impulse. Over the years he became a psychological fixture in the shabby suburbs where we grew up: the guy you couldn't trust whom everyone eventually made the mistake of trusting. Instead of being outraged, people were more often amused by his shady deals, trading stories about "Old Reggie's" latest scam.

An eighth-grade dropout resolutely ignorant of history, science, literature and all other intellectual and academic knowledge, Reggie had sharp native intelligence. He was a good mechanic, a clever horse trader of bike parts and stolen electronics, a well-informed gossip in the underworld of suburban crime. Most north-county cops knew him on sight. Many of them had arrested and questioned him repeatedly over the years. But he'd never done time.

When he was younger, he'd had a tough, muscular body, but he'd always been ugly, with kinky, brass-colored hair and a bloodhound face. Despite that, young girls flocked around him, beautiful fifteen- and sixteen-year-olds from good homes, attracted by his outlaw charisma and tendency toward silence and significant looks. I remember going over to his place on a humid weekday afternoon one summer during high school and finding two gorgeous lasses in tight shorts and T-shirts giggling across the kitchen table. When I asked where Reggie was, they said he was downstairs. This was his mother's house and his bedroom was in the basement. When I went down, I heard the typical moans and "please don'ts" of a girl getting it a little harder than she is used to but still liking it. Back upstairs, one of the girls had let a slim hand stray down between her legs, while the other one, a ripe Italian teen I recognized from my tenth-grade homeroom, paced back and forth from the refrigerator to the basement door, waiting for her friend to come up and tell her what it was like.

From his late twenties on, booze and bike wrecks had taken a toll on his body, reshaping it to match his face. He had always had fast, flashy choppers when he was younger, and was a skillful driver, winning cash, bike parts, even a runaway girl one time in nighttime races over the winding roads leading down into and back out of the Missouri River bottoms. At some point, the quicksilver machines started to get away from him, driving up the sides of vans or skidding like skipped rocks down the concrete streams of interstate highways. By the time I left St. Louis, he had the body of a man in his fifties, complete with wrinkles and a gut. But he was still pulling little biker chicks with nice asses. They weren't the beautiful angels he'd had in his twenties, but they were there and they still grabbed their big toes when he crooked his finger.

I had mixed feelings about finding Reggie snoozing on the porch. On the one hand, I was surprised how glad I was to see him. He was the older brother of a guy I went to school with, and I'd known him since I was twelve. I didn't have an older brother and he filled that role for me, showing me the ropes in the lower-middle-class drug culture I grew up in. He cheated and abused me occasionally during the first few years I knew him, taking my lunch money for beer, sending me on fool's errands and then laughing at me in front of other people. But after a few years that tapered off. He shoved the first girl I fucked into my arms, showed me how to shoot up heroin with an insulin syringe and sold me my first gun, a dinky little revolver that only shot .22 shorts but that made me feel in control of my life for the first time.

Nevertheless, for obvious reasons, I was wary. Reggie was a pathological con man and I knew he'd start trying to weasel something out of me as soon as he woke up. I wondered what his overgrown gnome's body had been up to, what secrets were crowded into his grizzled head. Over the years, I'd heard rumors about a darker side to his criminality, whispers about things worse than fucking a partner's girlfriend or selling heroin that was mostly powdered sugar. Some people said he stayed out of jail because he worked for the cops, which I never believed. Other people said he was protected by the barroom influence of the Italians who ran the north-county local of the laborers' union, men with beer-keg bellies and tiny eyes for whom he supposedly had done certain unspecified favors. His name had been linked to several unsolved fire bombings and at least two bodies in the woods. Reggie had always encouraged the rumors by denying them with a wink, but I never put much stock in them. Still, I'd seen a look in his eyes before that made me wonder.

I also felt sad looking down at the body huddled on the porch swing. Time was wearing away at his props and pretensions. His motorcycle boots were run down at the heels and his scraggly beard was streaked with gray. The sole of one boot was two inches thicker than the other, compensation for pulverized bone. The three-wheeled motorcycle parked at the curb didn't look like it would go very fast. The front tire was bald. There was rust on the engine.

# CHAPTER TEN

When I sh●ok Reggie, he woke up but pretended to still be asleep. I let him enjoy that secret-agent sensation for a few seconds, then shook him again. He sat up on the swing and rubbed his fists in his eyes with his elbows straight out, pantomiming the process of coming out of a coma. I waited. He looked over at me.

"What's happening, Robby?" he said, deadpan, as if it had been four hours instead of four years.

"You are, Reggie, same as always."

"Heh-heh." He laughed and stroked his beard. "I came to visit you."

"I'm glad to see you, man. How's St. Louis?"

"Fan-fucking-tastic," he said, elongating his face to indicate the opposite.

"What's up?"

"I got into it with Bob. The prick."

"What happened?" Reggie had never been the forthcoming type. If he had news, he wanted it pried out of him.

"He shorted me on some cars I sold, so I cleaned out the register."

For the past decade or so, Reggie had worked off and on at a salvage yard down by the river. It started out as something to do with stolen cars, but ended up being a semiregular job, Reggie's version of going straight in the aftermath of a near miss with the cops. At first, he'd worked the register, selling used parts to high school kids and farmers, but when too much money evaporated the owner stuck him out in the yard dismantling ruined machines. Later, he cooked up a scheme where he patched up junk cars that his boss towed in, then sold them in a dirt lot beside the salvage yard for much more than they were worth. He said Bob had tried to cut his percentage on those deals, charging him retail for the parts he used instead of wholesale.

"That prick's been fucking with me for ten years," Reggie said. "So I took the cash from two cars I sold plus the register and hopped on my trike. Decided to go sightseeing."

"How much did you get?"

"Fifteen big ones." That probably meant a grand, but at least he wouldn't be hitting me up for cigarette money right off the bat.

"You think Bob called the cops?"

"Naw—he don't want me talking to the cops. Not with the shit I got on him."

Reggie pulled two bulging garbage bags out of a homemade plywood luggage carrier bolted on the back of his trike. Each of us carried a bag as we climbed the outside staircase that led to my apartment.

The house I live in is a shingle-style Cape Cod built in the 1950s at the highest point on the bluffs, where the oceanfront cliffs turn to form one side of the entrance to Newport Harbor. After her husband died, Mrs. Pilly paid a contractor to remodel the attic into a spacious one-bedroom apartment with sloped ceilings and skylights. The contractor added a long shed dormer on the channel side of the building so that living room and bedroom both have views of the harbor. The front door opens at one end of the rectangular living room, picture window full of toy boats to the right. Beyond a pocket door at the far end of the living room, my bedroom occupies a continuation of the same, hall-like space. The kitchen and bathroom are to the left of the entrance, kitchen first, housed in a second, smaller dormer built onto the back side of the house. Light oak floors and kitchen cabinets, good-quality, cloth-upholstered furniture, muted plaids. I rent it furnished for twelve hundred a month.

"Ain't decided," Reggie said when I asked him what his plans were. "I'm keeping my options open. Considerin' opportunities."

I told him he was welcome to stay with me for a while, showed him the shower and foldout couch. I knew I was letting myself in for problems. He was trailing trouble behind him and he stirred up shit wherever he went. But I didn't care. Things were going good for me and I could afford to soak up some of his bad karma. You have to be loyal to the people who make up your life, and he was one of the people who made up mine. I knew what it was like to leave a wrecked world behind and come west with little or nothing, looking for a new start.

I'd only slept four hours the night before so I told Reggie to help himself to breakfast, then took a shower and went to bed, setting the alarm for one o'clock in the afternoon. Tension and consciousness slipped away like waves retreating down a beach as I stretched out on the cool sheets. I whirled down into deep sleep. After a while there were dreams. The first dream was tearfully happy. Walking with a girl beneath river trees, the thing that had always been missing suddenly supplied. The second dream left an aura of tragedy, but I couldn't remember the details when I woke up.

I woke up with a plan.

Out in the living room, Reggie was kicked back in the recliner, looking at the current issue of *Hustler* magazine.

"Well, if it ain't sleeping beauty," he said.

"I told you I was out late."

"Doing what?" A sharply inquisitive tone appeared in his voice.

"Counseling wayward girls. Where did you get the reading material?"

"Store at the corner. I was checking out the neighborhood."

There were no stores nearby that sold *Hustler*. He was lying just to keep in practice.

Taking a last lingering look at a nude black woman sucking two dicks while a white girl in a nurse's uniform licked her asshole, Reggie closed the magazine and put it on the end table between the chair and the couch. Sighing audibly, he began to look around the room like a pilgrim examining the Sistine Chapel. I ignored him and went into the kitchen to make coffee. When I went back into the living room, he was still at it, projecting the sense of crestfallen envy and admiration that was one of his most disarming forms of flattery.

"Where you getting all the moolah, bro?" he wheedled. The apartment was nothing special, but compared with the places I'd lived the last few years in St. Louis, and compared with his room in the basement of his alcoholic mother's house, which he had moved back into after his last bad accident, it was deluxe.

"Business is good."

"The remodeling business?" he said, balancing his tone between skepticism and sarcasm.

"What else?"

"I don't see many tools," he said.

"Did you look?"

"A little bit."

"I'm a salesman now."

I went back in the kitchen and poured myself some coffee. "You want a cup of coffee?"

"Milk and sugar."

I fixed him a cup and set it on a saucer on the end table, making a mental note not to wait on him again. He would get used to it real fast.

"I don't see a truck," he said.

"Salesmen drive sedans."

"What else do they do?"

"Drink your coffee."

"Yes, sir." Squirming around in the chair, rocking his torso back and forth, he brought the recliner into an upright position with a bump that almost ejected him onto the floor.

"You oughta put a seat belt on this motherfucker," he said. "Fucking thing's a death trap."

While he slurped coffee through his mustache, holding his cup with his pinkie finger sticking out, I grabbed my keys from the bedroom and went down to the car. My gun and my share of the money were wrapped up in a towel in a department store bag in the trunk.

"What you get me?" Reggie asked as I walked back through the living room.

"It's a surprise," I said.

After locking the bedroom door, I took the cover off the wall vent, lay on the floor and reached arm's length up into the ductwork, where a canvas bag hung on a screw I'd driven in with a little cordless driver. I transferred the gun and most of the cash to the bag, hung the bag back up, replaced the vent cover. The vent opening was too small for anyone to stick his head in and look up with a flashlight, and you had to get your shoulder in and stretch to reach the bag in its blind location. It was a good hiding place. I moved the armchair back in front of the grill.

Reggie had the magazine upside down, trying to get a better look, when I went back into the living room.

"Let's take a ride," I said.

"Where to?"

"I'll tell you on the way."

# CHAPTER ELEVEN

The Cadillac was parked at the end of the block. Reggie walked around it, checking the paint and trim, the tread on the tires, came back and stood beside me shaking his head.

"You ain't in the remodeling business anymore," he said.

"What?"

"That's a thirty-five-thousand-dollar car." Reggie knew vehicles. Motorcycles especially, but cars and trucks, too. He hit the base purchase price right on the nose.

"I bought it used for nine grand."

He made saucers out of his eyes and blinked them at me. It was his astonished expression.

"This car?" he said, pointing a stubby finger at the Caddie, as if there might be some confusion which vehicle we were talking about. "What did you have on the guy?"

"He was old. He didn't need it anymore," I said.

Reggie shook his head again. "You got a hell of a deal, Robby. It's a cherry ride."

"Thanks, Reggie. That means a lot coming from a connoisseur like you."

"A con-a-what?" he said.

In spite of myself, I was letting his flattery work on me. He was the guy who always had the fancy cars and flashy bikes when we were younger, the one I'd taken my cars to for appraisal when I bought them. In those days, he always told me I'd paid too much and pointed out flaws in the vehicle. I didn't need him to tell me the Cadillac was a nice car and that I'd gotten a great deal, and I knew he was working me, but his reaction gave me a glow, just the same.

"Leather, cassette player, factory alarm . . ." Reggie was ticking off the options as we rolled north on the Coast Highway. He stopped and unleashed another theatrical sigh, running his hand over the smooth burgundy dash.

"I always said you'd hit the big time someday," he said. I didn't remember him ever mentioning that, but it was nice to know he had been saying it when I was out of earshot, assuring everyone that I was on my way to the top. In fact, he had believed in me, hoped to make my book-learning pay dividends. I'd started out as his protégé but by the time I was eighteen we were partners. He asked my advice and listened to it, looking for the Yellow Brick Road that led from the small-time suburbs of petty crime up to the Emerald City of armored cars and limousines.

Just past the Arches, I turned inland on Newport Boulevard, took it to Harbor.

"Where we going?"

"I'm going to buy you lunch, brother."

Reggie gave an approving nod as we pulled into a just-vacated spot by the front door of Cow Town. He knew a low-price, large-portion steak house when he saw one.

The thought that had occurred to me as I woke up was that a restaurateur who had twenty thousand dollars in a lockbox at his place of business might have more cash at his house. Likewise, he might have other desirable things.

I didn't know who owned Cow Town but I had an idea how to find out.

I was so focused on that idea that it wasn't until we walked through the door into the clattering interior of the steak house that I realized I was making one of the classic mistakes of criminal life, doing something I'd never done before: returning to the scene of the crime.

I saw what I was looking for by the cashier's stand, but couldn't get a good look. A crowd of shrieking office girls blocked my view. A hostess in her fifties—age and waist size—took us to a table by the kitchen door. I wondered where the pretty Latina was. Sitting across from Reggie, I looked around the room. Waitresses were coming and going, people gabbing and gobbling. Normality had reasserted itself after the disruption of our crime. Through the small window in the kitchen door, I caught a glimpse of a cook chopping furiously at something on the stainless steel table, busting his low-paid ass to get the beef out. We ordered T-bones, baked potatoes and salad, and talked about St. Louis. I kept an eye out for Don and the busboy, but didn't see either of them.

When he had swallowed half his baked potato and two-thirds of the steak, Reggie signaled the waitress with a barely perceptible lift of his street person's head. She was a white girl in her early twenties with dull blond hair pulled back in a ponytail. A few wisps that had escaped from the rubber band hung down behind her right ear. She wasn't pretty, but she had long, finely sculpted legs and her skirt was stretched tight over an ass that turned heads when she wore her bikini.

"Yeah?"

Reggie pushed his massacred plate half an inch in her direction with a thick index finger.

"Shit ain't cooked," he said. She looked at the plate, then looked back up at him.

"Why did you eat it, then?"

"I didn't notice until I took a few bites," he said belligerently. "Look at that T-bone. That's raw meat. That shit will make people sick." He nudged his plate a quarter inch further in her direction. The stub of the steak was slightly pink on the inside. The girl looked him up and down, from his worn-out boots to his grease-stained denim shirt. I thought she was going to tell him to go fuck himself, or that he'd have to talk to the manager. But her plain face lit up with a conspiratorial smile.

"I'll get you another one," she said. "The potato, too?"

"Yeah. Make it a big one."

"Okay!" Pushing the front of her thighs against the table by his arm, the girl leaned over to pick up his plate. As an afterthought, she looked at me. "Is yours raw, too?"

"No. Mine's fine."

The guy was practically an old man. He was rude, ugly and dressed like a bum. But he still had the same old mysterious power over young women. It was body language or pheromones or some kind of psychic power—an image of a stiff dick transmitted to their subconscious minds—something I couldn't copy.

When the waitress came back, her hair was brushed and re-ponytailed, and she had a fresh coat of lipstick on her wide mouth.

"You want some more iced tea?" she asked after she set his plate in front of him.

"Sure, babe. Get my partner some, too." Reggie glinted his eyes at me through puffy slits.

"Nice ass," I said, as she walked away.

"Not bad."

The girl came back with a brown plastic pitcher and filled our glasses, then set the pitcher on the table, wholesaling another big smile in Reggie's direction.

"Do you need anything else?" she asked.

"I'll let you know, Cherry," Reggie rasped, reading the name tag pinned above her right breast.

"What kind of bike you got?" the girl asked.

"How did you know I ride, Cherry?"

"I just kind of figured from the way you're dressed, you know?" She had her legs pressed against the table again, standing as close to him as she could get without actually climbing in his lap.

"I got a trike I built from a seventy-eight pan head," Reggie said. "Plenty of room for two."

"Oh, wow, a three-wheeler! Who do you ride with?"

"I'm from out of state," Reggie growled, making that everyday fact sound exotic, significant, possibly dangerous.

"Cool! What state?"

Reggie shook his head, warning her away from the subject. He couldn't tell her exactly where he came from. That was classified information.

"Oh!" She was impressed.

"Excuse me for a minute," I said.

There was no one at the cashier's stand. I went over and stood in front of the short counter with its charity collection boxes and bowl of mints. I wondered how much was in the drawer. The hostess came back from seating some diners.

"Yes, sir?" She didn't see a check in my hand.

"I need change for the phone."

She held out her hand for the dollar I offered.

While she got four quarters out of the register, I took another look at the license on the wall behind her. Lewis McFadden. It was an old Newport name. The original McFadden brothers owned the Balboa peninsula before there was a Newport Beach or an Orange County. They built the first pier and the first railroad, a narrow gauge that hauled farm products down to the sea and manufactured goods back up to the farms in Anaheim and Orange. If the owner of the restaurant descended from those McFaddens, he might be very rich. Above and beside the license, there were half a dozen framed photographs. The same grim-looking old man appeared in all of them, clenching hands or posing side by side with politicians and entertainers. His wrinkled paws made me nauseous.

"Sir?" The hostess was holding out my quarters.

I went over to the pay phone in the alcove by the restrooms and called Switch's number, leaving a message for him to contact me as soon as he got back in town. There was no Lewis McFadden listed in the ragged directory chained to the phone. The page it might have been on was ripped out.

In the restroom, I washed the coating of cooked cow fat off my hands and mouth, combed my hair, looked at myself in the mirror. The precrime adrenaline was starting to flow. My eyes were bright, my mind racing from point to point, rummaging around for the steel puzzle pieces of a plan. At the same time, a voice was saying, "Stop." I was not a spur-of-the-moment criminal. I knew it was dangerous to leap without looking carefully. It felt dangerous to be back in Cow Town fifteen hours after we walked out the back door with loot. But I let the surge of epinephrine drown out the voice of caution, rushing over it like a whitewater river swallowing a raft.

When I went back to the table, the waitress was gone. Reggie was sipping a full glass of tea. His second plate of food was demolished.

"Let's go," I said, picking up the check. "I have a couple of stops to make before five."

"Go ahead," he said. "Cherry's giving me a ride back to your place. She's off at four and she wants to see my trike."

"The legend continues," I said.

"Heh-heh."

I took my wallet out and started to drop some ones on the table, but Reggie held up his hand to stop me.

"I'll tip her," he said.

I gave him my house key and told him to stay at the apartment until I got back.

"What time will that be?"

"Don't know for sure. Later. Make yourself at home, but be cool, all right?"

"Absolutely."

I paid the check on my way out, recycling one of the twenties from the stickup.

# CHAPTER TWELVE

Glancing in the rearview before backing out of my parking slot, I saw the restaurant entry door shimmer as if it had just closed. It struck me as odd because there was no one outside and I hadn't seen anyone crossing the lot toward the entrance. The afternoon sun reflected off the plate glass of the double doors and the wide restaurant windows, transforming them into coppery mirrors. One-way mirrors, like those in the police interrogation rooms where I spent some of my most memorable hours as a teenager. The diners could see out but I couldn't see in—an ironic reversal of the previous night when anyone who happened to be standing outside in the darkness could have looked in through the open blinds and seen me in the dining room while remaining invisible to my eyes.

My first stop was the Costa Mesa branch of the Orange County Library. In the reference room, I gathered up a pile of phone books that covered the entire county. There wasn't a Lewis McFadden in any of them, but there was an L. McFadden with an address in the city of Orange. I recognized the street, one of the shady, Victorian avenues near Chapman University. When I called, an old lady with the young name of Laura answered the phone. I told her I was in town on business, trying to look up a friend from college.

"Do you know a Lewis McFadden?" I asked her.

"Lewis?" Her voice was sharp. "I have a nephew named Lewis, but I haven't seen hide nor hair of him in thirteen years. Not since his father died." There was a country twang in her voice that reminded me of someone, but I couldn't quite think who.

"Do you have any idea where he might be living?"

"Last I heard, he bought a place somewhere down Newport way, by the water. But that was years ago."

"You don't know his address?"

"Oh no! And I don't know that I want to know it."

"Why's that?"

"I took care of him for six months one time when he was a child and his mother was sick. She was sick a lot, and then she died when he was only twelve. I tried to help him through that—not to take his mother's place, because no one can do that for a boy, but to make a place for him and be a friend to him. He used to visit us all the time. Many's the night he slept in this house and I cooked him breakfast in the morning, and he's never so much as called me in all these years. My husband, when he was living, always said Lew was a bad boy, that he took things from the house, money and things. I always felt sorry for him and stuck up for him, but I guess he didn't care about that."

"I'm surprised to hear Lew would act that way," I said, trying to keep her talking.

There was a long pause. "Did you know him well at Princeton?"

"We were roommates one semester," I said.

"Was he a good boy out there?"

"Sure," I said. There were several more seconds of silence.

"I guess you knew about the trouble he got in," the old woman said.

"Yes." I took a gamble.

"Do you think he did it?"

"No. I never believed it."

"I didn't, either—at the time."

"Do you believe it now?"

"I can't say one way or t'other. There were goings-on in that house that would make your hair stand on end. My sister-in-law went away when she was pregnant with Lewis. Supposed to been gone to a hospital back east because of some complication thing. Sounded strange to me at the time, and when she come back the baby didn't look a bit like her." Another pause. "Looked more like the little Ko-ree-an servant that had went with her on the trip. And he *was* a bad boy, even when he was little. Not bad inside, maybe, but did bad things. He set their house on fire one time, playing with matches. Killed a neighbor's dog with a bow and arrow his father got him. And then he hurt that boy in high school." She sighed. "It's funny you called today. I was thinking about Lewis this morning. I don't know why."

The old lady was starved for talk, and I nudged her to see if she would spill a little more information. "What happened when he was in high school?"

"He broke a boy's back playing football. Some of them said he did it on purpose. Said he tackled the boy from behind after the play was over because he was mad at him about some gal. I guess he didn't tell you about that."

"No, he never mentioned it."

"Well, it's all in the past now. But it makes me wonder some about that mess at Princeton, if maybe Lew did what they said he did. He was different when he came back. He changed when his mother died and he changed when they kicked him out of college. We hardly ever saw him after that. He went to work at his father's business up in San Pee-dro and that was that. Next thing we knew, he was running the business. I think there was trouble about that, too, but it was hushed up like everything else."

"You're talking about the restaurant business, right?"

"Not right off. He didn't start those restaurants till later, a few years before his father died. His father's family—my husband's family—was in shipping for years. They go way back in these parts. His father owned a steamship company. Later on he had a restaurant supply business, too, selling stuff they brought in on the boats. I guess that's where Lew got the idea for those cow whatchamacallit places."

"How old was Lew when his dad died?"

"Well—it was thirteen years ago, so I guess he'd of been thirty-seven."

The hulking, square-headed patriarch in the photographs wasn't the McFadden I was looking for. The old man was dying just about the same time the girl in the photograph was being born.

"Do you know anyone who might have Lew's address or phone number?"

"No, I'm 'fraid not. His sister's been gone six years now. She's the only one I know he stayed in touch with. There's not much of our family left anymore. I have a cousin lives down Newport way might know something about him, but she and I haven't spoken in years."

"Do you have her number?"

"I don't believe I do. Our family has all drifted apart, somehow."

"Well, thanks for your help. I appreciate you taking the time to talk to me."

"Well, that's all right."

"If I track him down, I'll make sure he gives you a call."

"Oh, I wouldn't bother. I don't guess it much matters now." I imagined her in a dim dining room full of dark wood furniture, replacing the phone in its cradle on a doily-covered table by the hall door, hearing the silence of her empty house solidify around her. I still couldn't think who her voice and manner reminded me of.

After inserting another quarter into the library pay phone, hearing the satisfying mechanical clatter as gravity pulled it down into the coin box, I dialed the Orange County Courthouse and got connected to the Hall of Records. They were open till four-thirty. It was a little after three when I left the library. Northbound 55 was already jammed so I took MacArthur over to Main Street and stoplight-hopped north into Santa Ana, speeding up and stopping, speeding up and stopping, a good metaphor for the futility of most socially approved activity.

That stretch of Main is run-down light industrial and commercial with working-class residential showing through the gaps. By the time I crossed Warner, 90 percent of the people on the street had brown skin and most of the signs were in Spanish.

A dozen blocks farther north, I made a left onto Santa Ana Boulevard, circled around and parked in the little pay lot behind the Hall of Records. Civic Center Plaza was spellbound in the afternoon glare, oddly empty and silent in the middle of the bustling city. A solitary homeless man slept on the grass in the shade of the four-story building.

The Hall of Records was deserted, too. To the right of the entry, the big lobby of the tax collector's office was empty, no one standing in the roped-off cattle shoots leading up to the counter. Turning into the long white hallway that leads to the elevators, I had a twilight zone sensation of being alone in an abandoned world.

Then an old man came out of an alcove, shuffling across the corridor on an angle toward an exit door without raising his eyes to me. He looked like he was in his late seventies, with stooped shoulders and withered skin on his face and hands. The rest of his body was covered with a bright blue Marine Corps dress uniform, complete with a double row of confetti over his heart. He carried his hat under one weak arm. I didn't catch his rank before he disappeared through the exit door, but I guessed he was or had been some type of noncom. It struck me how good the uniform looked considering how old it must have been. Glancing into the alcove, I saw a pebbled-glass door stenciled with black letters: TAX COLLECTOR: UNSE-CURED DELINQUENT COLLECTIONS. I wondered if he had come down to plead for relief in patriotic terms, citing his service to his country as a reason for mercy or mitigation. Or if he had offered himself, a worn-out carcass clothed in the resplendent uniform that represented the highest part of his life to him, as payment for a hopeless debt. In either case, it looked like he had been refused. I wondered if he'd shrug it off as he walked away from the public building, square his shoulders and look forward to breakfast at McDonald's the next day, or if he would show up on the evening news, a frail bundle covered with a blanket being loaded into an ambulance in front of a mobile home somewhere.

I took the empty elevator up to the first floor and went across the hall into the assessor's office. The double doors were propped open and there was a chubby Mexican girl I recognized from previous visits sitting at a computer terminal behind the counter. She looked up and smiled, brushing stiff red hair out of her face.

"*Hola!*" She put some friendliness in her voice.

"*Hola,*" I said. "Which plat book shows the lots on Balboa Island?"

She turned to face her terminal and typed in a few words.

"Book fifty. Right over there." She pointed to one end of a compartmentalized rack on a counter running along the opposite wall. Each big cubbyhole held four ledgers with numbers on the spines. To one side of the rack, there was a monitor and keyboard with an office chair in front of it.

"You know how to use the computer to fine information?"

"Type in the assessor's number and hit F3?"

"*Bueno,*" she said. "I thought I saw you here before. Are you buying another house already?"

"I'm thinking about it," I said, trying to remember my previous lie.

Pulling the ledger numbered fifty, I sat down and flipped through it. There were no names on the lots, just dimensions and lot numbers. Comparing the street names on the plat sheets with a Thomas Brothers Map of Central Orange County I'd brought with me, I figured out where the island started. Beginning with the first waterfront lot, I punched the eight-digit number into the computer. A second later, I was looking at a complete legal record of the property: owner's name and marital status, the bank that held the note, the value of the land and improvements, the date the lot was sold, and so on. Lot one didn't belong to Lewis McFadden. I punched in the number for lot two.

The Newport coast covers a lot of territory. It would take a long time to search all the plat sheets for a name that might not be there anyway. McFadden could have sold the place. He might have bought it under a corporate name. Maybe he never bought a house at all. Maybe it was just a rumor the old lady heard, a deal that fell through. I didn't think so, though. Laura McFadden sounded to me like someone who would have her facts straight, one of these old ladies with a powerful memory formed during the days of grammar school recitals, who can remember the color of the buttons on the preacher's vest at her wedding, what the weather was like on the day an older brother had a medal pinned on his chest by a proud commander.

I started with Balboa Island because of the word written on the back of the girl's picture and because of what Laura had said about the house being by the water. It was a long shot, but it gave me a manageable task. The island is small, half a mile in length by a quarter mile in width. I could cover half of it in the hour before the office closed, steadily typing numbers and glancing at names. If I had to, I'd come back the next day to finish Balboa and do Lido, work my way up the peninsula the day after that. I didn't have to. At four-twenty, I typed in 05020101 and "McFadden, Lewis" popped up on the screen. He owned a corner lot where the small channel that bisects the island meets the channel between the island and the mainland. The date in the change of ownership was March 1982: the same year his father died. He was single and the value of the land and improvements was listed at $536,000. If that was the value in 1982, it would be worth millions now. An outfit called Union Trust had financed the purchase.

I wrote everything down, thanked the clerk for her help and headed back to my car.

# CHAPTER THIRTEEN

Forty-five traffic-snarled minutes and about that many cuss words later, I drove across the arched bridge onto Balboa Island and parked in front of the seashell store on Marine Avenue. The sidewalks were crowded with bag-toting tourists wandering in and out of the resort-wear shops, restaurants and souvenir stores that line the island's main drag. When I turned left and walked across the little bridge that spans the internal channel, I entered quiet residential. The channel, which separates the eastern tip of the island from the main part, is called the Grand Canal, but that overstates it. It is twenty-five or thirty feet across, six or eight feet deep when the tide is in, lined with rickety little docks. There are no gondolas.

There aren't any tourist beaches on Balboa Island, either. At high tide, the bay licks the base of the concrete seawall that forms the perimeter of the man-made island. At low tide, there is a narrow strip of sand beyond the seawall where summer renters sit in lawn chairs with their feet in the water.

With miles of surf-washed sand stretching along the peninsula just across the bay, there is nothing to attract nonresident swimmers or sunbathers to Balboa. That keeps it insular, the way an island should be.

A wide sidewalk curves along the inside of the seawall. Waterfront houses edge up close to the sidewalk. Following the concrete path, I passed, on my right, a series of private docks—well-built walkways extending thirty or forty feet out from the seawall into the shallow bay, providing access to a menagerie of dinghies, yachts and sailboats. Some of the boats looked like kids' toys. Others could have cruised to Hawaii. Big and small, the boats rocked in the restless water, gear creaking and clattering in the breeze.

The houses to my left were typical waterfront architecture, bright pastel boxes with a hint of Cape Cod here and a glimmer of Key West there. Shallow terraces were decorated with potted palms and ships' bells, tiny flower patches and patriotic flagpoles.

McFadden's house was the nicest on the sea-bright block, a needle-sharp example of classic modern architecture, fieldstone and plate glass beneath four-foot eaves. It was built on the point where the Grand Canal connects to the channel between the island and the mainland, facing the mainland condominiums across 120 feet of shallow salt water. He had a double lot, and the back half of the compound was enclosed by a pale blue concrete-block wall with palm fronds and elephant ear plants peeking over it. My heart accelerated when I saw the wall. It was seven feet high, easy to get over, and would provide perfect cover for a break-in. Things that citizens intend for their protection often undermine their security.

The front yard was deeper than the neighbors' yards, twenty feet from the sidewalk to the house, carpeted with thick grass and enclosed by a low, decorative fence—fieldstone columns connected by wrought iron. The main part of the house was one story, built, by the look of it, in the fifties. To the left of the front door there was a newer, frame section with vinyl siding and small casement windows. It was two stories and came within three feet of the house next door. McFadden's substantial dock led down to a boat slip big enough for a small ocean liner. An octagonal sign stuck in the grass next to the wrought iron gate promised an armed response to intruders.

On my first pass, I approached the house along the main channel, turned left—the only way there was to go—and meandered down the canal to the toy bridge that connects the two sections of the island, the one I had crossed a few minutes before. I stood on the bridge for a while, doing my best to look like a tourist soaking up the local color, actually studying the houses along the canal. Pedestrians crossing the bridge nodded and smiled. It was a fine evening in a fantasy neighborhood. My skin and clothes looked like theirs.

I strolled back toward the house along the canal. The tide was out and small boats lay partly on their sides in the muck at the edges of the narrow channel. There was a rich marine odor in the air, a nostril-clearing tang of iodine and rot. As I approached McFadden's compound, I saw that his garage opened onto a dead-end street behind the house. Anyone arriving by car would have to come over the little bridge, turn left, drive two blocks and turn into the dead end. The bridge would be clearly visible from the second story of the house. I wished I knew what kind of car he drove.

Someone had left a Coke can at the base of the wall and I kicked it as I walked along the side of the compound, then tromped on it and ground it along the concrete, making as much noise as possible. Nothing barked. Better and better. Coming around the point, I noticed my shoelace was a little loose and stopped in front of the house to retie it, putting my foot on the top rail of the low fence. It was difficult to get it adjusted exactly right. It took me several minutes. While I fiddled with the lace, I examined McFadden's home carefully and methodically out of the corner of my eye. The drapes on the floor-to-ceiling picture windows were open, giving a museum-gallery view of the living room and dining room. Both rooms were furnished with valuable-looking Queen Anne–style furniture, antiques or high-quality reproductions. The dark, elegantly curved wood and fine fabrics contrasted brilliantly with the clean geometry of the architecture. The open drapes, along with the faint glow of several lamps, put a thrilling thought in my mind: McFadden was out for the evening.

Excitement built a rapid scaffold in my chest. Tiny Ferris wheels whirled in my bloodstream, and the carnival blood flooded my muscles and brain. Seeing the contents of the house on display and knowing that the restaurant owner thought they were safe *because* they could be seen brought out the pirate in me. It would take more than a Neighborhood Watch 101 precaution to keep me out of that house. The people who lived in the condos on the other shore were too far away to see what was going on in McFadden's dining room. If I chose to enter those two rooms, the only danger would be from chance pedestrians, and I'd see them as soon as they saw me. More important, only the front rooms were exposed. I'd be operating from the back of the house. The rear rooms in the main wing, and all the rooms in the two-story addition, including the bedrooms, where money, jewelry, guns and other valuable things would most likely be found, all were hidden from view. I imagined what the house would look like after dark, bright rooms shining like Christmas candles above the black water of the channel while I looted the place to my heart's content, uncovering all of McFadden's dirty secrets. I decided to go in that night.

# CHAPTER FOURTEEN

**The decision changed** the world like a colored filter slipped over the lens of a video camera, shifting me into the vital world of the crime. Hyperaware, I smelled hibiscus, decaying palm fronds and dog shit in the air, felt the angle of the sidewalk's slope beneath my rubber soles, away from the houses, toward drains at the base of the seawall.

I tasted adrenaline in the back of my throat and felt each thump of my heart like a boxer's fist hitting a heavy bag. The silver cables of social convention that held my fellow citizens in their appointed places, kept them cruising, for the most part, at exactly five miles an hour over the speed limit on the right side of the municipal and moral roadway, were not steel but gossamer. A deep breath broke them. I could be over the wall and in the house, rifle the bedroom drawers and be back out again before a cop could put his hat on. I felt the lust for potential treasure, more valuable than any actual material objects could ever be, whimpering to me from the unprotected interior of McFadden's home.

"Are you looking for Cagney's house?"

I jerked upright from my retied shoe to find a dapper little man wearing a blue captain's hat, seated in one of those miniature golf carts old people drive, observing me from the corner. The electric cart had rolled up silently on rubber wheels.

"That's it right there," he said, pointing with an arthritic finger.

"That's James Cagney's house?" I said, stupid from the guilty shock of being surprised at my surveillance.

"No! Cagney's dead a long time now, you fool. That's the house he built back in the forties when Newport was the playground of the stars. Did you know Newport was the playground of the stars?"

"I've heard that."

"There were wild times in this house back then, buddy boy. Booze and prostitutes. Dope, too." The little man thrust his head forward and bulged his eyes in my direction. "Opium, reefers—all of it. Boats like you never seen coming and going all night long, bands playing so loud you could hear them up at the Arches. This is the place where everything happened." I couldn't tell from his intense tone of voice if the old guy was censorious, telling me about dead sinners, or regretful, wishing the party was still going on.

"There you are." A middle-aged lady, heavyset, wearing a flowing white pantsuit, was coming down the sidewalk along the main channel. "Has he been bothering you with his James Cagney stuff?" Her pink nail polish and lipstick were neatly applied, her silver hair professionally finished.

"No bother," I said, wishing I wasn't talking to these people, wishing the lady, the daughter, I assumed, wasn't looking into my face with a memory that might or might not be good, possibly gaining the ability to say: *He was tall and he had light brown hair and blue eyes, Officer. He certainly didn't look like a burglar the way he was dressed, but Dad said he was hanging around in front of the house for quite a while so I guess he could have been the one.* "He was just telling me Cagney used to live in this house."

"I don't know how he got that idea in his head. They tore Cagney's house down twenty years ago and it was at the other end of the island, but he's convinced—"

"What the hell do you know about it?" the old man barked. "Were you ever at his house? Did you know him?"

The lady flinched at the harsh words. The mask of exasperated good humor, the face of a trouper coping with Dad's foibles, dropped off, exposing the weariness and worry beneath.

"He went to a party there once," she said. "He was a cameraman at Paramount, and he met Mr. Cagney on the set. Dad always knew a lot of jokes, and Mr. Cagney thought he was funny and invited him to come down for the weekend. Thirty-five years of marriage to my mother, our whole family life, all the trips we took together to Mexico and San Francisco, and that's all he talks about now. One lousy party where the band played loud and there were *prostitutes*." She turned her head to spit the bitter word at her father.

The old man shook his head violently and hit the throttle on his go-cart, taking off in the direction he had been going, the direction his daughter had come from, bumping my leg as he went around us.

"Where are you going, Dad? Be careful!"

"I'll goddamn son-of-a-bitch you," he said over his shoulder. "You don't have to worry about me anymore. I'll wheel out to the end of the dock and just keep going. I'm going on Jimmy's boat."

"Oh, Dad, don't say that!" The lady gave me a despairing look. "I'm terribly sorry about this." She hurried after him, jiggling down the sidewalk in her flowing white garb.

"You weren't there," I heard the old man say to the daughter he knew was pursuing him. "You didn't see those boats crossing the bay lit up like dreams. Cary Grant coming up from the dock with two starlets on each arm . . . and the champagne, my God, all you could drink . . . good stuff . . . steaks so thick . . ." His words faded as they disappeared around the curve of the island.

The interruption pulled the plug on my passion, restored me to a more rational frame of mind. I found myself back in the normal world. I would never actually have gone over the wall in the daylight, done a smash-and-grab on an island with only one land route out—unless I knew for sure there was another lockbox full of money, or something else worth taking the risk for, and knew exactly where it was. As the neurochemicals drained out of my brain tissue I felt a little depressed. The regret I heard in the lady's voice made me think of my own lost family. Her family was lost to time, an eight-by-ten photograph dropped in the wake of a ship that had sailed over the horizon; mine was drowned in ethyl alcohol.

It was the summer solstice, and the six o'clock sky was still bright and blue. The temperature had dropped a few degrees and the wind off the water had stiffened, freshening the air. A sleek-looking white yacht that cost at least a million dollars was moving south through the channel, headed toward the harbor entrance and the open sea beyond. The people on board may have been miserable, for all I knew, old and dying of cancer, but the ship reminded me of dreams coming true. Someone had wanted that boat and had managed to get it. A phone call to a stockbroker or forty years managing a factory had enabled him to sail out into the Pacific in style, entering the postcard of the Newport evening. For all I knew, the owner or owners were blissfully happy, a man at the peak of his career, a couple in love, enjoying good health and a keen awareness of their blessings. Small waves from the yacht's wake splashed on the sand below the seawall, a water gown trailing behind the wedding of the ship and the sea, the prow of the dream and its fulfillment. The old man's Shangri-la may never have existed, and was in any case gone, but mine was real, here, on the Newport coast, in 1995. The latest entrance to it was waiting on the other side of the silica force field that separated me from McFadden's private world. I walked back along the canal and over the small bridge to my car, putting the puzzle pieces of the job together in my mind.

# CHAPTER FIFTEEN

**Switch being out** of town was a problem. He'd worked for an alarm company for a while, selling security packages to nervous homeowners by quoting burglary statistics and insurance rates. He could tell simple contact systems from more elaborate ones with laser beams and pressure pads, knew how to deactivate the ones his company installed. I'd learned quite a bit working with him, and I was pretty sure McFadden's system was a basic window and door protector, something I could get around. But I wasn't completely sure. Switch was the alarm guy.

I thought about trying to call him in Vegas, but I didn't know which hotel he was at. He probably wouldn't like the idea, anyway. A spur-of-the-moment burglary that could link us to an armed robbery. So maybe it was better that he was out of town. I didn't want to get him riled up or help Mel convince him to go straight. I hated the thought of losing him as a partner. But I didn't like the idea of going into the house alone, either. I'd pulled solo jobs when I first came out, but for the past few years Switch and I had done everything together. I was used to his substantial backup. The guy I'd seen at McDonald's looked dangerous. If he was who I thought he was, there was a chance I'd encounter him in the house. I'd made those kinds of mistakes before, been sure no one was home and then found a deaf lady snoring in a back bedroom or met a shocked man emerging from the shower. Sometimes people came home unexpectedly. I wanted a second man for a lookout, if nothing else.

Then I thought of Reggie. Good old Reggie showing up at just the right time. He and I could do it. I knew he'd be up for it, and it would be a kick to work together again after all these years. He was reliable, too, in his own way. He might fuck your girlfriend behind your back or try to cheat you out of your cut on a drug deal, but he would never roll over on his partner for the cops. He subscribed to enough of a code, or had enough common sense, to keep his mouth shut about serious shit. The year after I graduated from high school by the skin of my teeth, some guys in army field jackets wearing ski masks and carrying M-16s robbed a bank in St. Louis. Afterward Reggie suddenly had money to burn. I was sure he was involved, but I could never get a word out of him about it.

Second thoughts came quick. It had been twenty years since we'd pulled a job together. I didn't know anything about what he'd been doing the last four years other than what he'd told me. I wasn't at all sure I wanted him mixed up in my business. Switch definitely wouldn't like it. And then there was his physical condition. Reggie had been athletic when he was younger, a good boxer and strong enough to carry a big color TV out the back door or lift a transmission into place without a jack, but he'd been smoking, drinking and drugging since grammar school. He had a big gut and a bad leg. I wasn't sure how much second-story work he'd be capable of, and I had serious doubts about his ability to flee the scene on foot.

I was weighing his pros and cons when I turned onto my street and saw a young woman come stomping down the steps from my apartment. I wheeled into a gap in the line of parked cars and jumped out. The girl was charging down the sidewalk toward me. As she came closer, I recognized her as the waitress who had served us lunch at Cow Town. She was wearing a pair of black stretch pants and a tight little T-shirt that showed every subtle curve and some that weren't so subtle. She recognized me, too.

"Hey!" she said. "Aren't you the guy that was with him at the restaurant?"

"With who?"

"That son-of-a-bitchin' sadist Reggie!" She stopped in front of me with her hands on her hips. Her face was furious, close to mine. I smelled alcohol on her hot breath.

"Calm down," I said, putting my hand on her shoulder. "What's wrong?"

"Don't touch me!" She jerked her shoulder back from my hand. "I'll tell you what's wrong. Look at what that bastard did to me." Turning halfway around, she jerked her pants down to the middle of her thighs, flashing a tanned ass with red welts on it, then jerked them back up.

"You shouldn't pull your pants down in public like that," I said, moving closer to her, looking up and down the street to see if anyone had noticed. "The cops might nail you for indecent exposure."

"He's the one better worry about the cops."

"What did he do?"

"What's it look like? He whipped me with his belt, the son of a bitch."

"Are you all right? Did he do anything else?"

"He wanted to."

"But you're okay?"

"No, I'm not okay. My ass is sore as hell."

"I'm sorry about that," I said. "He's not responsible for his behavior. He's only been out of the institution for a couple of weeks." Somehow, an outrageous lie seemed like the way to handle the outrageous situation.

"What institution?"

"You mean he didn't tell you about the asylum?"

"You mean he's crazy?"

"A little bit." That shut her up for a minute. She stared into the distance over my left shoulder, idly rubbing her butt with one hand, trying to remember the details of making it, or almost making it, with a crazy guy. I took three restaurant twenties out of my wallet. "Here," I said. "Don't call the cops on him. It would just make a lot of trouble for everybody."

"Especially him and you. It's your apartment, right?" She glanced down at the money, but didn't take it.

"For you, too, maybe," I said. "Do you want your name in the paper for going home with a guy you don't know and getting your ass whipped with a belt? And how about your work? You think your boss wants his restaurant in the news as a place where customers can pick up waitresses?" I saw her flinch when I mentioned her boss.

"You bastard," she said.

"Don't be that way, Cherry." I finally remembered her name. "I'm sorry he hit you, but he doesn't know what he's doing."

"He didn't seem that crazy to me."

"That's all part of his disease," I said. "He acts normal. Here, take this."

"What's this?" She took the money. "You think I go around letting guys beat my butt for sixty dollars?"

"I'm sure you don't. I'm just trying to make up for your trouble a little bit."

"What's wrong with him, anyway?"

"I don't know the exact name for it," I said. "He's had a lot of head injuries. You don't want to be around him."

"*You* must be crazy if you think I'd go out with him again. I gave him my phone number, but you tell him for me he better not call me. My brother teaches karate and he'll come over here and kick the shit out of him."

"I'll make sure he doesn't call you. You going to be all right now?"

"I guess so." She felt her ass again. "It doesn't sting as much now." As the fire went out of her eyes, I could see the blur of half a dozen beers there.

"Where's your car?"

"Right there." She pointed to a beat-up 325i parked across the street, red with what was left of a black vinyl top. I walked her over.

"So you're not going to call the cops?"

"I guess not."

"That's smart. Be careful driving home."

As I walked down the sidewalk toward my apartment, I saw Mrs. Pilly waiting for me on the front porch, white-knuckled hands clasped in front of her. I braced myself.

"I knew that man was trouble," she said, her face compressed and angry.

"What happened?" I asked, praying she hadn't seen the girl pull her pants down.

"I'll tell you what happened. Your friend showed up here two hours ago with a girl I wouldn't give ten cents for, both of them drinking and laughing real loud, carrying on as they went up the staircase. First thing they did after they got done stomping around like a herd of wild horses was turn the music up too loud. You know I don't like loud music. Not that you've ever been a problem. You haven't. But I don't like it, and I won't have it. My nerves can't stand it." This was not the first mention I'd heard of her nerves and I knew it wouldn't be the last.

"I know, Mrs. Pilly. I'm sorry if—" I tried to get a word in edgewise but she rolled over me.

"I went up there and told 'em to turn it down, and do you know what they did?" I was afraid to ask, but that was okay because she didn't give me a chance to. "They told me they were sorry, real sweet-like, that thing did, and then when I got back downstairs they turned it up *louder!*" She shouted the last word. I'd never seen her so upset.

For the most part, her nerves were actually pretty damn steely. Thirty-five years as a Marine Corps wife on top of a country upbringing had left her tough as an Irish trooper. She had a THIS GAL SHOOTS bumper sticker on the back of her big black Impala and a fast Palomino stabled out in Santiago Canyon. She played the Nervous Nelly routine to the hilt when it suited her, but I'd never seen her take any shit from anyone. Reggie had rattled her, though.

"They turned it *louder,* Mr. Rivers! So I went back up there and told them if they didn't turn it down I was going to call the police." She looked at me. "They turned it down then, by God. I was so upset I had to go back to my bedroom and lie down. They were quiet for a while—I pretty well knew what was going on up there—and then they started up again with more of their damn commotion. It sounded like one of them was chasing the other one. Something fell over and broke—it'll have to be paid for, whatever it was—and then the girl screamed. I thought it was murder, Mr. Rivers. The way she screamed, I thought he was killing her." She stopped to take in oxygen, opening and reclenching her hands to get a better grip on her anger. "I was so scared I couldn't move to pick up the phone. Then I heard her yelling and calling him names and him laughing, so I knew he hadn't done her in. They shouted back and forth and banged around some more and then the girl came tearing down the steps, cussing like you never heard, and took off down the street. Why any man would waste his time with something like that when there are decent women in the world is more than I can say. That was her you were talking to." Her eyes, which had been flashing around angrily, settled on me with a suspicious look.

"I saw her coming from your house," I said, still hoping she hadn't seen Cherry flash her ass. "She was upset, so I asked her what was wrong. They had a fight. No big deal."

"It's a big deal to me, Mr. Rivers."

"I know," I said quickly, trying to cap her before another gusher came in. "I'm sorry about the commotion. I'm going up there right now and read Reggie the riot act. I don't know what he was thinking of, but I promise you it won't happen again."

"I hope not. You've been a fine tenant and you certainly have the right to have a friend stay with you, but I can't have that type of carrying on in this house. I can't bear to think what the neighbors must be saying. We've never had any kind of trouble like that on this street, drunkenness and fighting. I'll call the police if it happens again, so help me I will."

"I understand, Mrs. Pilly. I'll take care of it."

"Who is that girl—the one you were talking to?"

"I don't know her. She's a friend of Reggie's."

"Where did she come from? Did she ride out here from St. Louis with him on that machine?" She made a woodpecker-like motion with her nose in the direction of Reggie's trike.

"No. She lives in the area."

"That was a mighty quick meeting-up." The suspicion in her gray eyes dilated. "Oh Lord! Is she a prostitute?"

I gave my landlady the most shocked look I could muster. "No!"

"What in the world men see in something like that I'll never know. Your friend is no prize catch but even he ought to be able to do better than trash like that."

# CHAPTER SIXTEEN

When I walked into the apartment Reggie was sweeping lamp fragments into the dustpan. He was wearing red boxer shorts and his boots, unlaced, shuffling around in them as if they were carpet slippers. His white belly hung over the elastic band of the shorts like bread dough.

"What's happening?" he said. "Thought you weren't coming back till later."

"You're fucking up, that's what's happening."

He made his saucer eyes and dropped his lower jaw.

"Funny faces aren't going to cut it," I said. "You cause a bunch of shit around here, your ass is gone."

His astonished look vanished into an old man's peevish face.

"Chill out, Robby. I'll buy you a new lamp." Besides the broken glass, there were empty Budweiser cans scattered around the room and dirty dishes on the coffee table. Through the open bedroom door, I could see tangled bedclothes hanging down onto the floor.

"I don't give a fuck about the lamp. I'm talking about your girlfriend causing a scene in the street in front of my house, threatening to call the cops on you, and my landlady being hysterical, also talking cops. I don't know what your problem is, but you better get one thing through your head." I put my face close to his. "I don't want cops around here."

"Take it easy, bro! Jesus. What'd Cherry do?"

"She pulled her pants down in plain sight of the whole neighborhood and showed me where you whipped her."

"No!" He started to laugh, thought better of it.

"Yes! I don't know if Mrs. Pilly saw her or not, but she heard Cherry screaming when you hit her. The only reason *she* didn't call the cops is because she was too scared to pick up the phone. You've stirred up more shit around here in two hours than I've had to deal with in the two years I've lived here. And look at this place—it's a fucking wreck. I wouldn't have given you the key to my apartment if I knew you were going to trash it."

"I'll have it cleaned up in a jiffy," he said. He scooted into the kitchen and emptied the dustpan into the trash can. "You want a beer?" he asked from the doorway. I gave him a dirty look.

"I thought you might have started again," he said as he came back into the living room, a fresh Budweiser in his hand. "Why you so worried about the cops? They cracking down on the remodeling business?"

"Just remember what I said, Reggie."

"Okay! Okay!"

I went in the kitchen and got a bottle of water out of the refrigerator. There were five beers left in a twelve-pack on the top shelf, another twelve-pack container crushed in the trash can. Reggie had about a dozen beers in him. That was some excuse, anyway. I went back into the living room, where he was putting the empty cans in a paper grocery bag. Watching him shuffle around like a deformed janitor, I started to feel bad about the way I'd talked to him. It wasn't sitting too well with him, either.

"I remember you making a few messes at my place," he said.

"I cleaned them up, too."

"Not all of them. And I never made no federal case out of it."

"I'm not making a federal case out of the mess, Reggie. Disturbing the peace, beating up on that girl, harassing my landlady—that's what I'm making a federal case about. You haven't been in town a whole day and you're already looking at a possible assault charge."

"That puss ain't gonna do a goddamn thing."

"Maybe not, but she could."

"Shit. She's the one wanted me to spank her ass."

"Why did she want you to do that?"

"Mr. Stiffy was being shy. The fucking doctor gave me some medicine to help me piss. Ever since then, it don't get as hard as it used to. She said her old boyfriend had the same problem but he always got a hard-on when he spanked her."

"Did she want you to use your belt?"

"I thought as long as I was doing it, I might as well make it sting."

"It stung, all right. It left marks, too. She's going to have bruises she could show to the cops a week from now."

"If you're so scared of the cops, you might want to pull back on some of your own sex trips."

"What are you talking about?"

"We saw the picture of the little slope in your bedroom. How old is she, about thirteen?"

Reggie had almost gone to Vietnam. In the summer of 1966, when the war was still seen by most Americans as a righteous tropical reprise of World War II, he and three of his buddies had gotten plastered and decided to enlist. They talked about it all night long, big teenagers guzzling Budweiser and bragging about how brave they would be and how many commies they would kill. Early in the morning they went downtown to a recruitment center to sign up. A block from the wide, limestone steps, Reggie, whose idea it was to begin with, ducked into a coffee shop to buy a pack of cigarettes. He told his friends he'd catch up with them. They walked off through the chatter of sunrise sparrows and went to Vietnam. Reggie went back home and slept off his hangover. Each of his friends had a girlfriend. Reggie dated all three and impregnated one while his buddies were overseas. The girls covered for him, and when his buddies came back, dazed by the sparklers and cherry bombs of war and addicted to heroin, Reggie joined up with them again, cruising drive-in restaurants and country lanes in a borrowed army field jacket, affecting the speech of the veterans. Vietnamese civilians were "slopes" or "gooks." Anyplace outside his mother's house was "the field." The enemy he began to imagine he had fought was "Charley."

"Did you search my room?"

"Cherry was looking for a condom in your dresser drawer. It looks like you were playing rough with your little friend, too."

"Fuck you, Reggie."

"Hey—it's no skin off my nose. What did I tell you years ago? If they are old enough to bleed, they're old enough to breed. That's the way they do it overseas. As soon as they are old enough to drop a litter, some old guy pops a dick in them. If you had to smack her around a little bit to get it, that's your business."

"I don't fuck children, Reggie. And I don't beat up women. I've never seen that girl before. I don't even know who she is."

"What's with the picture, then? You look at it when you beat your meat?"

"Yeah, that's it."

"Where did it come from?"

"It's part of something that's going on. I can't talk about it."

"What kind of something?"

"You still understand English, or is your brain completely fried?"

"Yeah, I understand English." He shuffled out into the kitchen with his bootlaces squirming after him like skinny snakes and stuffed the bag of beer cans in the trash. When he came back into the living room he flopped down on the couch, looking old and absurd. "I guess you don't trust me anymore."

"The shit you pulled today makes it tough."

"All I was trying to do was get a little leg, Robby. I didn't know she was going to start screaming."

"It was reckless, Reggie. That girl wakes up in a bad mood tomorrow, she could claim you raped her. She's got the bruises. Witnesses heard her screaming. We both know how the cops would feel about an out-of-town biker leaving skid marks on a local girl. You'd be in shit up to your eyebrows. I'd probably get kicked out of my apartment. Even if Mrs. Pilly let me stay, the cops would know my name and face. They'd be watching me, watching this house. I can't have that."

Reggie leaned forward with his elbows on his fat white knees and massaged his forehead with a big hand. "You're right, man." He looked up at me with bloodshot eyes. "I fucked up, same as I always do. I shoulda had more respect for your crib." I couldn't tell if he was acting or not. "I mean it, Robby. I'm sorry." He put more feeling in his voice. "It won't happen again. Cross my heart and hope to die." He made the Sunday school sign over the left side of his chest. "I'm tired of fucking up. That's the reason I split from St. Louis and came out here to find you. I wanna get my shit together and make something outta myself. Why don't you let me help you with what you're doing? You know I know my shit."

"I already have a partner, Reggie."

"Where is he?" He looked around the room. "I don't see him."

"He's out of town for a few days."

"Just let me help you till he comes back. Try me on one job and see how I do. I'll do whatever you tell me. Just give me a try." He could see I was thinking about it and bored in harder. "Even after your partner comes back, I'd come in handy. I could be your enforcer. Anybody gets in the way, I'll take care of them. Remember those phone calls I used to make?"

Years before, Reggie had built up a side business making threatening phone calls. If the uncle or older brother of a pregnant girl was after you, Reggie would call the guy up and warn him off for a slight fee. Likewise, if someone owed you money and claimed he absolutely couldn't pay, didn't have it, couldn't get it, Reggie would give him a call and, miraculously, he would come up with the cash. He might be hitchhiking afterward or listening to the radio instead of watching TV, but he paid up. When the owner of the liquor store in our neighborhood heard about Reggie's ability to project menace through thin copper wires, she hired him to collect on bad checks. He'd call the offending party and say something like, "You don't know me, but I know you. If you don't come down to Connie's and pick up that check this afternoon, I'm going to blow your brains out." Then he'd hang up. There was something in the sound of his growly, gravelly voice that scared people to their marrow. Within a few hours they would be at the liquor store with the cash, looking over their shoulder as they got out of their car.

"The phone calls were good," I admitted. "But we don't do business that way."

"You mean you never run across anybody scary?" He was intuitive for a biker. "Look at this." He hopped up and went over to his trash bags. Rummaging, he came up with a pistol. It was a little Junior Colt .25-caliber automatic that most Southern California criminals would consider too low-powered for their kid sisters to carry. It was almost invisible when Reggie wrapped his hand around it, the muzzle just peeking over his index finger.

"Anybody fucks with you—*ka-pow!*" He pointed it at an imaginary opponent and feigned a recoil.

"The only way you're going to kill anybody around here with that is if they die laughing."

"You might be surprised," he said in his menacing voice, moving closer to me, displaying the gun flat in his palm. I noticed some V-shaped marks cut into the plastic handle. "I got it loaded with hollow points. It works good at close range." I remembered rumors about him that had floated around in St. Louis and the fear his name inspired in certain quarters.

"I don't need anybody killed, Reggie. We try to keep the mayhem to a minimum. Brains instead of brawn, you know?"

"You always had a lot of brains, Robby. But you never know when you're gonna need some backup."

"What I need right now is someone who knows alarms."

"Alarms?" His eyes got big.

"Yeah, residential burglary alarms."

He walked over to the trash bags and put his gun away, came back and sat down on the couch. "You're looking at it," he said.

"You know alarms?"

"Yep."

"Since when?"

"Remember Fred?"

"From where?"

"He rented a room at the house the winter Fagey died."

"That tall, goofy guy with the thick glasses?"

"Yeah. He worked for an alarm company."

"You got him with you?"

"No, I don't got him with me, but he showed me everything about that shit. He wasn't supposed to talk about it, but I got him drunk a couple times and pumped him dry. He showed me how to install them, how to disconnect them, how to bypass them."

"How come I never heard about this before?"

"You didn't come around much when he was staying with us. That was back when you quit drinking the first time." He squinted at me. "You didn't have time for us north-side lowlifes."

"That was a long time ago. Alarms have changed since then."

"I can handle it."

I thought about McFadden and his pet ape getting the jump on me in a dark room. I thought about Reggie chasing Mrs. Pilly down the street in his red underwear, big belly flopping. I thought about the first restaurant we robbed together, the motorcycle and new clothes I bought with the money, the good times we had riding, taking suburban biker chicks for long cruises in the country. The vibration of a motorcycle between their legs was all the foreplay they ever needed.

"I might have something you can help me with."

# CHAPTER SEVENTEEN

I told Reggie I was planning to rob a house where there might be a large quantity of cash. We wouldn't be partners. It would be a one-time deal and he would be working for me. I'd pay him five hundred dollars or a third of the take, whichever was more. I wasn't sure how much cash there would be. There might not be any. I didn't tell him about the restaurant or the girl.

"You're the boss," he said. "Just tell me what to do."

"Do you think you can sober up by midnight?"

"If there's cash on the cooker, I'll be sober as a judge."

"Good, because I don't want to end up in front of one."

"I haven't done time so far," Reggie said, emphasizing the first word in the sentence.

After he got dressed, we drove down to a Mexican restaurant on the Coast Highway. While we ate, we put together a list of the tools and supplies he would need to bypass the alarm. The waitress was a big, masculine lady stealthily approaching retirement age on rubber-soled shoes, so there weren't any distractions. I paid. It was eight-thirty by the time we got back. The heavy food on top of the two gallons of Budweiser had made Reggie drowsy.

"Get some sleep," I told him. "I'll wake you up in a couple hours."

When I went into the bedroom a little while later to get a map of Newport Beach, he was sprawled on his back on the bed in his red boxers, snoring like Jack's giant with a head cold. His little gun was on the nightstand.

I wasn't sleepy. Precrime excitement made me as alert as if I had dropped a fat cap of Dexedrine. I studied the map, decided where to park the Cadillac and where to watch the house from. Doing the job on short notice, I didn't know the cops' patrol schedule. Newport police rolled onto most residential streets every two hours or so. If they cruised by at 10 P.M., they would be back around midnight for another routine drive-by, simultaneously protecting the taxpayers from criminals and suppressing their own tendencies toward crime. I planned to watch McFadden's house until the cops came and went, and then rob it in the interval before the next patrol. If we took our position at midnight, the latest we would be going in was a little after 2 A.M. The ferry to the peninsula is open all night during the summer and there is a fair amount of traffic on and off the island, so we wouldn't be conspicuous.

Bypassing the local hardware store where my face was familiar, I drove out to the Home Depot at Tustin Marketplace and bought the stuff we needed. Besides electrical supplies, I picked up two fresh pairs of cotton gloves and a small flashlight with a sheath extending past the lens to keep the beam tight. On a dark side street nearby, I stole the license plates off a Taurus and screwed them onto the Cadillac on top of my own. Back home I took another look at the map, and then went for a stroll around the neighborhood.

The air was marbled with the perfume of flowers foliating in the darkness. Scattered campfires sparkled on the beach below the cliffs, families or groups of kids trying to find their way into the magic of the natural world through flame and waves. The smell of cedar smoke drifting up reminded me of camping out in the summertime in the woods along the Missouri River. The rich aroma of burning wood made the darkness intimate and familiar. At the same time, the night was filled with the exotic feeling that California still evoked for me, surf shushing beyond the campfires, palm trees thrusting their composers' haircuts up into the starry sky, swaying with the symphony of the wind. I could sense the islands of Polynesia drifting far out in the mysterious ocean, emblems of the one thing everyone is always seeking as they slave in sealed office towers or drink cough syrup in alleys.

It was past eleven when I got back to the house. I made a pot of coffee and roused Reggie. Dragging him back into consciousness was like hoisting an engine block out of a well with a rope and pulley. The first few pokes and shakes had no effect. When I shook him harder and shouted in his ear, he came to a little bit but waved me off as if I were his mother trying to get him up to go to a school he hated that hated him. I kept shaking him.

"Yawright. Um up, man," he said, trying to focus his eyes on me. He was snoring again by the time I got to the door. Round two went better. I gave his beard a hard jerk and he came up swinging. I backpedalled, laughing at him, and before he knew it he was standing in the middle of the room, wide awake.

"Get dressed, Sleeping Beauty," I said. "We got work to do."

"That hurt," he said, rubbing his jaw.

"Sorry." I handed him his pants and shirt. "Get dressed in the living room. I have to change my clothes."

"I was gettin' up," he grumbled as he went out of the room.

I locked the door, changed into dark-colored clothes, got my .38 and a hundred dollars out of the stash. I put both guns, a pair of Celestron Regal binoculars and the stuff from the hardware store in a black leather briefcase.

The map was still spread out on the kitchen table. I showed Reggie the layout while we drank our coffee—where the house was, our route in and out, where we would be watching from. Walking out the door, it crossed my mind how much nicer my apartment was than an eight-by-ten steel box with no exit. I hoped I'd be sleeping in my own bed when the sun rose over the San Gabriel Mountains and lit up another seaside day. We went down the stairs quietly. Mrs. Pilly's apartment was dark.

McFadden's house was less than a mile from my apartment. The shoreline across from his compound is a flat shelf wide enough for Bayside Drive and a single line of waterfront buildings. The shelf dies into the bluff that defines the bay, rising as it curves toward the Corona del Mar promontory.

I parked the Caddie on Dolphin Terrace, a quiet subdivision street that runs along the edge of the bluff. The view side of the road was solid with expensive homes except for one lot where a foundation was being put in for a new house. I'd noticed piles of concrete forms and a small bulldozer from below earlier in the day. We strolled nonchalantly across the dark lot to the drop-off, putting a pile of dirt between us and the street. A crumbly path led down to a ledge.

During the daytime, anyone cruising the channel would have been able to look up and see us on the ledge. At night, in dark clothes, in the shadow of the overhang, we were invisible. We moved some empties out of the way and sat down with our backs against the flaky half-dirt, half-rock substance of the cliff. Fifty or sixty feet below us, one hundred and fifty yards across the lower road and the dark channel, the lights of McFadden's dock shimmered on the water. Looking through the binoculars, I examined the front side of his house from top to bottom. The glasses were powerful, pulled in details like window latches and alarm contacts. The drapes were still wide open. I studied the bright interior. The furniture was antique. An oil painting on the wall looked old and valuable. I wasn't planning on stealing the furnishings, but the evidence of wealth was exciting. On the sidewalk in front, I saw the Coke can I had flattened six hours earlier, kicked around the corner by a bored kid.

"He hasn't come home," I said.

"Bingo."

"Take a look." I handed Reggie the binoculars. "The house at the point, to the left of the canal."

"Whoa—these are nice," Reggie said, hefting the binoculars in his hand. "What they set you back?"

"Four fifty."

"They're worth it."

The bridge that led onto the island was one hundred yards to the right of the house, separated from it by the Grand Canal. Occasional cars crossed in both directions. Over McFadden's roof, I saw one end of the smaller bridge that connected the two sections of the rich archipelago. Beyond the glimmering expanse of the nighttime island, the cupola of the old pavilion on the peninsula was outlined with twinkling lights. We were in a perfect position. The only thing we couldn't see was the street behind the house that the garage opened onto.

"How long we gotta sit here?" Reggie asked after a while.

"Till the cops come and go, like I told you."

He yawned. "What time did you say they were coming?"

He was fucking with me because he was bored.

"What did I tell you?"

He looked through the binoculars again. "Where we gonna park?"

"On the street behind the house, a block back toward that little bridge."

"Couldn't you pick a house that isn't on an island?" he said.

"I didn't pick it at random, Reggie."

"Why did you pick it?"

"What did I tell you?"

"Might be a wad of cash."

"So why you asking?"

"Just wondering if there's any other reason."

"Like what?"

"Is this the deal that little puss is part of?"

Regardless of what his teachers had thought of him during the eight years between kindergarten and the day he walked out of school for the last time after laying the principal out with a sucker punch in the main hallway of Kirby Junior High School, Reggie wasn't stupid.

"She might be," I said.

"Is she in there?"

"Not as far as I know."

"But she might be?"

"It's possible."

"What if she is?"

"We take her, too."

Reggie whistled by way of exclamation. "Kidnapping?"

"No. We'd only take her if she wanted to go."

"Who is she, some rich guy's daughter?"

"This isn't television," I said.

"Well, who is she?"

I shook my head.

"It's a fucked-up place to make a getaway from," Reggie grumbled. "The cops could cut us off."

"That's why we're waiting until they come and go."

"If someone calls 'em, they'll come back."

"You having second thoughts?"

He treated me to several seconds of a deadpan stare. "Fuck those coppers."

"By the time the cops show up, we'll already be spending the money."

"Heh-heh."

A few minutes after one, twenty-four hours after Switch and I went through the back door of McFadden's restaurant, a Newport Beach patrol car drove across the bridge onto the island.

# CHAPTER EIGHTEEN

"When he comes off, we go on," I said. Two minutes later, the black-and-white crossed the second bridge onto McFadden's section of the island. Another ten minutes, at a quarter after one, he crossed back to the main section.

"Let's go, bro," Reggie said.

"No, we'll wait until he finishes patrolling the other side."

"Oh, yeah!" Reggie said a little while later. He was looking through the binoculars at a house four or five doors to the left of McFadden's. "That's it, sweetheart!"

"What is it?"

"Girl show."

"Let's see."

"Hold on a second. Heh-heh." After a period of time noticeably longer than a second, he handed me the glasses. Looking toward a yellow second-story window, I saw a young woman wearing a pair of white bikini panties and a white bra standing in front of a mirror with her back to the window. While I watched she twisted her hands behind her back and unhooked the bra. Turning sideways, she looked at the reflection of her profile.

"Nice," I said.

"My turn," Reggie said, tugging at the glasses. I let him take them. "There go the panties. Christ almighty! That's table pussy, Robby."

Past the house, I noticed the lights of a boat entering the channel between the island and the mainland. It was a quarter of a mile away to our left, coming toward us at the regulation five-mile-an-hour speed limit, the sound of its throttled-down diesel engines gradually getting louder.

"Let me see the binoculars."

"Wait your turn—shit! She turned out the light." He handed me the glasses. "I'd like to play Little Jack Horny with that."

It was a trawler-style yacht, a nice one. As it approached McFadden's dock, the sound of its engines changed, became throatier.

"Damn," I said. The yacht jockeyed lazily in the water and bumped into the boat slip.

"Who the fuck is that?" Reggie said. Through the glasses, I saw a young Korean in blue jeans and a white T-shirt making the boat fast to the dock. The Frankenstein I'd seen at McDonald's that morning came out the cabin door, elegant in gray flannel slacks and a white shirt. He had a highball glass in his hand, and his face, which the binoculars pulled in close and personal, had the glazed intensity of a heavy drinker tanked right up to the limit of his enlarged capacity, just a glug-glug away from slurred-word, cracked-head oblivion.

"It's the homeowner," I said.

"What now?"

"Looks like a no-go for tonight."

"I'll be goddamned. You gonna give me something for my time?"

"Yeah, I'll give you twenty bucks."

"Twenty bucks! For coming out here in the middle of the fucking night and hanging off the side of a cliff?"

"I'll pay you for your time, Reggie. Now shut the fuck up. I want to see what's going on here."

Standing at the stern railing, McFadden drained his heavy glass and slung it high into the air. It landed with a soundless splash in the dark water, sinking down among the other strange relics on the channel floor.

He lost his balance with the force of the throw, spun halfway around and caught himself on the railing. Laughing, he got his feet back under him and swaggered to the cabin door. His big loose grin made him look even more like a monster—a happy monster about to gobble someone up.

An older guy wearing uniform whites and a white captain's hat came out of the cabin. He was short and wide and well-groomed, with a close-cropped white beard covering the lower half of his face like shorn sheep's wool. They talked briefly. It looked like the captain asked McFadden a question that he answered in some detail. When he finished, the captain nodded and waved the deckhand over. They went back down into the cabin while McFadden looked around, up and down the shoreline. The neighboring houses were all dark. A few minutes later, the Korean came back out with a girl. She was barefoot, wearing a white T-shirt with NEW-PORT BEACH printed in bold black letters over her flat chest. The shirt hung down just below her crotch. The busboy came out of the cabin behind the girl, little ears sticking straight out, carrying a black plastic trash bag. He was still wearing the khakis and red shirt. McFadden slapped something into his hand, and he and the deckhand took the girl up onto the dock.

There was a slight swell in the channel and the boat was moving up and down. The busboy stepped onto the dock first, holding the girl's right hand, pulling her up from the boat. The sailor held her other hand, steadying her. As she stepped across, her arms stretched wide and the T-shirt rose up, revealing the bare skin beneath. She was turned three-quarters of the way toward me and I saw her face clearly for a moment before the blue-black curtain of her hair covered it again. It was the girl in the photograph.

Seeing her like that, with both arms stretched out and her cunt exposed in the glare of the dock lights, I remembered the content of my bad dream. I was a combatant in a tropical war scene, swooping down over a column of civilians in a living helicopter, pouring fire out of whiskey bottles onto the heads of the fleeing people. And then I was on the ground, kneeling with my arms spread to receive and protect a child running toward me. It was the girl in the news photograph that branded the world's retina in the midsixties, the little Vietnamese girl running down a palm-lined road away from a napalm attack with her clothes burned off and her arms stretched out like a miniature Christ. In the dream, her flesh had burned me like hot iron when she ran into my arms.

The girl being dragged, half-naked, up the gangway was older than the girl in the news photo, but she looked just as miserable. Up until that moment, I hadn't been sure what I would do if she turned up. It had seemed like a long shot. The picture could have been old. It could have been mere pornography. It could have been a lot of things. But my original idea had been right. McFadden had bought the girl from one of the gangs of sex smugglers that operate along the California coast. The number on the back of the photograph—62195, which I'd thought was an address or a zip code—was the previous day's date without the slashes. He'd been able to come up with another twenty grand. That could mean he had shoe boxes full of cash lying around, or it could mean he'd be strapped after paying for his illicit pleasure twice. I didn't much care.

After my wife left me the last time, her boyfriend molested my daughter when she was about the same age the Vietnamese girl was when the display picture was taken of her in some godforsaken refugee camp or whorehouse in Southeast Asia. He saved his life by skipping town before I found out about it. When I confronted her, my wife split, too, taking Sheila with her. There in the darkness on the bluff top, the anger and pain I felt at that time surged back to the surface and focused on McFadden. The sense of guilt came back, too. I knew this girl wasn't my daughter but it felt almost as if she were, and I decided to save her from the monster.

"What's happening?" Reggie asked in a stage whisper.

"They brought the girl in on the boat."

"Playtime."

"It's going to be a different game than they think."

The captain came back out on deck. McFadden took his hand and pumped it while the white-haired man looked off to one side. When McFadden slapped him on the back, anger flashed across the captain's face but the restaurant owner was too drunk on alcohol and anticipation to notice.

McFadden managed to get onto the dock without falling into the water and started up the ramp. The captain watched him until he disappeared into the house where the girl was captive, then shook his head and went back down into the cabin.

"Let me see the glasses," Reggie said. "Guy's got a nice boat." His love of machinery was emerging.

"It's a Sabreline 52," I said. "Half a million dollars' worth."

"How fast?"

"Twenty-five knots, something like that."

"What's that in English?"

"Thirty miles an hour."

"That all?"

"That's fast for a luxury boat that size. It's got twin Cat diesels — 320s, I think. Good range, too. They could go to San Francisco on one tank of gas."

Reggie looked over at me. "When did you find out every fucking thing about boats?" he said.

I shrugged.

"Sabreline 52, twin Cat 320s," Reggie muttered, still looking through the glasses.

I was trying to figure how we could take four guys without getting killed when the deckhand came back out of the house. He hurried down the dock to the boat and untied the two mooring lines. The yacht was already backing out of the slip when he jumped onto the deck with the second rope in his hand. After a quick look up and down the shoreline, he disappeared into the cabin. The boat cruised back down the channel past the coast guard station and disappeared into the light-flecked darkness of the bay. The odds were in our favor now. Two of them and three of us — Reggie, Robby and surprise.

"The job's back on," I said. "But it's going to be a stickup instead of a burglary."

"How many are there?"

"Just two and one's drunk on his ass."

"What's the plan?"

"Wait till the cop leaves the island, kick the door down and shout 'police' — take them by surprise."

"Seems kinda risky, don't it?"

"Don't worry about it."

"Don't worry about it?"

"Yeah. Don't worry about it."

"I'm worrying about it. What if they start shooting?"

"I don't think they will."

"He doesn't think they will." Reggie turned his head the other way and spoke to an implied companion, looked back at me. "Why not?"

"They know they're wrong, so it'll make sense to them when we shout 'police.' They'll buy it long enough for us to get the drop on them."

"How come they don't shoot the police?"

"They're not on that level. I don't know exactly what they could be charged with for the girl, but it would be some kind of vice rap they could plea bargain their way out of. McFadden has money. He owns businesses. No way he'd shoot a cop in his own house. He'd have no chance of getting away with it. He'd never even get off the island."

"If you say so," Reggie said.

Fifteen minutes later, the cop car drove back across the main bridge at patrol speed, leaving the island unguarded. We climbed back up to the construction site. I handed Reggie my keys as we approached the Cadillac.

"You drive," I said.

Following my directions, he piloted the car down to the intersection of Jamboree and Bayside, where we stopped at a red light. To our right, Jamboree curved up the bluff to the Coast Highway; to our left, it led immediately over the bridge onto the island.

"Driving this thing is like getting a hand job from a high school girl," Reggie said, smoothing his hand over the leather dashboard. He got a laugh.

"I never thought of it exactly like that."

Somewhere nearby, a block or two away, a siren woke up screaming and rushed toward us. Reggie looked in the rearview mirror, craned his head right and left. I couldn't tell which direction the sound was coming from until I saw the flashing lights coming down the hill to my right. The police car that had just left the island whipped through the intersection in front of us onto the bridge, spewing sparks as it bounced over the top of the arch. Reggie looked at me, inquiring.

"He must have forgotten his doughnuts," I said.

"Heh-heh."

"Let's see what's going on."

## CHAPTER NINETEEN

**The light turned green** and we made a left, following the cop onto the island. Two blocks down the neon-bright restaurant-and-shop-lined street, the patrol car had stopped with its jewels still sparkling, blocking the road. Beyond it, a white Mercedes 420 SEL sat at an angle in the middle of the intersection, rear bumper canted toward the bridge. A few people clustered on the sidewalk. Others hurried toward the scene. Behind us, on the mainland, more sirens joined the hunt.

"Pull over," I said. Reggie eased into a metered slot behind a silver Infiniti sedan.

"What now?" he said.

"Let's sit tight for a minute. Maybe it's something they can take care of quickly."

Behind us, the sirens expanded rapidly, filling up the space between the stars and the pavement with their piercing wail. In the rearview mirror, I saw an ambulance come over the bridge, blue lights blazing. A fire engine chased it onto the island, screaming and flashing, another wild thing descending out of the darkness to gather snarling around a wounded victim. Both vehicles cut their sirens as they squeezed in close to the intersection.

"Doesn't look like a quickie," Reggie said. The firemen and paramedics burst out of their vehicles and charged the Mercedes. I couldn't see what they were doing in front of it. There was a lot of running back and forth. Then the scene settled down.

"I'll take a look," I told Reggie.

A man who looked like an executive vice president or a successful stockbroker was sitting on a bench by the intersection with his head in his hands. A slinky black babe in Versace jeans and a yellow suede jacket that probably cost a thousand dollars was sitting next to him, patting him on the back absentmindedly and looking around with an alert expression on her erotic face. The cop was talking to one of the paramedics, a barrel-chested black guy with an aggressive manner who nodded his head steadily while the cop talked, as if he had heard it all, heard everything that could possibly be said at an accident scene, many times before. The other paramedic, a middle-aged white woman, was kneeling in front of the Mercedes. One of the firemen was kneeling beside her, hooking a tube with a mask at the end of it to an oxygen tank. The other fireman was standing on the running board of their powerful truck, talking on the radio.

The car had run over some kind of cart or scooter. The smaller vehicle was wedged under, and tangled up with, the front of the car. The person who had been driving the cart was part of the tangle. One skinned stick of a leg stuck out of the wreck. The rest of the body was caught beneath the Mercedes. There was a swath of scraped concrete glistening with blood in front of the car where the driver had backed up, trying to extricate himself from the horror. I heard the lady paramedic talking softly to the person under the Mercedes.

"Try to stay calm, sir. We'll get you out as quick as we can."

Going closer, I saw an old man's tormented face through a gap in the wreck. Looking over the lady's shoulder, his eyes focused on me with a look of desperate recognition.

"Jimmy!" he said in a strangled voice.

"Do you know him?" the paramedic asked, looking back at me, trying to cover up something like despair in her voice by speaking in a sharp, official tone.

"No," I said.

"You'll have to step back, then. We need this area to work."

When I saw the old man smashed on the street, blood trickling from his mouth as he spoke to me, the toes on his disembodied foot wiggling like antennas, my spur-of-the-moment plan to charge into McFadden's house with drawn guns suddenly struck me as insane. I felt sick. Something irrevocable might have happened in an instant. They might have been in separate parts of the house, one of them popping out behind us while we cornered the other. Drunk, McFadden might have fired even thinking we were cops. It was crazy.

"Step back, sir!" the black paramedic barked. I sensed the cop looking over, but the eyes of the dying man staring out of his steel cocoon held me with their desperate plea.

"Sir!" The cop's voice was brass knuckles inside a velvet glove, weighty with a controlled threat. "Step back away from the car. You're interfering with an accident scene."

I moved back, feeling the connection between me and the old man stretch like a rubber band and then snap.

"Why don't you give him the oxygen?" the lady paramedic said to the fireman beside her.

"There is something wrong with the valve," he said.

"He needs oxygen!"

"I know what he needs," the fireman said, stopping what he was doing to look at the lady kneeling next to him. "I don't need you to tell me what he needs. If you and your partner had the equipment you're supposed to have, we wouldn't have to use this piece-of-shit thing here."

"Hey—don't be yelling at my partner," the black guy said, turning his back on the cop and walking toward the Mercedes. "It's not our fault if someone on the day shift took our portable tank."

"Whose fault is it that you didn't notice until you needed it?"

"Oh, Jesus, he's hemorrhaging," the lady said. "Where's that rig with the torch?"

"It's on the way," the second fireman said. He was walking around the fire truck, checking the latches on various compartments, making sure all his equipment was secure. The black paramedic squatted by his partner, peering into the wreck.

"You might want to tell them to hurry up," he said. "This guy isn't going to last much longer."

"Screw you," the fireman with the oxygen tank said.

"No, screw you, asshole."

The cop shook his head and turned away. More sirens were approaching.

"Can't we start an IV on this leg?" the lady pleaded with her partner.

"No. The blood flow might be constricted."

I circled around the cop, heading back down the sidewalk toward the Cadillac. He had a notebook out and was questioning the man and woman on the bench.

"What's the nature of your relationship with Mr. O'Connor?"

"We business associates," the black girl said.

"Uh-huh." The cop looked her up and down. "And what business would that be?"

"Why did this happen?" the man said, looking up from the silky gray leather of his tasseled loafers with tears in his eyes. "I never meant to hurt anybody."

"It juss an accident, baby," the black girl said, rubbing his back.

"What was that old guy doing roaming around in the middle of the night with no lights on? There was no time to stop. Those things aren't allowed on public streets, are they?" The man looked up at the cop, hoping for absolution.

The cop shook his head. "Were you distracted by anything while you were driving, sir?"

Another patrol car and the second fire truck passed me as I walked back to the Cadillac. A third cop car flashed by as I got in.

"Let's get the fuck out of here," Reggie said.

# CHAPTER TWENTY

**The next day,** Tuesday, went fast. I pried Reggie loose from the fold-out couch a little before ten. After bacon and eggs, I sent him off on his trike to get a haircut and some new clothes.

"What's wrong with these?"

"Nothing, if you want every cop we see to give you a hard look."

"I ain't wearing a suit."

"You don't have to. Get some khakis and a nice denim shirt."

"Yes, sir." He saluted.

After Reggie left, I called Switch's number and left another message, then drove down to Newport Beach City Hall. I parked on 32nd Street and walked across the landscaped lawn to the building department. The interior of the building was a filled pool of light with more light pouring in through a row of clerestory windows that ran around the top of the two-story space. A contractor with a sheaf of blueprints was leaning on the counter, talking to a clerk while dust motes drifted in the air above him. A good-looking platinum blonde stood up and strolled over from her desk.

"Can I help you?" she said, giving me the friendly smile of an unattached woman in her midthirties.

"I'm thinking about buying a house that's for sale on Balboa Island and I was wondering if I could see the building plans. Are those a matter of public record?"

"They are, but whether we have copies here or not depends on when the house was built. Anything put up after 1950, we should have on microfiche upstairs. Do you know when it was built?"

"In the fifties, I think, but there is an addition that looks like it dates from the eighties. Would you have those plans, too?"

"Sure. They should be attached to the original prints. You have the address?"

"Four-sixty East Bay Front."

"Come on up. I'll see if I can find the sheet for you." She came out from behind the counter and led the way toward an open staircase on the right side of the big room. It went up to a gallery with a metal rail that projected partway over the desk space on the first floor.

"It must be nice to have money," she said as she went up the stairs ahead of me. She had a shapely ass, tightly sheathed in pink cotton pants.

"There are worse things," I said to her butt, which twitched pleasantly in my face.

"Are you new to the area?"

"Yeah. I was just transferred here from our Chicago office." I felt a little bit bad about lying to her, but I kind of enjoyed it, too. I sensed an alternate identity coming on.

"Who do you work for?"

"Merrill Lynch," I said.

"Big money!" She gave me another nice smile. The railed walkway was eye level with the clerestory windows. Looking out into the tops of the palms as we walked, I saw a big green and orange parrot mumbling into his feathers.

"Beautiful, isn't it?" the blonde said.

"I didn't know there were wild parrots around here."

"There aren't. That one must have escaped from its cage. It's been roosting out there for the last couple of months. Guess it got used to being around people."

"I like it," I said. "It makes the place seem more tropical."

"That's us," she laughed. "Exotic Newport Beach, playground of the stars."

In a windowless room off the gallery, she located the microfiche I needed and put it in the machine for me. "Just slide it around to find the address," she said. "Let me know if you need anything else."

She went out of the room with a light step, leaving the pleasant scent of gardenia perfume behind her. It took a few minutes to get the hang of the machine and find the plans I was looking for but it was worth the effort. The prints submitted by the builder of the two-story addition showed Celotex sheathing beneath the vinyl siding, exactly what I'd hoped for. I could break into the house with a sharp utility knife.

Up until the Second World War, frame houses were sheathed with three-quarter-inch boards and sided with another layer of wood. The walls were real, not imaginary, forming a substantial barrier between the silverware and the outside world. In the late fifties, most builders went to fiberboard sheathing. In the seventies and eighties, wood siding went by the wayside, too, replaced in most cases by longer-lasting aluminum and vinyl.

Self-important "security experts" interviewed on local news programs always talk about installing deadbolt locks and latch sheaths to make doors more secure, ignoring the permeability of the walls the doors are set in. The ironic thing is that most residential burglars believe in the illusion of walls, too. Walls look solid and substantial. Windows and doors look like easy access points. Commercial burglars—safecrackers, or people looking to heist jewels, drugs or computer components—don't think twice about going through walls, roofs or floors. It's part of their stock in trade. But 99 percent of the house robbers out there will spend half an hour fighting a reinforced door without ever thinking about the fact that the wall is made of fiber and plastic.

I'd fallen into the same trap myself. When I'd cased McFadden's house the first time, I was so preoccupied with the alarm problem and the fact that Switch was gone that I didn't think about going through the walls. It wasn't until the night before, during the long wait on the bluff, that the idea of going to the building department to check on construction details occurred to me. A twenty-foot section of the vinyl-sided back wall of the addition was in the area enclosed by the concrete block wall, which was shown as a double dashed line on the plans. If I made it over that ink barrier into the backyard without being seen, the burglary would be a walk in the park. Cutting through the wall with a razor knife would be quick and quiet, and would bypass the alarm system wired to the doors and windows. I checked the electric and mechanical plans and found a section of the wall with no electrical, plumbing or HVAC runs and put a mental bull's-eye on it. In my mind, I could see myself working quickly and carefully in the dark yard, slicing through another of the flimsy fantasies society depends on to function.

"How does it look?" the blonde asked when I came back downstairs.

"Just about right," I said.

"You going to buy it?"

"I haven't decided for sure."

"I'd love to see it sometime if you do."

Her open invitation stopped me in my tracks. I looked into her blue eyes and saw a warm, honest person. I would have loved to ask her out to lunch, to develop the Merrill Lynch persona and try to unbutton her pink pants, but I couldn't afford to get involved. City workers tend to know one another. She might know some cops. After the robbery, she might hear them talking, recognize the address, remember me. The less she knew about me, the better.

"You'll be at the top of the guest list," I said and walked out.

# CHAPTER TWENTY-ONE

I drove down to the end of the peninsula and took the car ferry over to the island. The blue bay was littered like the floor of a nautically minded child's room with sailboats and buoys. A big sea lion frolicked alongside the ferry as we crossed, swimming on his back with his front flippers spread out as if to embrace the summer morning.

"That'll be a dollar twenty-five." A surfer in his late teens with baggy board shorts and shaggy, shoulder-length hair stood at the window. He had a little tuft of hair in the cleft below his bottom lip and a palm tree tattooed on his forearm. There was no question that "Margaritaville" would blast from his car stereo when he turned the ignition key that evening.

"How are you?" I said, opening the armrest compartment to get five quarters, doing my part for the GDP by putting McFadden's money back into circulation.

"Great. Nice morning." He sounded genuinely content. The ferry cruises were a parody of a cross-Caribbean run, and someone had strapped a change dispenser to his waist, but he was out on the water all day, close to the waves. "What year is the Caddie?" he asked after I handed him the coins.

"It's a ninety."

"Nice one."

"Thanks."

"My old man's got one just like it. Same color and everything. Those are the smoothest-riding cars I've ever been in."

"Maybe you'll inherit it when he gets a new one," I said.

The young man's sunlit face darkened. "No, I won't," he said. "My mom divorced him last year. I never see him anymore. He's got a new family now, some skinny bitch with two kids."

"What are you driving?"

"I got a seventy-eight Eldorado I'm fixing up."

"That could be a classic."

"Yeah. Needs a lot of work, though. Take it easy." He moved on to the car behind me.

I felt a Jimmy Buffet mood stir inside of me as the Cadillac clattered up the wooden ramp off the ferry, a holiday mood rising like an audience standing up to applaud in an auditorium. There is something exciting about the simple fact of being on an island, and it was high summer on Balboa, the ferry lane crowded with vacationers buying souvenirs and taking the smiling photographs that would prove to them, when they were re-fossilized in their North Dakota or Columbus, Ohio, lives, that they had been to California and had a good time there.

It gave me a sense of control over the situation to know the construction details of McFadden's house. I now knew more about the structure than he did, probably. I decided to get fired up on caffeine and get some exercise by walking around the perimeter of the island, ending up with another pass by the house.

My holiday mood took a body blow at the intersection where the accident had happened. There were bloodstains on the pavement. Nobody else seemed to notice. They crossed the street laughing, eating ice cream bars and drinking sodas, not realizing there was a mini-Litchfield beneath their feet, the death place of a man who had known a lot of jokes and partied once, long ago, with Jimmy Cagney.

I downed a large coffee in Starbucks while reading a stained copy of the *Register*. The infusion of caffeine restored my spirits. I put the old man and my own permeability—the tentative way my blood stays inside me— out of my mind and went for a walk, starting along the mainland side and circling the big island at a pulse-raising pace, crossing the toy bridge and continuing around the perimeter of Little Balboa. The morning was all seagulls and diamonds, sharp caws and shattered light glittering around the white hulls of boats. Flags and pennants rippled in a shifting breeze. Metal tackle clattered against aluminum masts. Docks and hulls creaked. The tide was out, exposing the sloped band of sand around the island, and small children in bright-colored swimsuits played on narrow beaches in front of pastel cottages.

McFadden's drapes were shut. The boat slip was empty. After I rounded the point, I cut behind his house and peaked through a window in the garage door. There was a red BMW 720 inside that would be easy to spot coming over the little bridge.

Back at the Cadillac, I rolled all the windows down to let the bay breezes flow around me and drove a mile or so over to the main branch of the Newport Beach Public Library by Fashion Island. Upstairs in the reference section, I took a stack of antique manuals to a quiet corner table. The furniture in McFadden's living room was worth tens of thousands of dollars. He was rich, plain and simple. I put the idea of a rental van in my mind and left it there to rattle around.

Logging onto the Internet at a public computer, I tried to find some kind of database to check on McFadden's career at Princeton. One of the New Jersey papers had a Web page, but no archive. Going low-tech, I called the paper from a pay phone near the entrance and found someone willing to do a manual search of their morgue. It was pretty much what I expected. Accusations of statutory rape, then of intimidating witnesses, then nothing. The news reports stopped abruptly, the silence of dead presidents descending on the town in a ghostly legion. I wondered how he avoided the draft after he got kicked out of school.

## CHAPTER TWENTY-TWO

**Walking from the Cadillac,** I saw someone drinking iced tea with Mrs. Pilly on the front porch. He was sitting next to her on the porch swing, right arm resting on the back of the seat behind her shoulders. At first I thought it was the assistant pastor of her church, an old-lady charmer who came around every month or so to get warm and fuzzy. It wasn't until I started up the steps that I saw it was Reggie, clipped and cleaned and dressed in the nicest clothes I'd ever seen him wearing.

"What's happening?" he said casually. His beard was cut short and had a sharp edge. His hair, half the length it had been, was pulled back in a neat ponytail.

"What the hell happened to you?" Amazed by the physical transformation, I was even more surprised by his cozy posture with my landlady.

"Followin' orders."

"He looks a little different, doesn't he?" Mrs. Pilly said, smiling at my surprise.

"Didn't recognize him," I said, shaking my head. "You look sharp, Reggie!"

He gave me a half-inch bow with his barbered head.

"Would you care for a glass of tea, Mr. Rivers?"

"Sure."

After Mrs. Pilly went inside, I scooted one of the heavy redwood chairs that flanked the swing around to face Reggie and sat down. The thick cushions on the seat and ladder back of the chair sighed as I sank into them.

"How did you get on her good side?" I asked.

He moved his mouth a few millimeters in the direction of a smile and gave his head an almost imperceptible shake, indicating both the subtlety of his technique and the impossibility of communicating it to me.

Mrs. Pilly came back out with a glass in one hand and a pitcher in the other, elbowing the wooden screen door out of her way. I got up to hold the door back.

"Thank you, Mr. Rivers." The pitcher and tall glasses were heavy crystal decorated with a lemon slice design, the kind of set a person might receive as an anniversary present. Mrs. Pilly handed me the full glass and set the pitcher on the end table.

"Mr. England was just explaining to me about the trouble yesterday," she said after getting comfortable on the swing.

"Oh really?" I gave her my full attention.

"Yes. Apparently that young woman has a drinking problem and Mr. England was trying to stop her from overindulging. That's what caused the ruckus. She had her mind made up to keep on a-drinking and Mr. England was trying to restrain her. I know what that can be like. My oldest brother drank and my mother and he had terrible fights when she tried to take his bottle away."

"It can be rough," I said.

"She's the one who turned the music up so loud and broke the lamp," Mrs. Pilly said. "Because she was intoxicated."

Reggie had allowed his ghost of a smile to grow into a visible smirk. Mrs. Pilly took a demure sip from her tea.

"The only thing I don't understand," she said, "is why she pulled her britches down out on the street." The smirk vanished like a coin out of a magician's hand. My body, which had been lolling on the soft cushions, stiffened. She addressed the comment to me, accompanied by an innocent look. When I didn't answer, she swiveled her head to look at Reggie.

"A bee flew down her pants," I said. "She was trying to get it out."

"That must have been difficult for a bee to do, as tight as those pants were."

"Well—it flew under her shirt and then crawled down, I guess."

"Did it sting her?"

"I believe it did. That's when she—"

"I thought it must have. From what I could see, her backside was as red as this young man's face." Following her glance, I saw that Reggie was blushing. "I knew it didn't get that way all by itself." I kept my mouth shut.

"That's the only problem with all these flowers," Mrs. Pilly continued after a moment, nodding her head in the general direction of the neighborhood, which was lush with jacaranda trees, hibiscus bushes and hollyhocks. "They are lovely to look at but they attract those troublesome bees. There's a little girl lives three houses down who has been stung several times. Her mother had to take her to the emergency last time. She's gotten where she's allergic to the venom. I hope that young woman—what is her name?"

"Cherry." Reggie's mouth opened and closed.

"Yes—I hope Cherry isn't allergic."

"I don't think she is," I said.

"I believe you told me you don't know her."

"That's true, but she didn't say anything about an allergic reaction."

Reggie sat stiff as a cigar store Indian, eyes bugging out slightly, ambushed by Mrs. Pilly's flanking maneuver. She was relaxed and smiling, smoothing her flowered dress over her thighs. I waited to see if she was going to let the matter drop, holding the possibility of its renewal over our heads for the next six months or so, or if she was going to bore in.

"Isn't that Mr. Jackson?" she said. She was looking past me, down the street. Her voice was pleasant as the summer day, her nod affable. I twisted in my seat and saw Switch approaching along the sunlit sidewalk.

"You're back early!" I said, grateful for the distraction.

"Yeah, we won for a change," he said, smiling as he came up the steps. "Melanie talked me into leaving while we were ahead. How are you, Mrs. Pilly?"

"I'm about as well as can be expected, all things considered, Mr. Jackson," she said, signaling Reggie and me that we weren't off the hook. "How is your wife feeling?"

"She's feeling good. No problems so far."

"I'm glad to hear it. I don't suppose you'll be going on many more gambling excursions before the baby is born?"

"No, probably not." I saw by the look on Switch's face that my landlady had cast his weekend in Vegas in a new light in his own mind.

"When are you going to settle down and start a family like your friend here?" Mrs. Pilly asked me, shifting her field of fire. I had glossed over most of my past when I first met her. She didn't know I'd been married in St. Louis.

"I'll take the plunge one of these days," I said. "It would be nice to have a family."

"Don't wait too long. You never know what's going to happen. You don't want to end up alone like me."

"I've got time," I said, wondering if I did.

"It seems like you do, but you never know. I woke up the day Mr. Pilly died thinking we had years ahead of us, but he was gone by evening. It's awful lonely when you're by yourself, Mr. Rivers. All the friends in the world don't make up for family." I didn't like the serious tone the conversation was taking. It was reminding me of things I didn't want to think about.

"What about your cousin up in Orange?" I said. "Loretta, isn't it?"

"Her name is Laura."

"You should give her a call and invite her down for a visit."

"I reckon I should," she said. "And maybe I will one of these days. But it's hard to repair the breech when there's been trouble in the family."

"What kind of trouble?" I said.

"It was that boy, the one she was takin' care of, that caused all the problems," Mrs. Pilly said with a flash of anger that she quickly suppressed. It had sounded like she was about to launch into the recitation of a long-held grievance, but she shook her head, a negative to us and herself, deciding not to say more. "You boys don't want to hear a bunch of old history about my family. It doesn't much matter about me, anyway. I've had my life. You've still got your life ahead of you, and you don't want to miss out on having a family."

"This guy is the one who is working against the clock," I said, nodding at Reggie. "Maybe you could fix him up with one of the ladies from your church."

"I don't think those ladies would quite know what to do with Mr. England, but I may be able to find someone for him." Mrs. Pilly cast a sweet smile in Reggie's direction. His face got redder. She turned her own slightly pink face toward Switch.

"Can I offer you a glass of tea, Mr. Jackson?"

"Well . . ." He glanced at me doubtfully. He wanted to talk business, not chat with Mrs. Pilly. The hall phone rang during the pause.

"Excuse me," Mrs. Pilly said.

"Let's go upstairs." Switch mouthed the words as she went into the house.

"Hold on a second," I said, listening.

"Well, *hello*, dear. I was just thinking of you!"

"Let's go," I said. I didn't want to rile my landlady by ending the tea party abruptly, but it sounded like she would be on for a while. The musical tone in her voice suggested the start of a substantial conversation.

"We're going upstairs, Mrs. Pilly," I said through the screen door. She waved me on with her free hand, nodding and smiling a smile that knew we were escaping from her but didn't care because it also knew we couldn't go far.

# CHAPTER TWENTY-THREE

**"I've got something** for you," Switch said as we went up the stairs.

"What's that?"

"Your number hit."

"My number?"

"I put your C-note on number thirty-three and it clicked. You won thirty-six hundred dollars." He slapped a rubber-banded wad of cash on the coffee table as he sat down on the couch.

I sat down next to him, grinning. "I don't care what Mrs. Pilly says, you go to Vegas as often as you want to." He was looking at Reggie kicked back in the recliner.

"You remember this guy, don't you?" I said, unfastening the money with delighted fingers.

"He looks familiar," Switch said. "Have we met?"

"Once or twice," Reggie said.

"You remember Daryl England?" I said. "This is his older brother Reggie. They lived by Koch Park in Hazelwood. We used to buy pounds over there."

"You're Reggie England?"

"One and the same."

"You've changed."

"Turning over a new leaf."

"How long you been in California?"

"Just came out."

"On vacation?"

"You could say that."

"What else could I say?"

Reggie shrugged. Switch looked at me.

"Reggie wants to immigrate out here like the rest of us. He's crashing with me until he gets on his feet."

"He's staying here?"

"Yep," Reggie said. "Right here."

"What kind of work are you looking for?" Switch asked after a pause. "You're a motorcycle mechanic, aren't you?"

"I'm out of that now," Reggie said. "I'm going in the family business."

"What business would that be?"

Reggie shrugged again.

"It's nothing definite," I said. "We've been talking about him helping out on some of our jobs."

Switch stared at me.

"We need a third man sometimes," I said. "Like that grocery store in Palm Springs. That was a guaranteed forty grand we passed on because we couldn't find a driver in time. Reggie would come in handy in situations like that."

"Nothing is guaranteed," Switch said.

"It was your contact that came up with the figure."

"Can I talk to you in private?"

"Absolutely," I said. "Excuse us a minute, Reggie."

"No sweat."

Switch followed me into the bedroom and closed the door.

"What the hell is this?" he said.

"What?"

"Is this the same Reggie England who sold me ten pounds of highway department marijuana?"

"That was twenty-five years ago, Switch."

"The same guy who force-fucked your girlfriend the first week you were in the joint?"

"I was gone, man. She was going to fuck somebody. And as far as the force part goes, there were always two sides to the story."

"What about all the other shit—the rip-offs and double crosses? I can think of a hundred people he's screwed over the years. Nobody in their right mind would trust him."

"People change, Switch. You and I are different than we used to be, aren't we?"

"We were never like him."

"You never cheated on a dope deal?"

"I may have cheated a little bit, here and there, but I never out and out ripped anyone off."

"Look, I know what you're saying. But he says he's changed—he wants to change—and he sounds sincere to me. I had him out on a little job last night and he did fine."

"You had him out on a job? Doing what? What kind of job?"

"A burglary over on Balboa Island—but we didn't do it."

"Who were you burglarizing on Balboa? Where did this come from?"

"It was a spur-of-the-moment thing. I tracked down the guy who owns Cow Town." Switch's face contorted.

"You didn't tell England about the restaurant, did you?"

"'Course not. I didn't tell him anything about our business. All he knows is we were going to B and E some rich guy's house."

"This is too much," Switch said, running both hands through his graying hair. "That's like returning to the scene of the crime, Rob. Of all the houses in Orange County, why did you have to hit his?"

"I just told you, we *didn't* hit it. Something came up."

"But why did you want to hit it? And why did you take that basket case with you?"

"I took him because you were off partying in Vegas and I needed help. The house is wired and Reggie knows alarms. So I took him with me. End of story. I decided to hit the house because of all that cash we found at the restaurant. If McFadden had that much money at his business, he may have a wad at his house, too—right?"

"His name's McFadden?"

"Yeah."

"It doesn't make sense. The burglary could connect you—connect us—to the stickup, and you have no way of knowing if this guy has cash at his house."

"I think it is worth a look."

"It's not like you, Rob. You're Mr. Plan Ahead. Why didn't you wait till I got back?"

"The idea just grabbed me. Once I started thinking about it, I got on a roll—you know how it is. I wanted to tap him while he's still off balance. After losing twenty grand, he'll be more careful with his cash, and I want to get at him before he puts new precautions in place. I want to know what's up with the slave trading, too."

Switch stared at me for several seconds. "Are you looking for that girl?"

"That's part of it," I said. He kept looking at me.

"Does this have to do with Sheila?" he asked finally. Another intuitive guy. I was surrounded by them. I shrugged. He shook his head.

"I know that eats at you," he said, "but you can't start playing rescue ranger with every girl in trouble. You are a professional criminal and you have to act like one. Nothing you do for this girl is going to change what happened to your daughter."

"I know that."

"What makes you think she's still around, anyway? If he sold her, she's long gone. Even if he still has her and you take her away from him—what are you going to do with her? Pilly won't let you keep her here."

"He didn't sell her. At least not yet. We saw her at his place last night."

"So you did go there?"

"We were watching the house from across the channel. He brought her in on his boat. She's just a kid, Switch. We get her out of there, there's bound to be people up in Little Saigon who would help her."

"Are you kidding? Those people would turn her out faster than the guy who's got her. And how do you know he's going to treat her bad? Maybe she is like a mail-order bride or something."

"When you see this guy, you'll know what his plans are. He'll fuck that little girl to death."

"I'm not going to see him. I'm not robbing the guy's house, and you shouldn't, either. You're not Robin Hood. It's a tough break for the girl, but we can't—" A sharp rap on the door, followed by Reggie's abrupt entrance, cut off Switch's comment.

"This is our score," Reggie said to Switch. "It's already all planned out. We don't need any help."

"What are you doing, listening at the door?" Switch was furious. He shifted his posture slightly, dropping his center of gravity, and for a second I thought he was going to take a swing. He was three inches taller, and forty pounds heavier. Reggie didn't flinch. His wrinkled face was flecked with scars. It had been hit a lot. He knew a fist wouldn't do any serious damage to it.

"I could hear you in the other room," he said, putting some of the phone call menace in his voice.

"Take it easy," I said to both of them.

"I'm easy," Reggie said.

"Me, too," Switch said. "You want to start pulling jobs with this asshole, more power to you. Just make sure my name stays out of it."

"Why do I gotta be an asshole?" Reggie growled.

"Calm down, Switch," I said. "There's no need for name calling. Let's talk it over."

"There is nothing to talk about. I won't work with him."

"No one says you have to. It was just an idea."

"A bad idea."

"You're the asshole," Reggie said.

Switch looked at me and shook his head. "This is stupid," he said. "Melanie's right. I got a kid on the way. This shit's not worth it anymore."

"Hold on, Switch," I said, but he was already halfway to the front door.

"Don't sweat it, partner," Reggie said. "We don't need that scaredy-cat."

# CHAPTER TWENTY-FOUR

Switch was right, in a way. I couldn't blame him for not wanting to work with, or in the vicinity of, Reggie England. I had the sick feeling that I might have lost a good partner and gained a bad one. But I couldn't see turning my back on Reggie. I'd known him longer than I'd known Switch. At one time, we had been as close as Switch and I were now.

Reggie and I ate an early dinner at CoCo's on the Coast Highway. It was a little after seven when we got back.

"I'm going to take a walk down to the beach," I said as we got out of the Caddie.

"Mind if I tag along?"

"Since when do you like walking for exercise?"

"Since now. It's nice out. I can keep up." He put some giddyap in his limping stride, pulling ahead of me as we went down the sidewalk.

The sunlight flooding the promontory had taken on the pink and gold tones of evening. Coming out from among the houses to the edge of the vastness, we walked along the bluff side of Ocean Boulevard, looking down at the surf combing the curved beach. A few tiny people still walked in pairs along the lacy edge of the waves or lay on towels in the sand, but most of the summer crowd had gone back to motels and Craftsman-style bungalows to dress for dinner. The sea was dark blue. Catalina stood out sharp and clear on the horizon, looking like it was three miles away instead of thirty.

We stopped at the point above the entrance to the harbor to admire the view. Looking northwest, shading my eyes against the low sun, I could see the entire length of the palm-fringed Balboa peninsula: the old wooden pier at Balboa in the middle distance; farther north, the Newport pier with the bulk of its seafood restaurant perched at the end. Farther north still, forty miles away, the humpback of Palos Verdes was plainly visible.

"This place is far-out," Reggie said, and for the first time in my life, I heard a child in his voice. "It's like something out of a movie."

"Yeah."

"I always told people," Reggie said, turning his head slowly, scanning the horizon, "you'd hit the big time someday." He seemed to be under the impression that I had a proprietary interest in the thousand square miles of light-drenched land and water our eyes possessed. And I did, in a way. This place was part of me, the sunsets and soothing repetition of the waves stored in accumulating chemical layers deep in my brain, so deep that the memories would go with me when the chemicals were dispersed and I plunged in spirit form into the ocean that surges around the brief blips of our biological lives.

Boats were draining off the ocean, angling from the north and south toward the funnel of the harbor entrance. A single cruise boat plowed through cold salt water in the opposite direction, taking out a glass-lined gallery of tourists to dine at sea.

"Your buddy looks like he's done some boxing."

"He has."

"Does he still train?"

"Three times a week."

Reggie shrugged. "What's he got against me, anyway?"

I looked at him.

"So I fucked him around a couple of times. That shit's ancient history. How long's he gonna hold a grudge?"

I gave his shrug back to him.

"I'm turning over a new leaf, Robby. I swear I am." He looked at me with a solemn, mournful expression. "I'm even thinking about quitting drinking." I recognized a note of truth in the misery in his voice. He sounded like he was resigning himself to the amputation of his good leg or the loss of his firstborn child. I knew how he felt. "I don't want to die in a junkyard, Robby. I don't want to die under some piece-of-shit car with an engine block on my chest. I want to die out here, underneath these fucking palm trees."

I kept looking at him.

"I want to hit the big time, Robby—like you. I want what you have. I was made for this place—all this pussy and money. You know I know my shit. I can help you out in ways you don't even know. If your buddy can't handle it, fuck him. We don't need him. I'll box anybody needs boxing. You and me can pull jobs all up and down this coast and live like kings without his ass."

"Switch is family, man. We been partners a long time."

"I know, and I ain't saying against him. I'm just saying we don't need him. Whatever he was doing, I'll do. I'll take a lighter cut, too. We can split the shit however you say. Sixty-forty is fine with me."

"I know what he can do and I know I can trust him."

"You can trust me, Robby. Ain't we family, too?"

"Would you have given me the three grand? Or said my number passed?"

"I'd of give it to you, honest."

I couldn't decide what to do. Despite Reggie's touching monologue, I was tempted to tell him to forget it, that we couldn't work together. It would be stupid to lose Switch as a partner for his sake. I could give him some money and help him get a place to stay.

At the same time, I resented Switch for taking such a hard line and putting me in an awkward position. Why couldn't he wait and see how Reggie worked out? I couldn't tell Reggie he was no good without giving him a chance. Even if I did, Switch might quit, anyway. Then where would I be? I didn't want to be out there alone.

I even thought, briefly, about skipping the burglary. Maybe that would calm Switch down. Let him pick a job to try Reggie out on. But then I pictured the girl with that Frankenstein crawling on top of her, lead flesh crushing her into the bedsprings. Something had to be done. It wouldn't be right to shitcan Reggie because Switch didn't like him, but it was just as wrong to split with Switch to help Reggie. The burglary was reckless. There could be a lot of money or valuable information in McFadden's house but I had no way of knowing if there was. I didn't even know if the girl was still there. I might have missed my chance to save her the previous night. What was she to me anyway, really? Just because I felt sorry for her and she reminded me of my daughter didn't make her my responsibility. Yet I knew she was.

"Robby, check out this boat."

I was sitting on one of the benches at the point where the cliff makes a ninety-degree bend and runs inland, forming one side of the entrance to the harbor. Reggie was standing a few feet away, leaning against the woven trunk of a palm tree, looking out over the coppery bay. I saw the boat he was pointing at and jumped up. I went past him to the edge of the cliff and watched the yacht as it came out of the channel between Balboa Island and the mainland. There were two people on the aft deck.

"Give me a quarter," I said. Reggie had come up beside me and he produced a coin, magician-like, in his right hand. There was an observation telescope beside the palm, a brass tube fastened to a swivel on top of a metal stand. I put the quarter in the slot and aimed the scope at the trawler. One of the people on deck was McFadden, dressed in nautical-looking navy blue and white, Manhattan glass in hand. The big diamond on his right hand flashed as he took a swig, and the spear of light penetrated the murk in my mind. I knew what to do.

"Is that the guy?"

"That's him."

"What now?"

"Let's ride."

# CHAPTER TWENTY-FIVE

Based on the cop's one o'clock arrival the night before, there was a window of opportunity between nine and eleven. People would be out and about but that would work to our advantage. We would be less conspicuous. It would take only a second to duck into the passage between the two houses, another couple of seconds to get over the wall. Even if we had to circle around a couple of times to get a clear shot, it wouldn't hurt anything. Reggie looked respectable now. No one would notice us.

It was a quarter after nine when I turned left off Bayside onto the bridge, feeling through the tightness in my chest a flicker of the pleasure I always feel crossing to an island, the sense of adventure and escape. Looking to my left, I saw that McFadden's boat slip was empty. Light flooded out the big picture window.

Traffic was bumper to bumper on Marine, the sidewalks lively with people sporting expensive resort wear. Halfway down the brightly lit gauntlet, McFadden's big red Beemer passed us going the other direction. The busboy was driving, ears sticking straight out like miniature catcher's mitts as he slid by four feet to my left. A second intellectual rode shotgun. His-panic but not Mexican. Panamanian, maybe, dressed like the busboy in a dark sports jacket over an open-collared shirt. Both men's faces were in-tent. Neither of them glanced over. I guessed they were out for a night on the town, preoccupied with planning their smooth lines and tough moves. I wondered if the restaurateur knew the help was cruising for trim in his limo.

"That was McFadden's car and one of his guys," I said. Reggie turned to look at the back of the BMW.

"Coast should be clear," he said.

I was glad to see the busboy leaving the island. It meant the house would almost certainly be empty. We could do what we came to do. At the same time, it gave me a sinking feeling. The house would be empty.

I drove over the canal bridge and parked a block south of McFadden's on Abalone. We cut over to the walkway along the channel, strolled past the bright front of the house, took the sharp left at the point and continued along the side of the compound. The flattened Coke can had been kicked back around the corner and lay at the outer edge of the sidewalk at the base of the seawall.

I carried, strategically stowed in my pockets and belt, a small flashlight, two pairs of brown cotton gloves, a razor knife full of new blades, a minia-ture keyhole saw, a small flat bar and the Smith & Wesson. Reggie, who ac-tually whistled nonchalantly while we walked, had wire, clips and electrical tools, just in case we did have to deal with an alarm at some point. The notched .25 was in his back pocket.

A silver-haired couple were coming toward us along the canal, taking a romantic walk after dinner at one of the restaurants with no fear of being mugged. They were fifty yards away, snuggling as they walked. No one else was in sight. At the back corner of McFadden's garage, we made a casual left into the alley, crossed in front of the double-wide garage door, and, with a quick glance in all directions, disappeared into the gangway be-tween the two houses.

In the soft shelter of the shadows, we stopped to look and listen. I heard traffic crossing the bridge onto the island, classical music playing a few houses down, the reassuring slap and suck of water at the base of the seawall. It was a peaceful island evening. People were busy eating, drinking, worrying, thinking about mortgage payments and the past.

I linked my hands in a stirrup and boosted Reggie so that he could pull himself over the top of the wall. He did some grunting and made a thud when he landed on the other side. There was no one at either end of the passage and I scrambled over the wall after him, following my old mentor into the thrilling new world of the crime.

The concrete-block barrier was designed to protect McFadden's property, but we had reversed its polarity, punching through the hologram net of society's faulty expectations. Once we made the bold move of entering the yard, it protected *us*, gave us opportunity and security. Crouched in the darkness, smelling the scent of grass and earth rising from the scuffed place I had landed, I felt a wave of pure happiness wash over me.

"What now, boss man?" Reggie whispered. I glanced around. There were some sculpted yews growing by the gate in the opposite wall, the one that ran along the canal.

"Put these on," I said softly, handing him a pair of gloves. "Hide in those bushes and watch the back of the house to see if anyone stirs. Thump anybody who comes through the gate."

Light from the brightly lit front rooms filtered out the patio door but the back windows were all dark. I pulled on the other pair of gloves, walked straight to the back wall of the house and then along the wall to the edge of the sliding door, where I stopped and listened. The house was quiet. Stepping in front of the door, I looked in, nose to the glass, hands shielding my face to block out the glare of the ambient light that hovered above the island. There was no one in the breakfast room or kitchen.

I laid my tools out in the grass at the base of the concrete-block foundation. Using the heavy razor blade in the utility knife, I sliced away a three-foot-by-three-foot section of vinyl siding, exposing the blackboard beneath. Locating a stud, I made a plunge cut with the keyhole saw and hacked down to the subfloor with shallow strokes, letting the hidden two-by-four guide the blade, then cut across to the next stud, back up and across again. The fine-toothed blade ate through the soft sheathing with a barely audible panting sound. I popped the black panel out, exposing the cobwebbed hollow between the two-by-fours. Using both hands and leaning in, I scored the back of the drywall along and between the studs twice, and then kicked it out with a hard stomp. I listened to the silence for a few seconds, then looked back at Reggie, peeking gnomelike out of the bushes. He shook his head. I waved him over.

The Alice in Wonderland opening was fourteen and a half inches wide, about two feet high, with its bottom edge eighteen inches off the turf. Reggie bent down and peered into the interior darkness.

"That's slick," he whispered. "I never would have thought of this."

"Being a carpenter comes in handy."

"No shit!"

I wriggled through the hole and flicked on the flashlight, keeping the beam pointed straight down. The brown-carpeted room was furnished with a queen-size bed, a dresser and a nightstand with a lamp on top. It was neat and uncluttered. The dresser drawers were empty and smelled like wood. Reggie's head and shoulders came through the opening, followed, after a few more grunts, by the rest of him.

"You could have made it a little bigger," he complained.

"Let's find you a lookout post," I said. "Stay clear of the picture windows."

"Gotcha."

The bedroom door opened into a short hallway with four other doors, all closed. The doors opened into a linen closet stocked with clean sheets and towels at the end of the hall to our right, two small bedrooms opposite, and a bathroom to the left of the room we came out of. One of the front bedrooms was empty. The other was rank with the zoo smell of the busboy. There was some change and a couple of hard-core porno magazines on the dresser, dirty clothes on the floor. On the stand beside the double bed, a take-out box from a chicken place overflowed with bones and wadded napkins.

Opposite the bathroom door, a staircase led to the second floor, doubling back on itself at a landing halfway up. Beyond the base of the stairs, the hall opened into the breakfast room. The kitchen was beyond the breakfast room. The living room and dining room were visible through a doorway to my right as I peeked out from the hallway. The house was a sleeping world wholly open to our intrusions. We could search and pry and take anything we wanted. Each closed door and drawer hummed with white energy. I sensed that everything of value other than the illuminated antiques and paintings would be on the second floor.

Opposite the top of the stairs, there was another full bath, directly above the first-floor bathroom. The room next to it, which was above the one we entered through, was McFadden's office. The window behind his desk looked out over the roof of the detached garage toward the canal bridge.

"Keep an eye on the bridge while I check the front room. Yell if you see a cop or that red Beemer."

The master bedroom, which took up the space above the two front bedrooms on the first floor, was musty with the atmosphere of old money. Everything from the knickknacks to the Oriental carpet that covered most of a glassy hardwood floor looked valuable in the light of a low-watt lamp that had been left burning. The furniture and oil paintings that crowded the room were older than the island. The bed was huge, with an antique headboard and a luxurious, royal blue bedspread. The Vietnamese girl was tied spread-eagle to the bed.

# CHAPTER TWENTY-SIX

**She lay on her back,** blindfolded and naked except for a pair of boy's briefs, arms and legs stretched wide apart. Her feet were small and delicately shaped but callused, as if she had gone barefoot more often than she had worn shoes. Her legs were slender but strong-looking, sleek muscle beneath smooth skin. The underpants were very tight, showing not just the mound but the slit through the thick cotton. With her arms stretched out above her, her belly and chest were flat and taut. There was a large Band-Aid on her throat.

She raised her head when I came into the room, straining at the clothesline cord that fastened her wrists and ankles.

"It's all right," I said.

When I pulled the black silk blindfold up over her forehead, I saw fear, surprise and something that looked like physical pain in her eyes.

"Do you speak English?"

She shook her head. Her chest was heaving. She didn't know who I was or what I was going to do.

"Easy," I said, trying to soothe her with my tone of voice. "I'm taking you out of here." The first hand I untied shot down to hold her crotch. Likewise with the second hand. When I untied her legs, she rolled over on her side in a fetal position with her front toward me. Her eyes began to plead.

Something hard in my chest turned to water. I thought of my daughter, growing up without me, suffering all the pain and confusion of the world with no father to help her. I had gotten used to the loss of my wife, but when I thought of Sheila a frightening wave of sorrow still surged up in me, a sadness that twisted like panic. I missed her most on Sunday mornings. That was when I had taken her for walks along the river or to play on the playground at Spanish Lake Park. I missed her in early evening, too, at the hour when I used to read to her, doing the classic childhood characters in an alcohol-happy voice. We started with alphabet books and Dr. Seuss and got as far as *Narnia* and *Wind in the Willows*. For the first time, I hated McFadden and considered his death. At the same time I felt a strange stab of sympathy for him. He was broken and this was how he had tried to fix himself, and it was going to destroy him.

Kneeling beside the bed, I stroked the girl's upper arm, feeling the texture and heat of her skin. "Are you hurt?"

She moved her mouth as if she were speaking, lips shaping and forming rapidly, but no sound came out. Her dark eyes became more desperate. She began to make a panting sound, like a woman in passion. I looked around to see if there was anything near the bed they might have shoved up inside her, saw nothing but two empty water bottles. Her stomach moved in and out as she panted.

Taking hold of her shoulders, I pulled her upright. That didn't seem to hurt her, so I helped her to her feet, pulling her toward me. She didn't moan or wince as she got to her feet. There was no blood. Diagnosis would have to wait. "Where are your clothes?" She lifted her childish face, surrounded by a tangle of black hair, and looked into my eyes. The message of the look was plain. She didn't understand what I was saying. She wanted to do whatever I wanted her to do, but she didn't know what it was. When I let go of her shoulders to see if she could stand on her own, the look of pathetic compliance vanished and she sprang to one side quick as a fish turning in the water and darted toward the bedroom door.

Two long steps and I caught her in the doorway, wrapping my arms around her body, lifting her off the floor. She wriggled wildly for a few seconds, intensely alive, amazingly strong, daughter and granddaughter of jungle fighters, delivering sharp kicks to my shins with her heels. When she realized she couldn't get away, she tried a different tack, going limp in my grasp, completely passive, reminding me of Viet Cong fading into bush in the face of superior firepower and of the softness of water wearing down the hardest rock. I spoke to her softly. She panted. When I put her down, I held on to one arm. She stretched her other arm toward the bathroom door across the hall. I led her that way and let her go when she tugged. She shot into the bathroom, pulling her underpants down as she went, and sat on the toilet. Urine gushed into the bowl. She closed her eyes, and her face, which had been a complex mixture of war footage and nursery misery in the dim light, relaxed into an expression of extreme relief.

I guessed at McFadden's nasty game. After doing whatever he had been doing to her since he brought her home, he had forced her to drink the two bottles of water and left her with a growing ache in her bladder, continuing to torture her while he was gone. When he came back and found the bed wet, she would have been punished for soiling the sheets—spanked, whipped, subjected to painful insertions. Somewhere in the midst of the sniffing and beating he would have had his orgasm, mouth contorted to an anuslike O. Then again, a person who went to such extremes to feel sex might not be able to do the actual deed. Either he was stretching to stimulate severely jaded nerves or he was impotent, trying to achieve the impossible. If it was impotence, the girl would have been in deadly danger. Their romantic interlude might have ended with him crying, huge hands wrapped around her slender throat, squeezing it until it was as lifeless as his own penis.

When the girl finished she opened her eyes and looked over at me. They were soft with relief and filled with a frank gratitude and something that looked like curiosity. She was still afraid but she was taking this latest development in stride, waiting to see what would happen next, reaching out to me. She had grown up some since the photograph was taken. Her breasts, while still small, were fuller than in the picture, her face more mature. But when she stood up, pulling the briefs up a little slower than she might have, I saw that her mons was still smooth as a child's.

"Stay there," I said. She gave me a perplexed look. I went over, lowered the toilet lid and sat her down, gesturing with the flat of my hand toward her. "Stay there. Okay?" She nodded.

The bathroom window was too small for her to climb out of. After closing the door, I tied one of the pieces of clothesline she had been bound with around the doorknob and stretched it guitar-string tight across the hall, looping it around the middle hinge of the master bedroom door to make sure she stayed put.

Back in McFadden's office, Reggie was kicked back in the leather chair with his feet on the windowsill. He had found a box of cigars and was puffing on one while he watched the bridge.

"Check out my watch," he said. He held up a thick wrist decorated with the dress watch I'd seen on McFadden's arm at McDonald's. It *was* a Rolex. He probably wore a nautical timepiece when he was on his boat.

"Let me see that," I said.

"Finders keepers," Reggie said without conviction.

"Quit fucking around," I said.

Reggie held out his wrist.

"Take it off so I can look at it in the light."

Reluctantly, with a hurt look on his face, he slid the gold band over his gloved fist and handed me the watch.

"It's a President," I said.

"Huh?"

"It's a Rolex President." I examined the front and back of the case in the beam of the flashlight.

"How much?"

"Eighteen-karat yellow gold, ten or twelve years old, excellent condition." I went down a mental checklist.

"What's she worth?"

"Eight or nine thousand," I said, watching the impact on my partner's face. "That's retail." I took him down a notch. "We can probably get half that much."

"Not bad," Reggie said, caught between disappointment and delight.

"I found something, too," I said, handing him the watch.

"Cash?" He sat up ramrod straight.

"The girl."

"Where is she?"

"In the bathroom."

"Freshening up?"

"Probably. I put her there until we're ready to leave. Anything else in the desk?"

"Gold pen and pencil, address book, some computer shit, a picture album full of nekkid kids. You want me to check on the girl, make sure she ain't trying to get away?"

"No. She can't get out. Keep watching the bridge while I finish searching."

I looked out the front window of McFadden's bedroom to make sure the finger slip was still empty and cracked the window so that I would hear the boat if it approached the dock. Emptying dresser drawers onto the king-size bed, I rooted through the contents quickly, five or ten seconds per drawer, working the way most professional burglars do, making no attempt to conceal the fact that I'd been there. I found a packet of ten hundred-dollar bills with the bank band still on it, left like an afterthought in the bottom of the sock drawer. A jewelry box contained bulky gold cuff links, several gold and platinum rings, an emerald tie pin and a woman's diamond necklace that made my ears ring. I looked at the cut and clarity of the stones in the beam of the flashlight, made a deep scratch in the mirror over the dresser with the largest sparkler. Even at 30 or 40 percent, the necklace was worth a small fortune.

I turned the dresser over, tore the bed apart, looked under the mattress and carpet, took all the pictures off the wall, searched the walk-in closet. McFadden had an extensive wardrobe: a dozen suits worth at least a grand apiece, including the blue corporate costume I'd seen him wearing at McDonald's, cashmere sweaters, beautiful shirts, a camel-hair topcoat. There were shoes and ties and belts galore, all arranged neatly on racks, and a wooden case full of whipping implements—a paddle, a rattan that matched the welts I'd glimpsed on the girl's buttocks, a razor strap and a couple of braided leather things. Another case held a selection of dildos and handcuffs. The only item of women's clothing was an old silk kimono, the same color blue as the bedspread.

A deluxe set of black leather luggage filled one back corner of the closet. The largest suitcase had wheels and an extending handle. I packed my tools, the camel hair, the most expensive suits and sweaters and several small oil paintings of the California coast that looked valuable. The money and jewels went in my pockets. I took the kimono for the girl to wear.

When I went back into the office, Reggie made a face.

"Take lookout," he said. "I gotta go to the bathroom."

"Use the one downstairs."

"I just want to make sure she's okay." I could sense his concern for her.

"She's fine. We need to get done and get out of here. We've been inside fifteen minutes. If you have to piss, do it in one of his desk drawers. He'll like that."

"Heh-heh!" Reggie liked the idea, too. He whipped it out and took a long, loud piss in one of the bottom drawers, puffing on his cigar with a dreamy expression on his face, keeping an eye on the bridge.

The computer was protected by a password and I didn't try to get past it. Instead, I took the tower out into the hall and slammed it on the floor as hard as I could, then took all the disks I could find and tossed them in the suitcase along with his address book and a photo album. I had just found the wall safe, hidden behind some financial reference books in the back of a built-in bookshelf, when I heard a diesel motor out in the channel.

# CHAPTER TWENTY-SEVEN

I was sure there was honey in the safe. Intuition and intelligence flashed the fact in red neon. McFadden was a crook with good cover and a big cash flow. He had a lot to hide. Looking at the square metal front, I was sure I could dig it out of the wall and crack it open with tools I'd find in the house or garage. I'd done some research on safes for other jobs and McFadden's looked like more of a fire safe than a high-security model. He was counting on concealment as much as steel to protect his stash. The lock and door were solid, but a cold chisel and a five-pound sledge would probably punch through the rear panel. Failing that, we could drag it out through the garage and load it in the trunk of the Cadillac.

The only problem was the diesel motor getting louder in the channel. I ran to the front window. McFadden's yacht was almost even with the end of the dock. Two or three minutes of jockeying and throwing lines and the boat would be moored. Another couple of minutes and something big and ugly would be walking in the front door. It wouldn't be alone. If it had been Switch and me with such a complete drop on them, I would have ambushed McFadden, roughed him up and made him open the safe. When I thought of doing it with Reggie, the previous night's vision of a bloodbath flooded back into my mind, the misery and sirens and irrevocable karma. He was an old hand but if he got sloppy or trigger-happy, all hell could break loose on a permanent basis. That left one option.

"Get the girl and put this on her," I told Reggie, tossing him the kimono.

"Shouldn't we hose her down first? If she came from overseas she's probably crawling with bugs."

"We don't have time to give her a bath, Reggie. McFadden's parking his boat out in front right now. We have to get out fast."

Reggie's face went flat. Behind his old, expressionless eyes, mental activity took place. It seemed to me he was deciding if it was time to look out for number one, to take the watch and run, leaving me to deal with the complications. A second passed. He made up his mind. The situation was serious, but we could get out with what we had. He tossed his stogie in the desk drawer, and the mingled scent of cigar smoke and urine thickened in the air.

"How much time?"

"Enough. Five minutes. We'll be out the back before they come inside."

I closed and buckled the suitcase with trembling hands. Casting a last longing look at the safe door, I hurried from the room. A quick peek out the front bedroom window showed the bow of the cruiser just entering the boat slip. Back in the hall, Reggie was hustling the girl toward the stairs.

"Head for the hole in the back," I said.

"I wasn't planning on reading a magazine in the parlor," Reggie snapped over his shoulder. "Where are they?"

"Still on the boat."

"They better stay the fuck on the boat if they know what's good for them. I see them, I'm gonna start blasting."

We pounded down the stairs toward the exit. The getaway was looking good despite McFadden's surprise arrival. Then, halfway down the hall, the girl jerked loose from Reggie's grasp and dodged through the open door of the busboy's bedroom.

He hobbled after her, cussing. I grabbed his shoulder when he was halfway in the room, feeling his bull's strength as I pulled him back.

"Take the suitcase and cover the end of the hallway. I'll get her."

She was jerking open dresser drawers, searching through them frantically when I caught her from behind, wrapping my arms around her and carrying her toward the door. The silk kimono made her slippery and she struggled even harder than she had in McFadden's bedroom, spreading her legs and kicking at the door jamb with both bare feet, hurling us back into the room. Staggering backward, I tripped and fell onto the bed with an armload of wild girl on top of me. There was no way I'd get her out of the house in time if she kept it up, so I let her go.

She leapt back to the dresser, emptied the final drawer and tore into the closet. She found what she wanted as soon as she opened the door. It was the trash bag the busboy had carried up to the house. Clutching the bundle to her chest, she pierced me with a look of gratitude and came along quickly and quietly. A few seconds later, we were crossing the backyard, springy grass beneath our feet, ocean air filling our panting lungs.

I thought about going out through the garage. It would have been quicker and easier than climbing the wall. Also less conspicuous. But I was afraid of the alarm system. If a bell or siren went off on the premises, McFadden might send someone running to the back of the compound, triggering the blood scenario.

So we went over the rough, concrete-block wall, scraping our knees and bellies—Reggie first, then the girl, light and agile as I boosted her, then the suitcase and, finally, me. We made some noise landing in the gangway, grunts and gasps and a thump when the suitcase hit the concrete, but the opposition was still on the boat, too far away to hear. The engines revved up and died while I was straightening the girl's robe. Handel's "Water Music" was still playing nearby, the reassuring sounds of traffic still drifting over from the main bridge. As we filed out of the gangway and crossed the alley, I heard laughter from the dock in front. "They won't be laughing long," I said.

We didn't pass anybody on the brightly lit street. I put the suitcase in the trunk while Reggie and the girl climbed in the backseat. The big V-8 started with the first clean spark of ignition, and we rolled down the block and turned right onto the canal bridge. Everything seemed to be coming up roses. I shot Reggie a grin over my right shoulder.

"Good job, bro!"

"How much you think we cleared?" he said, voice tight with excitement.

"We did okay," I said. "There were some old diamonds in the—." The sudden whine of a siren close at hand cut off my remark.

We were sitting at the stop sign at the end of the small bridge, waiting to turn right onto Marine, the street that would take us off the island. The cop car was between us and the main bridge, crawling in our direction. The light bar was sparkling and the siren rose and fell again but there was no place for people to pull over. Parked cars lined both sides of the street and the drivers facing each other at the intersection weren't sure what to do. No one knew which way the cop wanted to go at the crossroads. It was dark and people had been drinking. There was pedestrian traffic.

The cop burst out of his car. Standing behind the shield of his door, he hit the siren a third time, waving traffic forward with a whiplike motion of his arm and index finger. The drivers in front of him got the idea and drove straight ahead through the intersection, slow and careful as a funeral procession, while the cars on the two side streets, including a 1990 burgundy Cadillac with low miles and no bullet holes in it, waited with idling engines.

"Get down!" Reggie pushed the girl down on the floor at his feet.

It was too early for the eleven o'clock patrol so someone must have called for the police, but it was hard to believe the cop was responding to the burglary. McFadden couldn't very well tell the police we stole his sex slave. Unless someone saw us come over the wall and called. But how could the cop have arrived so quickly? Passing by on Bayside. My heart was racing. There wasn't much room to maneuver. If he went past us onto Little Balboa, we'd be all right, cruise off the island like any other luxury car while he gnawed on his pencil at the crime scene. If he had a description of the car, we were fucked. He could block us in with his cruiser, get out the other side and point his gun. It would be shoot or surrender. Or back up onto the little island. I could spin the car sideways, blocking the other end of the bridge. If we fired some shots over his head and took off on foot, we might be able to hijack McFadden's boat and use it to get away. The harbor patrol would be on us, but if we could cross to Corona Del Mar we might make it back to my place on foot in the darkness before they lit the cliff top with helicopter light.

The cop was two car lengths away. I kept my face calm, squeezing the steering wheel small as a string. The intersection in front of us was the one where the old man was killed the night before. That seemed like a bad omen. I remembered one of Cagney's movies in which his character is cornered and machine-gunned to death by a gang of big-city police. Lights came up in my rearview mirror and I glanced back to see a bulky black SUV nosing my back bumper, cutting off retreat.

The cop was at the intersection. Pausing at the stop sign, he looked left, directly at me. I was reaching for my gun when he swiveled his head the other way and turned right, heading north toward the ferry landing. It wasn't us he was after. There was a heart attack or a fistfight or a fender bender at the other end of the island. The burglary was still private business.

As soon as his taillights were squarely in front of me, before they started to shrink, I turned right onto Marine, jumping in front of a silver Jaguar that started into the intersection from my left at the same time. We'd lost several minutes. I looked in the rearview mirror to see if McFadden was mounting any kind of pursuit. There was no sign of him.

In the backseat, Reggie was making saucer eyes for real.

"That was scary," he said. One hand was in his pocket, holding his gun. The other hand was on top of the girl's head, holding her face down in his lap.

"You can let her breathe now," I said.

"She's fine," he said, patting her black hair. "I don't want her popping up like a jack-in-the-box and scaring the nice people."

"Keep her on the floor, but let her lift her head up," I said.

As we crossed the bridge, I looked to my right and saw McFadden's stocky captain running bowlegged up the dock toward the house followed by two younger guys. We were getting away with it. We had the girl and some thrilling loot. Stuff that would fence for forty or fifty thousand dollars. But I ached for the contents of the safe.

Just in case there was any kind of tail on us, a nosy neighbor or a plainclothes Balboa rent-a-cop, I went straight ahead as we came off the bridge, climbing the hill to the Coast Highway, continuing inland on Jamboree for half a mile. At San Joaquin, I turned right, circling behind Fashion Island, crossing MacArthur and taking Marguerite back down toward the ocean. When I came to the Coast Highway again, I turned left and drove south to Poppy, entering my neighborhood at the point farthest from Balboa Island. Two blocks down, I turned right on Seaview and parked in the shadow of a jacaranda tree, watching the rearview mirror. No one followed us into the little lane.

Reggie looked around, checking out our location. "We gonna fuck her here?" he asked. He sounded disappointed, as if he'd been hoping for bright lights and a big bed.

"We're not fucking her." I felt a pang of dislike for him.

"What?" His voice was sharp and disbelieving. "Why'd we steal her, then?"

"We rescued her. Let her up on the seat, *now.*"

When he removed his restraining paw, the girl scrambled up onto the seat, crowding into the corner farthest from Reggie, watching both of us, shifting her eyes from one criminal face to the other. I hit the button that locked all the doors.

"Why can't we fuck her?" Reggie pleaded.

"She's just a kid."

"How do you know how old she is? Gook chicks look younger than they are. She could be twenty-five fucking years old for all you know."

"It doesn't matter."

"How old are you?" Reggie barked at the girl. She knew he was asking a question, looked to me for guidance.

"She can't speak English," I said.

"What fucking difference does it make how old she is, anyway? You know good and well she's broke in. They turn them out over there when they are about ten."

"We're not over there."

"This is fucking great," he said. "What are you going to do with her if you aren't going to fuck her?"

"I'll think of something."

We'd been sitting in the dark for ten minutes or so and the only car that had passed by was another Cadillac driven by a lady too old and shrunken to be chasing bad guys. I drove back to my end of the neighborhood and parked a block away from my apartment.

"Wait here with the girl," I said. "I'm going to make sure the coast is clear."

"No problem."

The girl grabbed my arm as I started to get out of the car, patting her chest with her other hand, begging with her eyes.

"I'll be right back." I squeezed her hand.

"Leave her alone," I warned Reggie. "I mean it."

# CHAPTER TWENTY-EIGHT

**The house was dark.** That was strange. Mrs. Pilly liked to snooze in her husband's old easy chair in front of the TV for a few hours before going to bed, listening to CNN from the NORAD installation of her subconscious, waking up to watch the loud parts. Ten-thirty was early for her to turn out the lights on a summer night.

Uneasiness sharpened to fear when I got to the top of the outside staircase. Behind the aluminum storm door, the entry door hung slightly ajar. The latch-side jamb was split from top to bottom. Someone had given it a hell of a kick. I had a pretty good idea who. The place was a wreck, furniture knocked over, cushions slit. The kitchen light was on and I could see pots, canned goods, broken dishes and the contents of the refrigerator scattered across the linoleum. A fast professional search makes a mess, but they had gone beyond that, intentionally destroying everything they could in a short period of time.

Just inside the door, I stood still and listened. Nothing but the refrigerator humming full steam ahead, trying to replace the cold air streaming out its open door. They were gone. How had they found my address? I checked the closet and bathroom on my way to the bedroom, holding the .38 with two hands like a TV cop. The medicine cabinet was wrenched from the wall, the shower curtain jerked down. The bedroom was a disaster, dresser drawers smashed and scattered. The girl's picture was gone. The armchair lay on its side in front of the vent. I shoved it aside, saw that the metal cover was still in place.

I was debating whether to leave the stash where it was or take it with me when the phone rang, jangling my nerves. Digging in the rubble, I found the handset lying in the corner by the door.

"Hello?" My voice sounded strange, unreal as the situation. It struck me what a strange word *hello* is.

"Hello? Could I speak to Robert Rivers, please?"

"Who's calling?"

"You don't know me. I mean, we've met, but—it's Don from Cow Town. That's you, isn't it? I recognize your voice."

"I don't know a Don from Cow Town." The world was reeling around me.

"I'm not trying to make trouble for you, Robert, I swear I'm not. You were nice to us and I'm glad you robbed that son of a bitch. I'm calling to warn you. My boss—my ex-boss—knows who you are. He knows where you live, what kind of car you drive, all kinds of stuff. I think he is going to try and kill you."

"Why are you warning me?"

"McFucken fired me. He said I must be in on it because I cooperated with you and I was lucky he didn't kill me and he *would* kill me if I ever told anyone anything. I know more about him than he thinks I do. I could have got him in trouble a long time ago, but I'm not like that. I just tried to do my job and keep my mouth shut. He is a very cruel person. I've always been afraid of him, but I made him money at the restaurant and never breathed a word when he did other things, and we got along okay until that bastard Snuff started working there last month."

"Who is Snuff?"

"That's Tim's nickname—the busboy you threatened. He says he got it in prison for killing a black man. He always makes trouble for everybody, throwing his weight around because he's the boss's nephew. I knew the job was just a beard for his parole officer so he could do other things for his uncle, and I didn't ask him to do very much work. I let him come and go during his shift even though I needed help. But he had to do some work or the other employees would be suspicious. They're always complaining about him—how he doesn't do his share. He started a fight with my best fry cook and tried to get Carla when she was changing her clothes in the restroom. I tried to talk to him but he just laughed at me. He hates me because I'm gay. He says all guys from prison hate *fags*. I put my arm around his shoulder one time, just to be friendly, and he punched me in the stomach so hard I threw up, and when I told his uncle he just laughed. They both hate me because I'm gay but I wouldn't want his ugly body, anyway, with those little stubby legs, but he thinks I'm hot for him and he told his uncle I tried to—"

"Slow down," I said, cutting off his torrent of words. "How does McFadden know who I am?" For whatever reason, I believed him. I remembered how eager he had been to help during the stickup, and it was too creative a scam for the cops.

"He has a surveillance camera no one knows about but him and me, one of those little secret ones, pointed at the cash register and entrance. He uses it to spy on the cashiers. It showed your face when you had your mask off, but he didn't tell the cops—I guess because of whatever it was you took from the safe. He showed the video to Tim to see if he knew you from prison or someplace. He suspected his little nephew, too. Tim was in the kitchen yesterday when you ate lunch. He saw you through the kitchen door and followed you out when you left and got your license number. McFadden knows a policeman who used the number to find your name and address."

"How do you know about their plans?"

"I heard him and Tim talking on the phone. He was waiting for me when I got to the restaurant this morning. He pushed me down and kicked me, pointed a gun at me. He asked me if I wanted to suck the barrel." I could hear the look of distaste on Don's face. "After he got done scaring me, he told me to get my stuff and get out. I've worked for him all these years and he kicked me out just like that. The phone rang while I was packing my stuff and I picked it up out of habit. He picked up the phone in front at the same time and didn't know I was listening. I was scared to death, Robert. I would have hung up if I could, but I knew they would hear me, so I listened to their whole conversation. I'm glad I did. I wouldn't want them to hurt you. As soon as they hung up, I took my things and ran out the back door. I kept looking back as I drove away, but they didn't come after me. They said your name on the phone and I looked you up in the book and tried to call you, but you weren't home and I was afraid to leave a message. I didn't know what to say, you know, in case somebody else played your messages. I didn't want to get you in trouble."

"What did McFadden say on the phone?"

"He told Tim that Sergeant Rojas—that's the policeman—called with your name and address. Tim wanted to know where you lived. He wanted to go after you right then. But McFadden told him to wait until tonight. He told Tim to meet him at his house later and they'd figure out the best way to fuck you up. He said he wanted his stuff back. He didn't care what Tim did with you as long as it was permanent."

"Where did he get the girl?"

"Which girl?"

"Is there more than one?"

"He's been smuggling little Asian girls into the country for years. That policeman helps him. Sometimes he keeps one at his house to use for a while before he does whatever he does with them. Is that what was in the box? Something to do with the girls?"

"How does he smuggle them in?"

"Sometimes they come on container ships, just the regular way. But he has other ways, too, with fake papers. I can tell you all about that. And that isn't all. He does other illegal stuff, too. Lots of stuff."

"How do you know so much?"

"Today wasn't the first time I picked up the phone when he was talking." Don made a sniffing sound. "I have to have some protection if the police ever come after me for anything."

"That's smart, Don. Did he say anything else on the phone?"

"No. But I can tell you other things about him so you can get him. I'll do anything I can to help you get him. I hate him."

"Do you know where the surveillance tape is?"

"I think he took it to his office in San Pedro."

"Can you help me get it?"

"I'll help you if I can," he said, his voice quavering. "But you have to swear you'll never tell him. Swear you'll never tell anyone. No matter what happens. I can't stand to think what he'd do if he found out."

"No one will know you were involved. Why don't we meet somewhere and talk in person?"

"Can I trust you?"

"Completely."

"Do you think he has anyone watching me?"

"I wouldn't think so, no."

"All right. My friend is coming over tonight, but I can meet you tomorrow morning. I want that bastard to get what he's got coming. The only way he'll ever leave us alone is if you get rid of him first. I think I know a way we can get some of his money, too."

"Where do you live?"

"In Santa Ana, but I don't want to meet you here."

"You know where Hof's Hut is in Belmont Shores?"

"Yes."

"Why don't you meet me there at nine tomorrow morning? We'll have breakfast and talk things over."

"I'll be there, Robert. I'm glad you're okay."

"Thanks, Don."

"Be careful."

"You, too."

I left everything the way I found it, pulled the door as shut as it would go behind me. The cops would have to be called at some point because of the damage to Mrs. Pilly's house and furniture. But not when my car was parked around the block with a biker, an illegal immigrant and a bundle of stolen goods inside.

Mrs. Pilly's front and back doors were locked, and there were no broken windows. I peeked in from a couple of angles, but couldn't see anything in the darkness. Her Impala was in the garage. I didn't knock because I didn't want anyone to know I'd been there. There was no way my apartment could have been trashed without her hearing it if she were home. I hoped she was out with a friend.

Back at the car, the girl was huddled at one end of the backseat, legs tucked up under the deep-water-blue kimono, trash bag cradled in her arms. She looked relieved when she saw me. Reggie was dozing in the other corner. He sat up with a jerk as I got in.

"You were gone long enough," he said, trying to cover the security lapse with an irritated tone.

"You all rested?"

"I wasn't asleep," he snapped. "What's Pilly doing?"

"She's not home."

"Good. Let's take your girlfriend and the rest of this shit upstairs and get something to eat. I'm starving."

"We can't. The apartment's been burglarized. We have to get the girl and the goods out of here before the cops come."

"Are the cops coming?" Reggie looked out the back and side windows.

"Not now, but they'll be here eventually."

"Who did it?"

"Take a guess."

"The guys we hit, hit us?"

"I think so."

"Where we gonna go?"

"Long Beach."

# CHAPTER TWENTY-NINE

"Your buddy ain't gonna be too happy to see us."

"He won't be happy to see you." I looked over at Reggie. "But he'll back us up a hundred percent. Just behave yourself."

"Maybe we should go to a motel."

"Too risky with the girl. Young as she looks, someone sees us taking her into a motel room, they might call the cops."

"Is your buddy gonna want to fuck her, too?" Reggie was great at wearing down resistance to what he wanted by pretending that none existed. An hour or a day after you used up a big block of emotional energy arguing and explaining and apparently convincing him of a point, he'd puncture your confidence with an offhand comment that ignored all your earlier efforts and started the discussion over again at square one. It could be very discouraging if you didn't know his MO.

"How many times do I have to tell you—she's not pulling any trains."

"Does he have an old lady?"

"Yeah, why?"

"Just wondering. He probably won't try and get in on the girl if his old lady is around."

"Good thinking." When I didn't bite the second time, he started in on something else.

"Ain't his old lady gonna bitch if we show up in the middle of the night with a nekkid girl and a suitcase full of hot shit?"

"No."

"She knows what you do?"

"Yeah."

"Sounds risky."

"Why's that?"

"What if she blabs to one of her girlfriends, or they have a fight and she runs to the cops?"

"Don't worry about Melanie. Don't get friendly with her, either."

Reggie was quiet for a mile or two.

"I'll behave myself if he behaves himself," he said. "I'm not taking any shit from him. I don't care how good he thinks he can box."

It was past midnight when we bounced into Switch's driveway on 3rd Street in Belmont Heights. TV light flickered in the picture window.

"Wait in the car," I told Reggie.

Switch was lying on the couch watching the Vietnam War movie with the two sergeants. He got up and unlatched the front door when I rapped on the glass.

"What's up?" he said, looking past me at the car.

"We did McFadden's house. It went okay, but someone burglarized my apartment while we were gone and tore the place up. I need someplace to regroup."

"Who hit you?"

"I'm not sure." I didn't want to get in a big thing about McFadden.

"Who's in the car?"

"Reggie and the girl."

"You got the girl?"

"She was tied to his bed."

Switch raised his eyebrows. "Where was *he*?"

"Out on his boat. You want me to bring them in the side?"

"I'll unlock the door."

The girl looked around swiftly and methodically as I took her up the driveway to the side porch, noting the details of her new environment, the lay of the land. Switch was standing in the door, looking bulky in a pair of black boxer shorts and a black T-shirt.

"Come on in," he said congenially, like a good host. "How you doing, Reggie?"

"Fine as frog's hair," Reggie said, coming up at the rear with the suitcase. "We hit the jackpot at that house." His voice was boisterous.

"Glad to hear it."

"How much you think the shit will fence for, Robby?" A little more boisterous.

"Keep your voice down," Switch said. "My girlfriend is sleeping."

"Sorry," Reggie said in a stage whisper. "Think we'll clear ten grand?"

"Something like that." I didn't want him to know just yet how rich the score actually was. It might go to his head. I didn't want to rub it in Switch's face, either. The burglary had turned out to be more lucrative than the armed robbery.

"Two-way split, that's five Gs for me," Reggie said, looking at Switch, the sixty-forty concept forgotten.

Switch ignored him, locked the back door and padded into the living room to shut the blinds on the front window. Reggie flopped down on the couch where Switch had been laying.

"You got a beer?" he said.

I took the girl into the middle bedroom. When she saw the bed, she looked at me for a long moment, eyes dark, deep, unreadable, then lay down, stretching out on her back. She let me look at her wrists and ankles where the ropes had burned her skin. When I turned around, Switch was watching from the doorway.

"What are you going to do with her?"

"Right now, I'm going to put some aloe on her rope burns and see if she wants something to eat. Can she borrow some clothes?"

"What's she need?"

"Socks, panties, a pair of sweatpants and a T-shirt."

"What are you going to do with her tomorrow?"

"I don't know."

Reggie came through the swinging door from the kitchen with a green longneck in his hand, saw us standing by the bedroom door and did a Chester giddyap into the hallway to join us, trying to crowd past me to see into the bedroom.

"What are we doing?" he said, stretching to look over my shoulder.

"You're not missing anything."

"I'm not planning on missing anything, either." He took a long drink from his full bottle of beer, got a sour look on his face, checked the label. "What is this, fucking near-beer?"

"I told you to keep your voice down," Switch said.

"It's nonalcoholic," I said.

"Ain't you got any real beer?"

Switch got the clothes from his bedroom while I plucked a leaf off the aloe plant in the dining room. Reggie wandered back to the couch grumbling about the beer.

"What do you have to eat?" I asked Switch when he handed me Melanie's clothes.

"There's most of a pizza on the stove," he said. "You want me to stick it in the microwave?"

"Do you mind?"

I closed the door to keep Reggie from peeping and went over to the bed. The girl looked up at me, waiting. I dropped the clothes on the floor, split the aloe leaf with the penknife on my key chain. She stiffened when she saw the blade but gradually relaxed when I began to spread the soothing gel on her skin.

"This will make your legs feel better," I said. When I finished with her left leg, she pulled her foot in toward her, raising her knee, to feel the sore spot. The blue silk slid down her thigh. I could smell her then, a faint scent of urine with a pungent female smell behind it and another odor behind that, a hint of sandalwood. I was kneeling on the floor beside the bed and when I looked up her face had changed. The girl was gone, replaced by a sophisticated Saigon lady. Looking into my eyes she put a delicate hand on my shoulder, turning her sexuality on as if with a switch, flooding the room with subtle energy. However old she was, she was no child.

Taking her hand from my shoulder, I held it in my own while I rubbed slippery aloe on her raw wrist. The skin on her forearm was soft and smooth and golden in the lamplight. She seemed surprised that I didn't take what she offered. She kept looking into my eyes, but the seductive look turned sleepy.

There was a soft knock at the door and Switch came in with a Coke and two pieces of pizza on a plate. The girl pulled the kimono down over her thighs and sat up, looking at the food. She still hadn't spoken.

We left her alone to eat. Back out in the living room, Reggie was gobbling the rest of the pie, three bites to a slice, not being too careful about where the crumbs went. The guy never did have any manners.

"Thanks for saving me some," I said.

"I thought you were eating in the other room," he sniggered, taking another big bite, dripping sauce.

"Watch what you're doing," I said, feeling another flash of dislike for him. "You're getting shit all over the couch."

He made a prim face at Switch. "Miss Manners," he said, jerking his head toward me. Switch's face stayed blank. Reggie turned to me. I saw his eyes glance down from my face and back up again. "You got a rise in your Levi's, son," he said, making me aware of the ache in my groin.

"That tell you anything?"

"Yeah. You want to hose her same as I do."

"Skip it."

Reggie shrugged. "You got someplace lined up to fence our stuff?"

"I'll make some phone calls tomorrow."

"When can I get the moolah?"

"As soon as I do."

"Can I get a grand on Front Street?"

"Sure. Tomorrow."

"All that money's going to come in kind of handy," Reggie said, looking at Switch again, gnawing on a crust.

"It usually does," Switch said.

"Don't talk to him about money," I said to Reggie. "He's got more than God."

"Oh yeah? How come you got so much?"

"That's just the way I am," Switch said. "You through with this?" He took the pizza box from the coffee table.

"Just about." Reggie tossed the remains of his crust into the box. Switch walked back to the kitchen shaking his head.

Vietnam was still on TV, Viet Cong soldiers flitting through the jungle around a U.S. Army encampment.

"How much has he got stashed?"

"Half a million," I said, fucking with him.

"Lotta dough," Reggie said casually. "He doesn't keep it here, does he?"

"What do you think?"

"Don't know, don't care."

"Why'd you ask, then?"

Reggie shook his head, reached over and picked up the remote. "What we watching these gooks for?" He started punching buttons with his spatulate thumb. A rerun of an L.A. cop show flashed on the screen, then a priest saying something about sexuality, and then the war movie again. Fumbling with greasy fingers, Reggie hit the volume button and a row of green bars dominoed across the bottom of the screen. Simultaneously, the sound of automatic weapon fire filled the house.

"Turn it down!" I said.

"That's what I'm trying to do!" Reggie said, pushing the volume higher. A mortar shell exploded among a group of terrified GIs, who screamed and cursed as Switch came charging through the swinging door from the kitchen.

"What the hell are you doing?" he said, snatching the remote out of Reggie's hand and turning off the set.

"Fucking thing don't work right. I was trying to change the fucking channel."

"Who told you to change the channel?"

"A little birdie."

"What's going on?" Melanie came into the dining room rubbing her eyes, wearing a T-shirt and panties.

"Nothing, babe. Go back to bed," Switch said.

"It sounded like shooting."

"It was just the TV."

"Hi, Robby," Melanie said, resting her drowsy eyes briefly on me before shifting them to Reggie.

I nodded. "Hi, Mel."

"We'll be quiet," Switch said. "Go on back to bed. You need your rest."

"I'm up now," Melanie said.

"Well, put some clothes on if you are staying up."

"I was planning to." I could tell from her tone that they had been fighting. She turned her butt toward us and twitched back into the bedroom.

"Nice ass," Reggie said.

"You think so," Switch said evenly. He was about ready to throw Reggie out. I was beginning to think there was a flaw in my idea of the three of us working together like a band of brothers.

"Sorry about that," I said to Switch. "Reggie's a little amped up by the score. He's been out of commission for a while."

"I got your amped up right here," Reggie said.

# CHAPTER THIRTY

Melanie came back out wearing a pair of yellow sweatpants. She was barefoot and hadn't bothered to put on a bra.

"Sorry we woke you up," I said.

"S'awright. Who's this?"

"Reggie England, a friend of mine from St. Louis. Reggie, this is Switch's girlfriend, Melanie."

"Hello," Melanie said.

Reggie nodded without smiling. "You didn't have to get dressed on my account, Mel," he said.

Melanie laughed. "I can tell you and Robby are friends. He's the only other one who calls me Mel."

"We go way back," Reggie said in his growly voice.

"How long are you out here for?"

"Permanent."

"Oh really? You're moving out here?"

"Don't worry," Switch said. "He's not staying here."

"I wasn't worried about it."

"Good."

"So why are you guys up here so late?" Melanie asked, half to me, half to Reggie.

"Trouble at the homestead," Reggie said.

"What kind of trouble?"

"Someone broke into my apartment," I said. "The place is trashed and we had some stuff we didn't want the cops to see so we came up here. Switch said we could crash here tonight."

"Yeah, sure. What didn't you want the cops to see?" Her eyes lit up with the memory of our haul two nights before. She had some larceny in her young heart.

Leaving out the restaurant connection, I filled her in on the day's adventures, leading up to the part about the girl in the bedroom.

"You mean she's here?"

"Just for tonight," I said.

"Can I see her?"

"I can't introduce you," I said. "She doesn't speak English. I'm not sure she can talk at all. They may have done something to her to make her mute."

"What do you mean?" Melanie said.

"She has a bandage on her throat and when she tries to talk, no sound comes out. They may have done something to her vocal cords."

"That's horrible. Why would they do something to her vocal cords?"

"They wouldn't want to cut her tongue out, would they?" said Reggie. We all looked at him.

"To keep her quiet, I guess," I said.

The girl was sleeping when we went in the room, breathing slow and deep. She was wearing Melanie's panties and T-shirt. The kimono was wadded up in a corner. We stood by the bed.

"She's a doll," Melanie said.

We were standing close together, watching the girl's chest rise and fall. When Melanie bent over to cover her with the blanket, her hip and thigh brushed mine. Our bodies were still touching when she straightened up.

The sexuality the girl had exuded hung in the bedroom air along with her sandalwood scent. I could feel the heat of Melanie's body through her sweatpants. She leaned against me.

"They were using her for sex?"

"Yeah."

"How old is she?"

"I'm not sure—sixteen or seventeen, maybe." I was revising my estimate of her age upward to match the look she had given me earlier and the way it had made me feel.

"I'm glad you got her out of there."

Switch and I took the stolen goods out to his office and put them in his stash. He had a compartment behind a false wall that I had helped him build, which held a floor safe for money, jewels and guns. Very well concealed.

Switch was a careful guy. He had a detailed evacuation plan in place. If the shit ever came down, he could split at a moment's notice and be at a safe house in Mexico in a few hours with enough money to live for a year.

When we came back in, Reggie and Melanie were sitting at the dining room table drinking the last two nonalcoholic beers. She was asking him questions about the robbery—was he scared when the guy came home? Of course not. How did he know so much about alarms? It came with the territory. Melanie was leaning over the table toward him, looking impressed. It had to be pheromones.

I felt Switch harden as we came into the room and saw them talking. Reggie noticed the dangerous look on his face. He pushed back from the table and stood up, leaving Melanie's last question unanswered.

"Where can a guy find some action around here?" he asked.

"What kind of action?" I said.

"Some nasty floozies and real beer."

I didn't like the idea of him wandering around Long Beach feeling like a gangster, but it seemed smart to get him out of the house before he and Switch started fistfighting.

"There's a biker bar up on Fourth Street," I said. "You can find a boozy floozy there."

"Don't send him up there," Melanie said. "That place is a dive."

"It'll be perfect for him," Switch said. "Come on, we're going to bed. Lock up after he leaves, Rob."

"How am I supposed to get back in?" Reggie said, belligerent. Switch started to swing around, his shoulders rising.

"Knock on the side door and I'll let you in," I said. "I sleep right by the door."

"Oh, you get the bed. Where am I supposed to sleep?"

"You can crash on the couch," Melanie said from the hallway as Switch herded her out of sight.

"Keep the noise down," he said over his shoulder, giving Reggie a mean look. "And don't bring anyone back to the house."

"He won't," I said.

"What's his problem?" Reggie said, after the bedroom door closed. He didn't expect an answer. I walked out to the sidewalk with him. He held out his hand.

"What?"

"Car keys."

"No."

"What?" Saucers.

"No."

"How am I supposed to get pussy without a car?"

"You'll manage."

"Come on, partner!"

"No way. I don't want my leather seats jizzed up and I don't want my Cadillac wrapped around a palm tree."

"Oh, so you don't trust me to drive your car?"

"The bar's two blocks straight down the street," I said. "Try and stay out of trouble."

"What's trouble?"

Watching him limp briskly down the street toward the smear of neon in the distance, I felt the old craving creep up in my chest. I envied Reggie his access to the loud oblivion we used to share, the numb glow of alcohol and warm chatter, the crush of bar music, breath and bodies in a dim unreality lifetimes away from the daylight on either side of it.

Shaking off temptation, I went inside to check on the girl. She was still sunk in profound repose, completely relaxed after who knew how long. I lifted one of her warm hands a few inches off the cover and dropped it. She didn't stir. The lumpy trash bag she had been desperate to find in the busboy's feral pen was under the covers beside her. I slipped it out and carried it to the dining room table.

The way she had clung to the bag made me think there might be something of monetary value in there—smuggled currency or jewels—but when I peeled back the rustling plastic there wasn't much. Just an old Ao Dai—the slinky national dress of the Vietnamese, form-fitting with slits up the sides—the Newport Beach T-shirt and two photographs stuck inside a Vietnamese-language paperback book. The dress was a medium-red with darker wine-red flowers embroidered on it, made of a light, airy fabric, some blend of silk and cotton. It was torn and stained. The pants that usually go with an Ao Dai were missing.

The first photograph was of a man in his late twenties or early thirties wearing the uniform of an ARVN officer. He was leaning against a jeep with a military barracks in the background, smiling at whoever was holding the camera. The second picture was of a beautiful young Vietnamese woman standing on the bank of a wide brown river beneath a willow tree. A little girl of four or five was clinging to her red-sheathed thigh, laughing up at her.

This was all she had left of the life she had come from. Two pictures and a ruined dress. It was more than some of the Vietnamese came to Orange County with. But it wasn't enough. I wondered if her father was living, carrying the memory of his lost daughter like shrapnel in his heart, or if he and the slim, laughing woman were among the four million Vietnamese soldiers and civilians killed during the war and its aftermath.

I put the bundle back beside the girl and trudged to the guest room by the side porch, where I lay down alone in the cold, narrow bed of my own exile.

Stealthy tapping on the six-light door at the foot of the bed woke me up sometime later. It was still dark. I unlatched the door and swung it open on the same hinges it had been swinging on since the 1920s. Reggie was in his secret agent mode, holding his finger over his lips.

"I found out some shit," he said in a drunk whisper.

"What shit?"

"Thurz lotta pussy peddlin' going on 'round the met'politan area."

"Pussy peddling? You didn't bring a hooker back here, did you?" I leaned out the door and looked around the corner for a drunk chick.

"No, man. Big score. Met these guys." He was getting louder.

"Quiet!" I shushed him. "Tell me about it in the morning."

## CHAPTER THIRTY-ONE

Reggie was drinking coffee and reading the newspaper at the glass-topped table in the dining room when I got up at eight. He looked at his wrist as if there were a watch there, glanced up at me over the top of the sports section with red-rimmed eyes and shook his head. I went through the swinging door into the kitchen, got a cup, put an ounce of milk in it and poured coffee on top, then went back and sat down across from him.

"Nice to see you up and around again," he said.

"It's nice to be here."

We drank our coffee. Melanie came out of the bathroom, dressed for work.

"Morning, Robby," she said, giving the table a nice smile.

"You're looking good," I said.

"Thanks. I gotta run. You still have your key, don't you?"

"Yeah. Where's Switch?"

"He had an early appointment. He said to tell you he'll be back around one. See you guys later."

"Bye," I said.

"Don't do anything I wouldn't do, Mel," said Reggie.

It got a laugh, musical and feminine, as Melanie went out the front door into the blue summer morning. Gold-tinted light poured in the windows along the driveway, filling the long room. I could smell mimosa and salt water in the breeze that came through the open door.

"If you don't need me later, I got a side job to do," Reggie said.

"What's that?"

"Confidential," he said. "Can't talk about it."

"Very funny," I said. "Let's hear it."

"I met a couple of skulls at the bar last night. Got a little deal going down tonight they need help with."

"Skulls?"

Reggie made a sour face. "Buccaneers," he said. "The motorcycle club?"

"Oh, yeah." I felt fourteen again, my ignorance of biker essentials exposed.

"They got a couple of cunts they traded scooter parts for at a rally in Arizona. Plannin' to sell 'em to some Asians at a pussy auction but they need extra muscle. They don't trust the gooks. I'm going along for backup."

"Have they seen your piece?"

"They've seen enough."

"What are they paying you?"

"Five hundred."

"Why don't they trust the Asians?"

"Why you think?"

"Where's the auction at?"

"Melonhead said something about someplace called San Peedro. You interested? You could unload that little piece in the bedroom for some heavy jingle. Melonhead says the gooks shell out for young ones. Claims he'll get ten Gs apiece for his and they both been around the track a couple times. One of them looks like she's about twenty-five. That little slope would bring top dollar. You want to go over and talk to them? They live right down the street. We could get our dicks sucked while we're down there and then go out and get some breakfast."

I shook my head. "I have to meet someone at nine. You didn't tell Melonhead we have the girl here, did you?" He had to hook up with Switch's one enemy in the neighborhood.

"I'm not stupid."

"So you didn't?"

"Hell no. Guy's a lowlife. I wouldn't tell him our business."

"So why you getting involved with them?"

"It's easy money. I can handle them. Who you meeting?"

"A guy who works for McFadden."

"That guy whose house we knocked off?"

"Yeah."

"One of his guys stabbing him in the back?"

"It looks that way."

"You want me to come with you in case it's a double cross? You never know who you can trust nowadays. Sometimes little guys get big ideas."

"No. I need you to stay here until I get back. I won't be gone long. Can I trust you to leave the girl alone?"

"I'm not going to bother your girlfriend. That little blond at Melon-head's sucks a mean dick. I'll go up there after you get back."

"Did you tell Melonhead where you are staying?"

"Yeah, why?"

"Don't let him or any of his buddies in if they come down here."

"Why's that?"

"Because of the girl, Einstein, and because Switch doesn't like them."

"Big fucking surprise."

I washed my face and combed my hair and checked on the girl. She was still sleeping. I borrowed an aloha shirt from Switch's closet and got my gun from his office, tucking it in my belt beneath the shirttail.

The sea view dilated as I drove down Temple to Ocean, opening up to include the *Queen Mary* and the hills of Rancho Palos Verdes, beautiful above the old seafaring town of San Pedro across a corner of the bay. Turning left on Ocean, I soaked up half a mile of the bright vista on my right before the road veered away from the water, cutting over to Second Street. There were empty parking places in front of Hof's Hut but I parked two blocks down and walked back along the alley, circling behind the restaurant before going in the front door. No sign of the blood-colored BMW or the busboy. Entering the 1960s interior of the diner—all glass and chrome and turquoise vinyl—I saw Don nibbling on his lip in a booth by the windows that overlooked Granada Avenue.

# CHAPTER THIRTY-TWO

I walked along the right side of the restaurant and took a quick look through the kitchen door before cutting over to the booth.

"I was afraid you weren't coming," Don said. I looked at my watch. It was a few minutes before nine. "Oh no. You're not late. I just worry too much." His sandy thatch hadn't gotten any thicker since I saw him last. The hangdog look was a little droopier, as if he'd been beaten for chewing on a slipper. Conspiracy didn't agree with him.

"I wouldn't worry," I said, sliding in across from him. "If McFadden wanted to hurt you, he had his chance."

"What if he finds out about us meeting?"

"He won't find out from me."

A burly hausfrau of a waitress brought me a cup of nasal-clearing coffee and took our orders.

"What's McFadden up to, Don?"

He squared his thin shoulders and leaned toward me. "He hurts people, Robert. He's killed two people that I know of. And I think he may have done something to Carla."

"That pretty Latina?"

Don nodded. "She didn't come to work on Monday and her sister called me at home this morning asking if I knew where she was. She was crying. He may have thought she was in on the robbery and done something to her."

"Why would he think that?"

"He may have thought she did it to get even. He raped her at the Christmas party last year and had someone beat her up to keep her quiet. She tried to quit but he threatened her family to make her stay. Snuff hates her because she kicked him in the balls when he tried to get her in the restroom last month. And now she's missing. I'm so worried about her."

Another layer of anger and dislike formed on top of the reservoir of ugly feelings I already felt toward McFadden and the busboy.

"What else is he involved in?"

"He smuggles girls and drugs into the country. He hires illegal immigrants and cheats them out of their money. He's into extortion and money laundering. He's a horrible person."

Over scrambled eggs and link sausages, Don told me everything he knew about McFadden. He knew a lot. His father had worked for McFadden's father, and he had known McFadden most of his life. The original McFaddens—the brothers who came to Southern California in the 1870s—were traders and merchants. They built the first pier in Orange County in 1890, extending the rickety wooden structure far enough out into deep water so that coastal steamers could dock to load and unload cargo. From there, the McFaddens shipped the produce of the local farms and ranches to San Pedro and San Francisco, and brought in lumber and manufactured goods the farmers needed, carrying the freight inland on a small-gauge railroad. McFadden's father was the grandson of the older brother and he had carried on a similar business, adding to the family fortune by becoming the biggest food wholesaler in Southern California. He imported Asian food products, among others, and bought fish from American, Mexican and Asian fishermen. McFadden grew up in the business, watching boats come and go with strange cargos, hearing sailors' stories about what went on along the dark streets of port cities around the world.

"I used to go down to the dock with my father sometimes, and when

McFucken was down there he would get me off to the side and tell me about the stuff they did overseas. I have a younger sister, and when he saw her one time, he asked me if I ever did those things with her. It made me sick. I hated the way he talked but I couldn't tell because his dad was my dad's boss. He always treated me like crap, like he was so much better than me because his dad was the boss. But he's the one that got kicked out of college and I finished my degree at Cal State–Fullerton."

"Why did he get kicked out of college?"

"Rape. Him and three other big, tough Princeton men forced a high school girl. His dad got him off somehow but they kicked him out of school. He tells people he has a degree but he doesn't. He came back home at the end of his junior year. His dad put him to work in the seafood business doing all different kinds of jobs to get to know the business. Then he turned it over to him. Just like that. Twenty-three years old and he was a big businessman."

Somewhere along the line, McFadden had started smuggling illegal immigrants into the country. After his father died, he switched from charging voluntary immigrants outrageous fares for passage on his boats to buying girls in the refugee camps and slums across the water. He got them for practically nothing in Thailand, Vietnam and China, and sold them for huge profits in Los Angeles. Some went to men—and women—who wanted a girl slave. Most went to businessmen who ran the Asian whorehouses operating in nondescript bungalows and apartment buildings in subdivisions and city neighborhoods from Santa Barbara to San Diego, young women cut adrift from their lives and cultures by the whirlwind of war.

With the money he made from smuggling and slave trading, McFadden had started buying restaurants. According to Don, he was a good businessman. He owned three Cow Towns plus half a dozen Thai and Chinese places. He used them to launder smuggling money, but he made money out of them, too. His bottom line was bolstered by cheating his illegal kitchen help. He drove them hard and paid them little, pocketing the dividend.

"Tell me about his office in San Pedro."

"That's where he runs the seafood business from. His personal office is there. His big, fancy personal office."

"Have you been there?"

"Oh yes. He makes the restaurant managers come up there to be reviewed. Which means being cussed out and told you are lousy at your job. He always wants more money. Serve cheaper food, charge higher prices, cheat the Mexicans a little bit more."

"What makes you think he has the videotape up there?"

"He keeps all of his records and important papers there."

"Do you have time to take a ride up to San Pedro?"

"Why?" Don looked stricken.

"I have to get that tape back."

"I can tell you where it is. I'll give you the address. It's called Seastar, his business. It's at 5972 East Bay. You go over the toll bridge and turn left on—"

"It'll be easier if you come with me, Don. It won't take long. We can be up there and back in an hour."

"I can't let him find out. What if he sees us? He'll kill me!"

"Do you think he's there now?"

"I don't know, but I can't take a chance."

"If he's there, we won't stop. We'll just drive by. If he's not there, you can show me where he parks, where his office is, where to go in. I need your help on this, Don. Once I get the tape back, we can do whatever we want to him. What would you like to do to him?"

"I'd like to smack him in the mouth, but I could never do that. I'm too afraid of him." Don looked at me with anguished eyes. "He used to take me down to the end of the jetty where the water is deep and throw fish guts in the water to attract sharks and threaten to push me in. He'd make me beg him not to. I want him to get in trouble, bad trouble, so he'll go to jail for a long time and I won't have to worry about him coming after me."

"We'll do it," I said. "You know his operations and I know how the cops think. I'll make them want him bad enough that his friends won't be able to help him. We'll set him up to be busted by the whole alphabet: LAPD, FBI, INS and anyone else we can think of. If he did something to Carla, we'll make him pay for that, too. How does that sound?"

"It sounds wonderful." Don reached over and put his hand on mine, looking at me with eyes that were a little too sparkly. "I'm so glad I don't have to go through this alone."

"I know what you mean," I said, patting his hand briefly before withdrawing mine. "So you'll ride up there?"

He took a deep breath, compressed his pale lips and gave a quick nod.

"Great, let's go." When I looked up to signal for the check, I saw Brunhilda watching me with a grim look of disapproval on her extra-large frying pan of a face. She trudged over and slapped down the ticket. She knew we were up to no good. I left 20 percent to distract her and headed for the door.

"This is a beautiful car," Don said, sliding his hand over the leather dashboard of the Cadillac as we headed north on Ocean. "I always wanted a luxury car. Of course, I could never afford one with what he paid me. And now I'm out of work."

I looked over at him in his Wal-Mart clothes, remembering his shabby office and economy sedan. "Maybe you'll be able to afford one now," I said. "I'm going to rob his office to get the tape and I'll give you a share of any money we get. That would be sweet revenge, wouldn't it? Riding around in a Cadillac he paid for while he's making the license plates for it?"

Don laughed for the first time since I'd known him, a feeble staccato I'd never hear again.

# CHAPTER THIRTY-THREE

The grimy brick building sat in front of a row of old fish houses half a mile south of the Vincent Thomas Bridge. The red Beemer was parked in front, in between a cream-colored Continental and a black Mercedes with a vanity plate that said IMPORT. Don didn't recognize the Lincoln or the Mercedes.

"They can't belong to anyone who works for him. He doesn't pay anybody worth a crap."

One of the dilapidated waterfront structures behind the building had the Seastar name on it. The area looked like it would be dark and deserted at night. My pulse hardened. Don said the first employees arrived at four in the morning. There would be long hours of opportunity in the inky night. On our second pass, he showed me the window of McFadden's second-floor office and pointed out the jetty where he had been terrorized. I couldn't get anything else out of him. He had a hard time breathing while we were close to McFadden. He kept taking big, sudden, sucking breaths, trying to take the air by surprise and get some oxygen out of it.

I dropped him at his car on Second Street and drove back to Switch's house. When I went in the side door I heard muffled grunts coming from one of the bedrooms. The sounds got louder in the couple of seconds it took me to sprint from the door to the hall. There was a harsh cry and a cackle of laughter.

Reggie's broad white ass greeted me when I opened the door of the middle bedroom. He had the girl on her back on the floor. All I could see of her were her brown legs angled up behind his planted arms. His burly body was wedged between her thighs, splitting her in half. His pants were down around his ankles, his buttocks clenched.

He was off her in a flash, wiggling his pants up and whirling toward me at the same time. I nailed him while he was still hunched over, a hard overhand right to his nose, then did a sweep kick with my left foot, turning into him, catching him in his right knee. When he howled, stumbling sideways against the bed, I realized it was his bad leg, the one broken three times and pinned together with steel. A sucker punch surge of guilt stained my fury, stopping me from following through with another right. In all the years we'd known each other, I had never hit him and it made me a little sick, as if I'd slapped my father's face.

The girl had scrambled into the niche between the bed and dresser. She was naked. That seemed to be her fate. I wondered how long it had been since she'd laughed like the girl on the riverbank.

Reggie was smiling when I looked back at him, adjusting his nose with two thick fingers.

"I'll take that one," he said. "How'd yer meeting go?" He was trying to carry it off as a prank. He got caught with his hand in the cookie jar and deserved a swat.

"I told you to leave her alone, Reggie." His smile was dispelling the guilt.

"Hey, take it easy," he said, shifting his position, turning his left side toward me and dropping his right hand.

"You said you'd leave her alone."

"It's okay, man. She ain't no kid. She's nineteen. She just looks young." He backed up a step as I moved toward him.

"How do you know that?"

"Gook has a store at the corner. I went down to get a pack of smokes and heard him talking that gobbledygook and got him to come back up here and talk to her. She's from Saigon. Her name's Song."

"She talked to him?"

"No, you were right. They did something to her throat, cut a nerve or some fucking thing to keep her quiet. But she knew what he was saying. She scribbled some of that shit they write to answer him."

"What else did she say? What did he say?"

"Not much. I told him what to ask her. I just wanted to find out how old she is to get you off my back."

I looked at the girl, crouched small in the corner. She didn't look traumatized. Her face was alert and surprised. When our eyes met, she let hers melt, opening up to mysterious depths.

"See? She's fine. You think she's young 'cause her pussy's bald, but it ain't really bald. Run your hand over it, you can feel the stubble. Them guys shaved it."

I held my hand out to the girl and she grasped it firmly with her small, strong hand. As I pulled her to her feet, she moved in close to me for protection or something else, pressing her nude body against me. Reggie raised his eyebrows at me. Someone had folded the kimono and put it on top of the dresser. I wrapped it around her and took her to the bed. She lay down the same way she had the night before, looking at me, waiting.

"Run your hand over that puss," Reggie said. "You'll see what I mean."

"Just because someone shaved her doesn't give you the right to rape her."

"I didn't rape her. She liked it."

"How the fuck do you know she liked it? Because she was too scared to fight back? You took advantage of her."

"Try her yourself, if you don't believe me. This ain't no innocent little girl you got yourself here. She's well broke in. She was nibbling on my dick last night when I pushed her head down in my lap in the car. She was aching for it."

"She's used to being treated that way, you asshole. Because she let you do it doesn't mean she wanted you to do it."

"You think I can't tell the difference between a girl that wants it and one that doesn't? How many girls you seen me fuck in the last thirty years? You ever hear any of them complaining?"

"Yeah, I have. Teresa complained a lot."

"Don't start that shit again. She wanted it and so did this one. I guarantee you that. She has a little body, but she's a big girl, and that's what big girls want. If you haven't figured that out by now, you must have a hole in your head."

"I must have a hole in my head for trusting you."

"So don't trust me."

"I don't. How long was the guy from the store here?"

"Ten minutes."

"What did he say when he left?"

"Sigh-a-nara or some fucking thing."

"Did it cross your miniature excuse for a mind that he might call the cops, or come back here with some of his people to get the girl?"

"He ain't gonna do shit."

"How do you know that, Reggie?"

"Because I gave him twenty bucks and told him I'd kill him if he told anybody she was here."

"Which means he knows something's up, and if he comes back, he'll come back strapped. You ever hear about the Vietnamese gangs out here? They're ruthless killers. They'll chop your fat ass up and serve it as sushi."

"Fuck you, too. I'll chop those little pricks up. And that old guy ain't in no gang. He's sixty if he's a fucking day. What's he want this skinny little chick for? Even if he can still fuck, there's gook chicks all over the place out here with more ass and tit than she has."

"He might want to help her, you ignoramus—or take her away from us to use her for the same thing McFadden was using her for—that *you* used her for."

"You jealous or something?"

"Of what?"

"Of me. Because I did what you want to do but don't have the balls for. I've always gotten more pussy than you and now I fucked this tight little twat before you did and you're mad about it. But you don't need to worry about me. She's not my type. I like 'em a little riper. She's all yours, as far as I'm concerned. I just wanted to try it out for you and let you know how it was." He was over his chagrin at getting caught, starting to resent getting hit and kicked and yelled at.

"How was it?" I asked, going nose to nose with him.

"Tight."

"Touch her again and I'll put you in the hospital."

"In your dreams, motherfucker."

"Try me and you'll wish you were dreaming."

"I'll fight two of you any day of the week. I fought everybody in Mattingly's in '85 and kicked every one of their asses. I'm sure as fuck not worried about you."

"That was before you were old and crippled up, Reggie. How many fights you won lately?"

"Enough."

The tension steadily tightening the atmosphere in the bedroom was scaring the girl. Her eyes darted back and forth between us as we argued.

"Let's go in the other room," I said.

"After you." It was his classic line whenever anyone asked him to step outside. A lot of times, it had meant the fight was over before it started. I'd seen him kick guys in the balls from behind, shove people down outside staircases. I went out of the room with my head partly turned, watching him from the corner of my eye.

Switch was coming through the front door as we entered the living room.

"What's going on?" He was grinning and his voice was jovial. Something good had happened. I shook my head. The smile dropped off his face. He looked from me to Reggie and back again. "There a problem?"

"I came home and found him fucking the girl."

"You fucked that little girl in my house?"

"She ain't no little girl. She's a little woman and she's been fucking for years."

"How do you know that?" Switch's voice was cold.

"A little birdie told me."

The muscles in Switch's back and shoulders contracted and his hands closed. "Why did you leave her alone with him?" he asked me.

"I'm stupid," I said.

"You're stupid, all right," Reggie said. "Making a federal case out of fucking a gook whore. How many girls have I given you to bang? Huh? I don't know what your fucking problem is unless you turned queer or something."

"I told you not to trust him," Switch said.

"You were right."

"Fuck the both of you," Reggie shouted. "I don't give a fuck if you trust me or not. You don't want me working with you, that's fine and fucking dandy. I got other options."

Switch and I stayed silent, looking at him.

"I don't believe this shit," Reggie said, changing his tone. "I could help you, Robby. I'll do anything for you. You know that. I didn't know you were serious about the girl or I'd have left her alone. I told you I won't mess with her no more. Give me another chance." He was talking to me as if Switch weren't there, putting a pleading note in his voice. "Come on, man! Didn't I do good last night? And what about those gangsters from Balboa? I'll take care of 'em for you anytime you want me to. Just say the word, and they're fish food. What do you say, Robby? Aren't you gonna say something?"

"We'll handle the guys from Balboa," Switch said. "You pursue your other options."

Reggie kept staring at me, a look of disbelief creeping out from beneath his beard, taking over his deeply lined, drooping face. In his mind, fucking a pass-around was expected behavior. It might be worth a punch in the nose if someone was trying to take her exclusive, but not a breakup of old partners.

"You gonna let him run me off?" he said.

"You should have left her alone," I said.

The slack folds of his face tightened. He grabbed his jacket off the couch and stomped toward the front door, his right shoulder rising up and collapsing awkwardly with each angry step. I remembered him stomping out the door of the house in Hazelwood years before when both his legs were good, on his way to deal with a guy who had sold me a kilo of shitty weed. He'd come back with bloody knuckles, a black eye and all my money. Later, he and I turned around and sold the key to some hicks in a farm town outside of St. Louis, and used the money for a three-day party, staying drunk on tequila and taking turns bumping a plump, jolly biker chick he picked up at a bar in St. Charles.

Reggie spun around on the porch. "I'll be at Melonhead's if you change your mind," he snarled. "I'll be back for my money." His face was red and twisted. The fury I'd felt when I caught him with the girl had jumped to him, and he took it with him as he clumped off down the street.

"Melonhead's?" Switch said. "Why's he going to Melonhead's?"

## CHAPTER THIRTY-FOUR

I filled Switch in on Reggie's other activities.

"The guy from the Paris Market?"

"That's what it sounded like to me."

"You think he is telling the truth about how old she is?"

"The Vietnamese or Reggie?"

"Both of them. You think she's really nineteen?"

"I don't know. She could be. Right now I'm more concerned about what the old guy might do. Who knows what kind of screwy impression he got from Reggie. He may think we're holding her against her will."

"He won't cause any trouble. He knows this is my house, and I've been doing business with him for years. I'll stop by and talk to him. Melonhead's the problem. I don't like the idea of him knowing about the girl or anything else around here. It figures Reggie would hook up with him."

"He said he didn't tell them about the girl."

"Not yet."

"You think they might try something if they find out she's here?"

"I don't know. I broke Melonhead's nose and arm when I kicked his ass last summer. His head is pretty much mush but he probably remembers that. Same time, if they're messing in the slave trade, they'd have to be tempted. We need to get her out of here. I don't want any kind of trouble that is going to bring the cops around."

Switch paused for a minute and then went on. "Speaking of which, I went by to see a customer of mine this morning to check on a dishwasher I sold him. He's Vietnamese. I thought about him last night. I asked him who might help a refugee and he gave me the number of a church in Little Saigon. I went ahead and called them—hope you don't mind—the lady said you can bring the girl down there tomorrow morning." He paused again, gauging my reaction. "It's up to you. I just happened to think of this guy and he had the number because his niece came over illegal last year. As long as I was there, I went ahead and called. He said they're nice people."

"Did you tell them we were bringing her down?"

"I didn't tell them anything. I just asked if they could help and they said they could. The lady wanted specifics, but I kept it theoretical."

I thought about the girl lying in the next room, the child or young woman, waiting to see who would come through the door. I had rescued her, but she seemed to be slipping away from me before I had a chance to know her.

"It's probably the best thing," Switch said. "Pilly will never let you keep her at your place and she can't stay here."

Genuinely Christian in most of her attitudes, my landlady had adopted her husband's dislike of the Vietnamese. She viewed them as interlopers in the county of her youth and referred to Little Saigon as "a den of iniquity." "She needs to be with her own people," Switch said. "They'll help her get some kind of life going. That's what you want, isn't it?"

"Sure," I said, but I wasn't sure.

"So what's going on with your apartment?" Switch changed the subject. "You going back down there today?"

"Yeah. I need to get the place cleaned up and secured. Make a police report."

"I have to go back out to place an order at one of my suppliers. It's a big one and I want to talk to him in person to make sure everything goes smooth. When I get back I'll ride down there with you and help you clean up—if you want some help."

"I could use some help."

"Good. I'll be back in three or four hours. Melanie should be home about the same time. We can leave her with the girl and cruise down in the Caddie. How is she, anyway? She need a doctor or anything?"

"No. He didn't beat her up. She seems to be all right. I'll check on her in a little while."

"You want a cup of coffee?"

"Not right now."

Switch went through the swinging door into the kitchen. I heard the rush of low-class municipal water extending in a foamy bar from the tap to the drain, a splashing sound as he rinsed the coffeepot, gurgling as he filled it with middle-class water from a plastic bottle. Through the picture window, I saw a tall black girl wearing bright red shorts and a pink halter top Rollerblading down the sunny street in the direction of the Pacific. I wondered if she was headed for the oceanfront path that stretches from downtown Long Beach to the mouth of the San Gabriel River. I wondered if Song would like to take a walk. A stroll down to the beach; half a mile along the water and back would probably do her good. I wondered if she came from the coast of Vietnam or the interior.

The phone by the hall doorway rang as Switch emerged from the kitchen. He snagged the handset and kept walking back to the bedroom.

"*Hola, mi muchacha,*" he said. It was Melanie, his young love. The house was quiet and I heard his end of the conversation distinctly through the thin wooden panels of the closed door: "I got home a little while ago. Okay. Reggie's out of here. Yeah. He was messing around with the girl and Rob kicked him out. Things aren't always what they seem. You're too trusting. I don't know. We may have a place lined up. I know. Hey, listen, I had a three-thousand-dollar morning! That's right. Ng is going to buy another dishwasher for his other restaurant. He gave me the name of two other restaurant owners who need equipment, too—a cousin and an uncle." He was silent for a few minutes. I heard him opening and closing dresser drawers. "You're right," he said finally. "We probably could. This might be the right time. We'll talk about it later. Love you, baby."

After a few minutes, Switch came out of the bedroom wearing a dark blue suit, cut across the corner of the dining room into the kitchen, came back through the swinging door carrying a steaming green mug with a chemical company logo on the side of it.

"There's coffee if you want some," he said. "I'll be back by four."

"I'll be here."

Strutting out the front door, he looked much more like a businessman than a crook.

Song was stretched out naked on top of the covers, lying on her stomach. She stirred when the door opened, buttocks contracting and then relaxing as she wiggled down deeper into the nirvana of sleep. A bolt of lust wobbled my legs. I knew at least some of what Reggie had said was true. The way she had looked at me the night before. I could have her if I wanted her, bending over to kiss the back of her neck and sliding my hand between her thighs, but I had been thinking of her in the same mental and emotional frame as my daughter, and I wasn't sure how to go from seeing her as a child to seeing her as a woman.

So I didn't disturb her rest. Her life had made her very tired. I closed the door softly and wandered back into the dining room. I was sleepy, too. All the activity of the last two days was catching up with me. I thought about drinking some of the coffee Switch had made, trying to think through some kind of plan. I had to decide what to do about the girl. I was worried about Mrs. Pilly. The thought of the apartment made me cringe in half a dozen different ways at once, as if I had multiple bodies in which to feel emotional and psychological discomfort. The work of cleaning up. The loss of possessions. The sense of having screwed up. The damage to my life. Dealing with the police. I wasn't looking forward to that. And then there was the tape. Until I got it back, I was in real danger. McFadden was gunning for me. Reggie had let me down. Now he was gone. And Switch. And on and on. I needed to think everything through, but I didn't have the mental energy. Like Song, I wanted not to think for a while. Take a shower and sleep for a couple of hours. Rest.

The hot water pounded against the back of my neck and shoulders, relaxing the deep muscles around the spine, melting sharp nodes of tension and anxiety. By the time I dried off, I was so relaxed I could hardly hold my eyelids up. They kept slipping down, obscuring half my view of the bathroom, hall, Melanie and Switch's room. I pulled a clean T-shirt and a pair of sweatpants out of a drawer and staggered into the bedroom beside the kitchen. When you are really, really sleepy, drifting off into unconsciousness is as pleasurable as a heroin nod. That heavy narcotic magnetism clutched me when I flopped on the mattress. I dropped the clothes beside the bed, pulled the light blanket up to my chin and disappeared from my own radar screen, dispersing and breaking up in the erotic hum of deep sleep.

Out of the blackness, a garden slipped into my dreams, secret as a child through a hidden gate. It spread across the hills and valleys of my subconscious. I could smell the perfume of purple and yellow and the sweet scent of green. And then it was an herb garden as well as a flower garden and I smelled the heart-lifting scent of mint rising out of the tangled stalks, the silky grass, the long, smooth strands of a girl's hair. A shampoo smell and a warm body rubbing mine. I opened my eyes and saw her face close for a second, close as an image in a mirror, her eyes huge with Eros behind a last thin layer of fear, before she turned her head, nuzzling my neck. She had crept under the blanket and was lying on her side next to me in the crook of my right arm. I slid my hand down the back of her body, over the hard curve of her buttocks, feeling her smooth skin, her heat. She snuggled closer, sliding one thigh over the top of my hairy legs. I clenched her tighter with my right arm and she put her mouth on mine, pushing her tongue between my lips. She tasted like peppermint and I wondered whose toothbrush she had borrowed. The first touch of her hand made me hard as a steel bar. That pleased her. She stroked it with her thumb and two fingers, while I slipped my finger into her from behind, pushing against the cheeks of her ass with each deep thrust. It was tight like Reggie said. A flash of hatred dispersed quickly, like a cup of ink spilled in the sea.

She began a gentle descent, kissing my neck and chest, sucking on both nipples, not just briefly, but for a while, like a baby nursing, going lower, probing my navel with her tongue, finally arriving. She teased it gently with the wet tip of her tongue, pushing it back and licking from the base to the tip, circling the rounded edge of the head. She nibbled on the side of it like she was eating an ear of corn, using her lips instead of her teeth. She popped the head in and out of her mouth, kissed it, licked some more, harder, with her whole tongue, and then I don't know what she was doing, sucking and licking, moving her head up and down, turning wild, taking the whole thing into her mouth and throat then coming off of it to smear her tongue and lips across my nerve-filled lower belly, sending shivers everywhere, and then back on it, up and down and off to lick the insides of my thighs and back to the erection again, the hard ache.

It ranked right up there among the top ten blow jobs of my life. And I'm not just saying that. Each time I was about to come, she sensed it and slowed the tempo down to prolong the pleasure. The energy that had seemed already to be exploding like a slow-motion film of a man diving through plate glass paused, trembled, receded while she browsed just outside the magic circle. Until the last time, when she didn't stop. She was sucking hard and wild and I could feel myself gathering, the rubber band stretching, the water balloon filling, fuller and fuller, stretching to a molecule-thin membrane separating me from pure delight, and instead of stopping she sprang on top of me, holding it upright between her legs as she slid down on it, encompassing me, clenching it deep inside her as I started to come.

I don't know if it was the tightness of her vagina, the series of near climaxes that came before, the thrill of her youth, or what, but the orgasm was overwhelming—slow-spreading, bone-deep, fine-grained pleasure radiating through my ass and thighs and up my back in a warm wave that changed my body from a physical to an emotional substance.

She was straddling me with her right hand on her own breast and her left on mine, rubbing us both while my hands squeezed her ass and the pleasure kept spreading, across my stomach and chest, through my shoulder and neck muscles to my scalp, down through my calves to my feet and toes. I seemed to feel it through her body, too, running my hands up and down her back and sliding them along the goose-bumped skin of her thighs as she rode my hips lightly, rising and falling above me, focusing the exotic beauty of her face on me like a searchlight. The physical sensation was as good as it was the first time, masturbating in the ten-by-twelve bedroom I grew up in. There was the same sense of extraordinary revelation, of gratitude for the body's unexpected and unbelievably generous gift, the same delight and anticipation of future pleasure. But so much better because Song was not an unreachable dream torn from a magazine in Miles O'Reilly's basement but a living being giving herself to me completely.

As the physical thrill subsided into a deep physical peace, I pulled her down and kissed her, putting my whole tongue in her mouth, probing the back of her throat, hugging her body against my chest, trying greedily to squeeze a few last spasms out of the moment. She folded her feet back along my thighs and clung to me tightly. In that moment of mutual surrender, the world opened up in a new way. My heart opened completely and I felt young again, as if my life were still before me. I started crying. At first, I thought I was laughing but then I realized I was crying and then it was beyond my control, like another person inhabiting my body, and I laid there and cried while she comforted me. She kissed my ear, my eyes, my lips, rubbed her cheek against mine, wept a little with me.

I'm not sure what I was crying about at first but it was a tremendous relief. Maybe I was crying about losing my wife and daughter, finally letting them go. Or about my life, the way it had gone wrong for a long time. Finally, I was crying the way soldiers do when they come down the gangplank or airplane steps, amazed to be alive, and see the towns and farms and women they thought they would never see again. Song made me feel like I was coming home.

When she had started her sexual routine, nibbling and breathing, she had managed to seem curious and surprised in a childish way, even as her actions made plain how experienced she was in giving pleasure. She seemed delighted to feel my dick get hard, surprised and excited at all the details of a man's body. Then she had seemed like an equal lover, passionate and knowing, giving and receiving lustful pleasure. Now, she seemed more like my mother comforting me when I was a child, making me safe with her acceptance and love. I flashed powerfully on my mother's face, voice, emotional aura, remembered for the first time in many years the huge love I'd had for her. And in a way I can't explain, she was my daughter, too, that missing part of my life restored.

I went back to sleep with Song stretched out against my side, her head resting on my shoulder, her hand holding me.

# CHAPTER THIRTY-FIVE

Switch woke me up banging in the side door. He stopped and stared when he saw me in bed.

"Can I get you anything?" he said. "Extra pillow? Peeled grape?"

"You caught me," I admitted.

"I'm not going to let you forget, either," he said, looking at his watch. "Robert Rivers sleeping at three-fifty in the afternoon. You better drag your ass out of there if we're going to get your place straightened out today." He went through the swinging door into the dining room, shaking his head, making an old lady's dismayed clucking sound with his tongue.

I put on the black sweatpants and white T-shirt lying on the floor beside the bed. Someone was doing something in the kitchen, running water, clattering. I pushed through the swinging door and saw Song, dressed in Melanie's black sweatpants and white T-shirt, doing the dishes. My heart accelerated.

She looked over her shoulder and smiled. I liked the smile. For the first time, she looked grown-up to me. Standing behind her, I put my hands on her shoulders and kissed the top of her head. She pushed her butt against my thighs and kept scrubbing.

Switch came through the door from the dining room while I still had my lips pressed against her thick, shampoo-scented hair, sized up the change.

"What time you want to go to Corona?"

"Whenever Mel gets home."

"She's here," he said, rummaging in the refrigerator. "You probably didn't notice her coming home because you were asleep. In the middle of the day."

"Let me get dressed and grab a cup of coffee and I'll be ready to go."

"No hurry." He went back into the dining room with two glasses of iced tea.

I reached under Song's arms and covered her breasts with my hands, feeling her small, hard nipples through Melanie's T-shirt. When I made a pot of coffee, she watched the procedure closely. I kissed her neck and ears and felt her up some more while the coffee brewed. She accepted my attentions as if they were the most natural thing in the world. She liked me touching her and I couldn't keep my hands off her.

I had known the girl less than twenty-four hours, but the intense physical connection of our sexual union seemed to have broken through some kind of barrier, changing both of us and the world. Everything about her was precious to me, the shape of her hands, the midnight color of her hair.

I'd been head-over-heels in love only one time in my life, with a sultry brunette named Gabriella when we were both fifteen. It was love at first sight when she walked into my driver's education class wearing platform shoes and a red miniskirt. Her last name was Robierre and mine was Roberts, so we sat next to each other and learned to drive in the same car, laughing after class at the absentminded instructor, holding hands in the hallway, kissing in the parking lot. She made me happier than I had ever been before, and, eventually, much sadder.

The way I felt toward Song reminded me of Gabriella, made me think of her for the first time in the longest time. Who can explain the mysteries of chemistry and karma? Maybe Song had been my daughter or sister or lover in another life. Maybe I had finally met that perfect person whose pheromones matched mine. Maybe it was anima projection. Whatever it was, it was wonderful. We fit together like a key in an ignition switch or a coin in a slot machine poised for a jackpot. The difference in age and background seemed as irrelevant as a feather blowing by in the wind.

I drank a cup of coffee while leaning against the counter, watching the deft movements of her hands as she worked, the sway of her hips, basking in the unexpected and unexplainable joy I felt just standing near her. When Switch poked his head in again and cocked an eyebrow, I went and got dressed. When I came out of the bathroom, Song and Melanie were sitting at the dining room table looking at pictures of clothes in a fashion magazine. Switch was lying on the red velvet couch, watching CNN.

"You ready?" I said.

"Sure." He got up and came over to the table. "We're going down and get Rob's place straightened out," he said. "Keep the doors locked while we're gone and don't let anybody in."

Melanie looked up from the magazine. "Why, what's up?"

"Nothing. Reggie hooked up with that brain-dead biker down the street last night. He headed that way when we ran him off. If either of them show up, don't let them in."

"Okay. See ya." She tilted her head back to be kissed. Switch gave her a husbandly peck.

"You know where the Glock is, don't you?"

"Yeah."

Without thinking about it beforehand, I kissed Song, too. She put her arms around my neck and clung to me a little. I kissed her again, disengaging, and looked up to find both Switch and Melanie watching. I shrugged and smiled.

"Let's go," I said.

"I guess you decided she *is* old enough," Switch said as we walked to the car.

"All grown-up."

"You going to take her to Little Saigon tomorrow?"

"No. Let's stop by the Paris Market and see what the old guy knows about her."

"I already talked to him."

"What did he say?"

"She's nineteen like Reggie said, almost twenty. She was born in Saigon nine months after the communists took over. They locked her father up because he was in the other army but her mother shacked up with a commie bigwig who protected her and the girl. She grew up with more than most of those people have because of the politician, but her mother died when she was twelve and the old guy started in on her. When she complained, he sold her to what sounds like a high-class brothel in Hue.

"Tran only talked to her for a little while so he wasn't clear on all the details, but it sounded like they took pretty good care of her—kept her for special customers—until this summer when they sold her. The owner was in some kind of trouble with the government and needed money. She came over on a freighter with six other Vietnamese women. McFadden picked her up on the boat at sea. He knew the captain."

"What about her throat?"

"Tran's English isn't great and he started crying when he was talking about it so it was hard to understand him. The best I could make out, a doctor cut all of them while they were on the boat to make them seem more submissive and to make it harder for anyone to get information from them. It makes them more valuable."

"How did you leave it with him?"

"He's fine with her being here. He asked her if she wanted help getting away from our house and she said no." We were standing by the car and Switch paused, smiled. "Apparently she thinks pretty highly of you. She said you save her good."

I pushed through the afternoon traffic in Belmont Shores and Seal Beach, coming out onto the open stretch of the Coast Highway at Bolsa Chica a little before five. It was high summer in Southern California. The beach that had been empty two mornings before was covered with a bright confetti of bathing suits. Cars on the highway and in the beach parking lots had license plates from dozens of states—big Lincolns that had made the cross-country cruise from New York piloted by old men who could barely see over their steering wheels, convertibles from Arizona driven by lush Chicano women dressed in brilliant colors, cheap family sedans packed full of Midwestern children defying their red-faced parents, shrieking for the ocean. They competed for space in the dream with hoards of local surfers rushing seaward after the workday in pickups and old station wagons, bodies starved for the lift and sting of salt water as if for a drug, and with the tribes of sun-slowed high school students who drifted down from the Orange County hills when school ended each summer and stayed, with brief intervals of sleep in their messy rooms, till the first day of the next academic year.

Traffic clogged the commercial strip in Huntington Beach and we had to sit through the light by the pier three times. That kind of delay usually makes my skin crawl, but I didn't mind that afternoon. It was hot and it felt good to sit and sweat and watch bikini-clad girls scampering across the highway when they were activated by the electric signal, jiggling tanned breasts and buttocks. People are strange. The girl's presence and affection had magically lifted the weight of the future and the past from my shoulders. Despite the serious problems I faced dealing with McFadden, I was lighthearted. The happiness I felt seemed immune to any disaster.

# CHAPTER THIRTY-SIX

A motorcycle was going around the corner two blocks down as we turned onto my street. I only caught a glimpse, but it looked like Reggie on his trike with a passenger. The second person looked like a woman.

Mrs. Pilly's car was still in the garage, the front door still closed up tight.

"They got you good," Switch said when we went upstairs. "You have any idea at all who did it?"

"It was probably some of McFadden's guys."

"He knows where you live?" Switch was shocked.

"Evidently."

"How?"

I told him about my conversation with Don, explained about the hidden camera and the crooked cop.

"That's fucked," Switch said. "Wait a minute—he doesn't know where I live, does he?"

"I don't see how he could. Your car wasn't there and you never took off your mask."

"So what now? Are we at war with this guy?"

"I think I know where the tape is and I'm going to try and get it back tonight. When I do, I'm taking him out."

Switch looked at me with Reggie's favorite expression. "What's that mean?"

"Don's going to help me set him up. They go back a long way and he paid attention over the years. He knows a lot of shit McFadden doesn't know he knows. With his information, I can motivate the cops to snap a bear trap on McFadden's ass."

"You sure he isn't a plant?"

"Pretty sure. McFadden smacked him around and fired him for cooperating during the robbery, accused him of being in cahoots with us. He threatened to kill him, too, and Don thinks he might go through with it. He's helping me to protect himself and to get even with his ex-boss. McFadden's been abusing him for years and there's some resentment built up."

"The worm has turned."

"Exactly."

"If McFadden gets popped, he'll send the cops after you."

"I don't think so. If I get the tape, there won't be any evidence, and he knows I have Song. Sending the cops after me would bring her into it and get him another charge."

"What about his guys?"

"I don't think he has much of an organization. It's him and four or five flunkies. A couple of them will get busted when he does. The others will scatter when he goes down. If it looks like there's going to be trouble, I'll get this place equipped with a good alarm system, maybe go to Mexico for a few months. I'm not worried about his guys."

"Has Pilly seen this yet?" Switch had tuned me out since I was disagreeing with him. He was looking around the living room, taking stock of the damage.

"Not that I know of. I'm worried about her. She wasn't here last night and it doesn't look like she's been back today."

"So?"

"There were gangsters here last night. They might have hurt her—or snatched her."

"What would they want with her? She's sixty-something years old. She's probably visiting someone. Didn't she say something yesterday about a cousin she hasn't seen for a while? Maybe she went up there."

"She's never gone away before without telling me."

"How could she tell you? You haven't been here. Anyway—from what I've seen, she can handle herself. She's pretty good with a gun, isn't she?"

"Yeah, she can shoot. Her and the general belonged to a gun club at El Toro."

"Then quit worrying. What I'm thinking, if she's been away, she doesn't know about the burglary. We can clean it up and pretend like it never happened. No cops. If McFadden's guys did it, we don't want them caught. It could drag us into the whole restaurant thing."

I had planned to call the cops before we touched anything—acting like I'd just come home and found the break-in. But Switch was right. I could fix the door jamb myself and replace her furniture. It would cost me a few bucks that my renter's insurance would have paid, but it would be much better than having the Newport Police Department practicing their TV-imitative arts inside my perimeter. Most of them were nothing but faux-Columbos, mouthing thirdhand wisecracks and walking on the evidence, but every once in a while there was a sharp guy blended in with the group. I didn't want that guy looking in my eyes, asking me a lot of offhand questions. Mrs. Pilly would instantly detect the aftermath of a mess the first time she came up, but I could tell her Reggie got drunk and busted the place up. She'd be a handful. I'd have to hear quite a bit about how she and the marine had slaved and scrimped and "worked like dogs" to have a decent home, but the emotional wound would heal when I replaced everything with newer, better stuff.

Digging in the back of my tumbled bedroom closet, I found the remnants of my tools. Using a backsaw and sharp wood chisel, I carved out the split section of the jamb. There was a piece of one-by-six pine in Mrs. Pilly's garden shed. I sliced it into two strips with a circular saw and fit the wider piece in between the unbroken sections of the jamb, using shims to bring it flush, number-eight finish nails to fasten it to the two-by-four frame. The narrow strip filled in the missing section of stop.

It felt good to find that the old skills were still ingrained in my hands despite an ocean of booze and years of nonuse. I remembered how it felt when I first began to develop those skills in my late teens, remodeling houses in St. Louis, how happy I'd been when old men started looking at my work with approval, slapping me on the back and saying, "You're a purty good carpenter, son!" always sounding surprised as well as pleased.

I imagined myself in the future, building big houses overlooking the ocean during long California days, returning tired and dirty to bathe with Song in the red evening. It was obvious Switch was getting out of the business. Maybe I would, too. I had enough money to start a small construction company, and the rough stuff with McFadden was casting a new light on our profession. I was an outcast like Song, but if she married me she would become a citizen. I would, too, in a way—a member of normal society again with a wife and family of small, golden children. At the same time, I would remain enough of an outsider to be safe from society's psychic Novocain, married to a dark skin with blood tainted by communism.

I swung the door shut and marked the location of the striker. Using my cordless drill and a one-inch paddle bit, I bored a hole for the latch, screwed the latch plate over it and tried the door again. It closed tight and locked. With some sandpaper, wood putty and paint, it would look fine. If Mrs. Pilly wasn't happy with it, I'd put in a new prehung door, something with a crystal window.

Switch worked inside while I fixed the door. Most of the time, he was lazy about domestic chores, liked to be waited on by his lady of the moment. But he came through in a pinch, pitched in and got the job done. By the time I finished, he had the place squared away. The scattered food and lamp fragments were bagged. The undamaged stuff was put away. My bed and dresser were reassembled, the rest of the furniture upright in approximately correct positions.

"Thanks a million, bro," I said.

"De nada," he said, standing in the middle of the room, looking around. "Let's grab something to eat."

He hadn't said a word about the bad consequences of going through with the robbery. Or about the fact that I had lied to him the night before.

"I'll buy," I said.

It was dusk by the time I sparked the Cadillac's big engine. There was an accident in Huntington Beach that caught us in a place where we couldn't turn out. We were stuck just south of the pier for a solid half hour, inching forward in the fast lane. When we finally made it through the intersection, we saw broken glass in the street and what was left of a vintage

'68 Mustang being hauled off by a platform tow truck. It was turquoise with a white vinyl top, a sea-colored car built the year of the Tet offensive.

Since it was getting late, we decided to hit the drive-through at In-N-Out Burger on the corner of 2nd Street and the Coast Highway. The place was packed and it took us twenty minutes to get double cheeseburgers, fries and chocolate milkshakes for four. It was ten-thirty when we arrived at Switch's house. We didn't notice anything until we were on the porch.

# CHAPTER THIRTY-SEVEN

The front door had a grid of glass panes centered between wooden top and bottom panels. The pane next to the doorknob had been smashed out completely. Because there were no jagged edges, the damage wasn't noticeable from the street. The door was unlocked. Switch charged into the dark living room before I could stop him. My gun was in the Cadillac. I ran back to get it. When I returned to the house, Switch was standing beneath the beam that marked the location of the old wall between the living and dining rooms with the Glock clenched in his right hand. Mel hadn't had time to get to the gun. His chest was heaving, his eyes bulging with a combination of fear and rage that resembled panic.

"They're gone," he bellowed.

Two of the dining room chairs were turned over. There was a broken glass on the floor by the kitchen door, shards glinting in the light shining from the hallway. The television was on, playing the local news at normal volume.

"I'll check the office," I said. It had been violently ransacked. Remnants of Switch's hobbies—oil paintings, framed black-and-white photos, wood carvings and pieces of stained glass—were scattered everywhere. Several guitars lay in splinters on the floor. They hadn't found the stash.

When I rushed back inside, Switch was gone. The front door was standing open. I was on my way out the door after him—I knew where he was going—when the television froze me, sucking the will out of my muscles.

"This was a particularly brutal crime," the male half of the news anchor team was saying. His consort made a serious face and shook her head.

"The man, who was found in a drainage ditch in Irvine earlier this evening, apparently was beaten to death with an iron bar," the newswoman said, reading her half of the dialogue from the electronic scroll. "And apparently . . . the bar was forced down the man's throat at some point. Is that right, Jim?" You know the news is bad when local newscasters, the chief cheerleaders of the apocalypse, can't spit it out without verbal stumbles.

"That seems to have been the case, Jill."

"Do we know if the man was alive when this occurred or did it occur subsequently to him being beaten to death?"

"That we don't know, Jill. Police are only saying that the man, who has been identified as Donald Parker, a restaurant manager, apparently was beaten to death with the same piece of iron that was found at the scene."

"A shocking crime, indeed," Jill said through the death mask of her multiple face-lifts. "Police say they have no leads at this time. We will keep you updated as developments occur."

Murder and mayhem were flowering around me. Don's fears had been well founded. He was horribly dead. Our homes had been invaded. Song and Melanie were gone, maybe raped and murdered. We had violent enemies in unknown places who would have to be found and incapacitated. Blood and prison beckoned. I shook my head violently. Tried to think. Switch. I was out the door and down the steps, running with my gun in my hand toward the biker's dilapidated house. As I crossed Melonhead's front yard, Switch came bursting out the front door.

"They're not here," he yelled.

"We'll find them."

"I'll kill him!"

"Who?"

"That son of a bitch Reggie!"

"Reggie wouldn't do this."

Switch was standing in front of me in the middle of the biker's yard, panting, swinging his head back and forth to scan the street. He jerked his red face back toward me.

"You saw the way he looked at Melanie. He wanted her. He already raped the girl. What the fuck are you talking about? He did it!"

"Shut up," I said. "Calm down. He might have said something to the bikers about Song, but he wouldn't break into your house and take the girls." Even as I said it, a rapier blade of doubt punctured me. I remembered the look on his face as he left, the bodies on the mud floor of the forest along the Missouri River.

"Who then?"

"I don't know. The bikers, maybe. They could have done it behind his back."

"I'll kill them all," my good-hearted friend brayed at the black sky. "I'll hunt them down in every lowlife hangout in this city. So help me God. If they hurt Melanie, I'll kill them!"

"There's another possibility," I said and swallowed hard.

"What?"

"It could have been McFadden."

"You said he doesn't know where I live," Switch roared.

"I don't see how he could, but this is like him. His guys broke into my house, now someone hit your place. I wouldn't put anything past them." I paused. We were looking into each other's eyes. "They killed Don," I said.

"The manager?"

"Yes."

"How do you know?"

"It was on the news. Maybe they had a tail on him when we met earlier. Maybe someone followed me from the restaurant."

"You led them to my house?" The hand not holding a gun clenched into a brick.

"I don't know. We have to consider it. And we need to get off the street with these guns."

His barrel chest was pumping like a bellows and his eyes were popping out of his head, but he put his gun in his belt and stalked back down the block with me. He looked like a bull with the first pic in it, head down, feet stomping the pavement, fierce and powerful enough to butt heads with an economy car and win, grabbing it by the bumper and flipping it over to clear his path.

Back at the house, I spread a map of Southern California out on the dining room table. If McFadden had the girls, we would have to hunt him at his office, restaurant and home. I marked the locations on the map: San Pedro, Costa Mesa, Newport. If we found him we might find the girls. If they weren't with him, we'd make him tell us where they were.

The second possibility was that the bikers had snatched them, with or without Reggie's help. Switch was sure it was the bikers, especially after I told him about the auction.

"Where did he say it was?"

"San Pedro."

"Where in San Pedro?"

"He didn't say."

"We have to find it."

Something clicked in my mind. "If there's a girl auction in San Pedro, McFadden probably knows about it," I said. "He may be involved. The computer disks from his house are in the safe. Maybe there's information that will help us find him *and* the bikers."

Someone knocked softly at the front door before Switch could answer. I cat-footed into the hallway and waited with my gun drawn. Switch jerked the door open.

"Is everything okay?" I didn't recognize the voice, hoped it wasn't a cop responding to a report of men in the street with guns.

"Yeah, Pony," Switch said. "Why?"

"I thought I heard some noise down here earlier and then when I came back from the market I noticed the glass broken out of the door." The voice sounded concerned. The name clicked. It was the fem half of the gay couple who lived in the apartment above the garage.

"What did you hear?"

"I thought I heard someone scream, but then I didn't hear anything else and I thought it must have come from Jack's TV next door."

"What time was that?"

"Around ten o'clock." I gnawed the inside of my cheek, tasted blood. We had been sitting in the line at the drive-through, less than three miles away.

"Did you see anyone?"

"Not then. But earlier there was a guy beating on the door and walking around the house. I thought Melanie was home but she didn't answer the door."

"What did he look like?"

"He was about five-eight or -nine, stocky, with a beard."

"What was he driving?"

"One of those three-wheel motorcycles. Is Melanie okay? How did the glass get broken?"

"She's okay," Switch said in a choked voice. "I forgot my key and had to break in. Thanks for checking."

Switch closed the door and looked over at me as I stepped out of the shadows.

"If he hurts Melanie, I'll gut him with a broken bottle."

I didn't say what I was thinking. Just because he was here earlier in the evening didn't mean Reggie was with the guys who broke in.

"Let's get the disks," I said.

There were three of them. The first contained fifty or sixty Word files, mostly business letters and sets of business letters addressed to restaurant suppliers, shipping companies and miscellaneous associates. Most of them were full of complaints and threats. A few were congenial. All were laced with a Richard Nixon level of profanity. I printed several that had San Pedro addresses. The second disk was financial data—spreadsheets and long lists of figures. The third disk was labeled "My Life." It contained a single Word file with the same title—a seventy-five-page autobiography in progress. I skimmed it while Switch canvassed the other neighbors to see if they had seen or heard anything. The picture that emerged wasn't pretty.

McFadden was the offspring of rape. His father, Marshall, had molested a Korean servant and gotten her pregnant. Marshall's wife, Lucinda, had helped him cover it up but hated him from then on. The girl was banished to Korea and Lucinda raised McFadden as her own child. She drank heavily and alternated between lavishing affection on him and savagely beating him. His father despised him. He was an ugly, Mongoloid-looking child, tormented at school until he began to outgrow his classmates and pass his home beatings on to them with bloody relish. He found out the secret of his birth rooting through his mother's papers after she drank herself to death while he was a sophomore at Tustin High School, turned even more savage, broke the boy's back. He dwelt on that incident at some length, recalling the satisfaction it gave him. His prose was crude but clear. A sense of rage and self-loathing ran through the document. He never meant for anyone else to read it. It was a private record of hell. I stopped reading after the first twenty pages, just glancing at the rest of it. There were lots of rape vignettes, real or imagined, him forcing Asian women to do a catalog of degrading sexual deeds. Lots of descriptions of young girls, what he had done or wanted to do to them. Nothing that could help us. I blocked my mind from thinking about Song and Melanie.

# CHAPTER THIRTY-EIGHT

Switch came back as I was returning the disks to the safe. We got the sawed-off shotgun, a blackjack and three boxes of shells out of the stash, one for each weapon. I double-checked the .38. Switch put the blackjack in his back pocket, the Glock in his belt. He carried the 12-gauge.

We stopped at O'Reilly's at Temple and 4th, where Reggie had met the bikers the night before. Leaving the shotgun under the seat, we walked in heavily, looked around. No one had seen Melonhead or his crew. We tried two more bars on our way north—one on 7th Street, one on Broadway. There was no sign of Reggie or the bikers.

We were almost through downtown, heading for the bridge across the harbor, when I spotted Reggie's trike in the parking lot of a dive one block off Ocean. I backed the Cadillac into a spot close to the street so that we could peel out if we had to. Switch found a dark spot between the bar and the building next door where he could cover the door. I went in.

There were two guys in leathers at the bar with a skinny junkie between them. Her stringy blond hair needed washing and she had missed her lips the last time she touched up her red lipstick in the ladies' room. Obnoxious motorhead music played on the jukebox, guitars strangling at high volume. I checked the booths and found an old man with a gray ponytail and tattooed arms drinking whiskey by himself in one, a fat biker chick rubbing a guy's dick in another. There was no one in the filthy men's room.

The bartender was surly at first but he loosened up when I asked about Reggie.

"Oh, yeah, old Reggie was in here earlier bothering the barmaid," he said with a grin that showed teeth that shouldn't have been shown. Old Reggie. The bartender couldn't have known him any longer than two nights, and had probably only known him for one, but he talked like they'd been in the same cottage in reform school thirty years before and been pals ever since.

"Is he still around?"

The bartender swiveled his shaggy head back and forth and then looked at me with a comic face. "Do you see him?"

"His scooter's in the parking lot."

The bartender shrugged.

"When did he leave?"

"You taking a survey?"

"No."

"You buying a drink?"

"Sure. Give me a double shot of Wild Turkey."

He grabbed a bottle with a Wild Turkey label, poured and set a large shot glass deftly in front of me. I picked the glass up and sniffed. It smelled like dirty feet.

"It's Wild Turkey," the big man said defensively, trying to block out the mental image of himself with a siphon, pouring rotgut from a gallon jug. I nodded and set the glass down.

"Four bucks," he said belligerently. I handed him a ten.

"Keep the change."

"Thanks." He jangled the cash register and came back over. "What did you want to know about Reggie?"

"When did he leave?"

"Hey, Angelina." The barmaid was lounging at the other end of the bar, talking to the debutante between the two bikers. She looked over. "What time did Reggie leave?" The girl shrugged. She was a tough-looking little redhead with the surprising good looks that a lot of biker chicks start out with.

"Around nine-thirty," she said.

"You know where he was going?" the bartender said.

The barmaid said something to the junkie that made her throw her head back and howl like a coyote, then walked over to us, swinging her junior-high-school-size shoulders like John Wayne.

"Who wants to know?" she said.

"This guy's a friend of his. Trying to track him down."

The girl looked at me, mentally chewing gum, appraising. Then she smiled. A wide, warm, winning smile with movie star charisma that lit up the bar and made me forget the mess I was in for part of a second.

"He left with Melonhead," she said. "I don't know where they were going. Melonhead said something about picking up a couple of *bitches*." She mocked Melonhead with the emphasis she put on the last word. He wasn't as bad as he thought he was.

"Thanks," I said.

"Anytime." She let her eyes linger on mine for an extra moment, challenging and inviting, then sheathed her amazing smile and walked back down to the other end of the bar.

I nodded to the bartender and headed for the door.

"Aren't you going to drink your whiskey?" He sounded hurt.

"No."

"Come back and see us," Angelina called as I was going out the door.

Switch waited till I was at the car before he came out of the shadows.

"He left with Melonhead a couple of hours ago," I said. "They talked about going to pick up some girls." Switch's torso swelled like a prairie chicken's, his face got mean like a rooster's. "They could have been talking about Mel and Song," I said. "Or they could have meant the two girls they already had."

# CHAPTER THIRTY-NINE

McFadden's office was dark, the parking lot deserted. We drove along the San Pedro wharf, looking for his BMW and Melonhead's van. The parking lot by the fish restaurants was full of cars, mariachi music and drunken laughter drifting over from the waterside patios. Past there, out toward the point, the fish-packing houses were closed up, gates padlocked, floodlights illuminating dilapidated buildings.

We turned around in the rutted lot where the road peters out, grinding the muffler on a gravelly hump.

"Shit," I said.

"What now?" Switch asked, grim.

"Let's hit his office," I said. "If we don't find anything there, we'll try the addresses on the letters."

"Right. There might be something there. And you need the tape."

"I don't care about the tape now. I only care about getting Melanie and Song back. Everything I have is on the table, Switch."

I knew he blamed me for what had happened and I couldn't argue with his reasoning. Whether it was McFadden or the bikers, I'd brought the trouble to his door. But I didn't want the conflict in the open. We had to work together, now more than ever. For one more night at least, we had to be a team.

We parked in the shadows between the office and the waterside buildings where they unloaded the fish and packed them, silver on silver, in boxes of ice. When we got out of the car, I heard the black water slapping at the pilings, thought about all the bodies in the ocean. Out at sea, a container ship coming into the harbor blew two long, sad blasts.

Switch ghosted through the alarm system. Upstairs in McFadden's personal office we found his third and largest safe. It was a McGregor 2000, a massive steel box manufactured for small banks and savings and loan companies in the 1940s and fifties. First glance, I knew we couldn't open it.

We ransacked the rest of the office quickly. There was a can of lighter fluid in one of the desk drawers. I thought of torching the place. He would be notified when the alarm went off. He might show up. We could grab him and make him talk. Fire also appealed as a form of vengeance, a way of getting back at him for the trouble he had caused us. I couldn't do it, though. It seemed too much like Vietnam, escalation after escalation. If we kept escalating with this guy, everyone was going to end up dead. Everyone might, anyway, but I didn't want the mayhem lit by chemical-scented flames that came from my hands. I'd been a lot of things in my life, but not an arsonist.

My chance to get the tape was gone. He'd know we had his office, move the tape, maybe turn it over to the cops, who'd try to hang two burglaries and an armed robbery on me, long gray years of misery if convicted. I pushed that thought to the back of my mind.

We used a Thomas Guide in the outer office to locate the three local addresses from McFadden's business correspondence. The chances of him being at one of them were slim, but we didn't have any other leads. It made sense to check them while we were in San Pedro. If we didn't find him, or someone who knew where he was, we'd race south to Balboa.

The first two were dark warehouses with padlocked parking lots. The third was a tavern halfway up the hill on 9th Street. As we rolled toward it, the black Mercedes with the IMPORT license plate came out of the alley beside the bar and passed us, heading back down the hill. I bounced into the alley, waited a couple of beats, backed out and followed.

"That car was at McFadden's office this morning," I told Switch. He pumped a 12-gauge shell into the chamber of the sawed-off.

Staying well back, I tailed the big sedan down 9th to Pacific Avenue, then along Pacific to Paseo del Mar, the road that curves and climbs along the shoreline of the Rancho Palos Verdes peninsula. A couple of miles outside town, the Mercedes's taillights lit up as it slowed at the gate of a walled compound. A figure swung the wrought iron open for the idling car as we passed.

The front of the compound stretched for a couple hundred feet along the right side road. The house, half hidden in a grove of palm and eucalyptus, was a two-story stucco with a flat, Italianate roof, probably five thousand square feet. A steep slope went up behind it. Across the road, the land fell toward the water, fifty feet below. The front of the house was dark. There was a For Sale sign on the concrete block wall, red letters on a white background.

A quarter mile from the corner where the wall of the compound made a right angle and started up the hump of the peninsula was a turnoff into a new development. Past one jury-rigged streetlight, the raw concrete street disappeared into ink. I parked on gravel behind the construction trailer. We loaded our pockets with extra shells and took all the guns. All the jobs we'd pulled, we had never taken extra bullets before. I got my binoculars out of the trunk.

It was a beautiful summer night—midseventies with a breeze off San Pedro Bay. A thick smear of stars shone down on us as we started up the slope along the seven-foot-high wall, picking our way through the weeds and cactus in the heavenly light.

Two hundred and fifty feet up the slope, the wall made a ninety-degree angle and ran along the back of the property. Climbing a little higher, taking cover in some wild sage, we were able to look down into the walled area. Light leaked from half a dozen curtained windows in the back of the bulky house. There were seven cars and a van parked around the perimeter of the asphalt square where the driveway ended. The black Mercedes. McFadden's blood-colored Beemer. Melonhead's van. One of the three overhead garage doors was open, showing the back end of a cream-colored Continental.

The biggest Korean I've ever seen came out the back door. He was six-

six, 350 pounds, minimum. Beneath a bright yellow aloha shirt with palm trees and purple flowers, he had the boulder belly of a Chinese Buddha. His droopy face was Buddha-like, too, sleepy and pacific, more suited to chuckles than gangster growls. The most un-Buddha-like thing about him was a light machine gun that hung from a strap over the bulk of his right shoulder. He stopped outside the door to light a cigarette with a flip-top lighter. After looking up at the stars for a little while, smoking, he walked with a rolling sailor's gait across the asphalt and disappeared around the garage corner of the house. A commercial-size air-conditioning unit kicked on at the other end of the building, filling the vacant backyard with a useful hum. We waited.

Five minutes later, the yellow shirt and baggy chinos came back into view around the far corner of the house. After grinding out his cigarette butt on the patio, he went back inside. I had the binoculars trained on the door as he opened it, saw the interior of a kitchen with stainless steel appliances, the foot of a staircase in a hallway beyond.

The yard sloped down about a hundred feet from the wall to the back of the house. Floodlights lit the parking area. The other half shaded off into darkness. We could have waited for the guard to come out and circle the house again to gauge the frequency of his routine patrols before going down, but I didn't know how much time we had.

"You cover me from here," I said. "I'll go over the wall on the other side and see if I can get a look through the windows."

"You think the girls are in there?"

"I hope so."

I followed the back wall to the corner and skidded down even with the house. The big compressor hid my scuffling sounds beneath a calm mechanical *om*. I scraped a knee going over the wall, dropped down into a bed of irises, crunchy and slippery. There were two tall windows on the end of the house, flanking the rectangular bump-out of a chimney.

I crawled to the closest window and peeked through a crack in the curtains. A dozen men in business suits and expensive sports clothes sat in folding chairs facing the fireplace. Their faces were as intent as those of medical students watching a complex operation. I couldn't see what they were staring at.

Standing behind them, watching the action in front of the fireplace or talking in small groups, were another half dozen men, less well dressed. Reggie and Melonhead were talking with the big guard by a doorway that led back toward the kitchen. It looked like Reggie was telling a joke. He stood back from the other two and put his right hand on his hip, wagging the index finger of his other hand. Melonhead smiled grudgingly and shook his head. The renegade Buddha laughed, rocking back and forth, belly and heavy jowls jiggling. There was another Korean with another machine gun in the opposite back corner. Buyers and sellers and security guys. It looked well organized, two-thirds Asian.

I slipped around the corner to the back of the house. The curtains on the window by the air conditioner were closed tight. The next window showed a bright crack. Peeking in, I saw a tiny Korean man in a black tuxedo standing in front of the fireplace facing the buyers with his hand on the shoulder of a naked brown woman. The old man's black hair was slicked straight back above a lively face. The wrinkled hand that touched the girl was small as a child's. The girl's body was voluptuous, thighs swelling above her knees and curving back into her crotch, grapefruit-size breasts riding high. A swollen eye disfigured her pretty Mexican face and it took me a moment to recognize her.

In his right hand, the little man held a white wand like a conductor's baton but longer and thicker. After saying something that brought smiles to the watching faces, he slid the wand between the girl's thighs at a downward angle, moving it back and forth to define the slit beneath her curly pubic hair. Her wounded face stayed blank while he probed her and he didn't seem to like that. Twining his left hand in her thick hair, he struck her sharply across the front of her thighs, making her mouth twist with pain and fear.

Moving the wand up from her thighs, holding it flat against her body, he traced the curve of her stomach and breasts, working the nipples a little as he passed, continuing up over her throat and chin to her lips. Moving the stick back and forth, he worked it into her tattooed mouth like a bit. She closed her eyes and clenched her hands at her sides. He gave her another welt on her thighs and spoke into her ear. She opened her mouth and let her tongue hang out, then pulled her lips back to show small white teeth.

Beside me, the compressor made a loud click and stopped with a sigh. When the auctioneer spoke again, I could hear him, faintly but distinctly.

"Show your butts now," he said to the girl, smiling in a grandfatherly way, pointing with his baton to a sawhorse with a wide, padded top sitting in front of the fireplace. She turned so that her back was to the audience and looked at him, frightened and uncertain. "Spread your pretty butts," he said sharply. When the terrified girl draped herself over the device, her fingertips and toes just touched the hardwood floor and her private parts were fully exposed. The Korean slapped her butt with his hand, and pushed her legs wider apart with a tiny foot encased in black patent leather.

"Bidders only making inspections now," he said.

Several of the men came forward to examine her. I don't know if they were looking for signs of venereal disease or checking her for fit. The last one, a thin white man who looked like the first Darrin on *Bewitched*, was unsteady on his feet. He had removed his suit jacket and the tail of his white dress shirt hung out in back. He knelt down behind the girl, putting a silver hip flask on the floor. After looking closely, he took a long sniff. Several of the seated men laughed, turning their heads sideways to look at one another. Encouraged, the man leaned closer and licked the girl's genitals and anus. The girl bucked up, the crowd roared and the auctioneer struck the man lightly on the head with his wand. It was a raucous moment in an otherwise sedate affair.

"Must buy before kissing," he said. The smaller, machine gun–toting Korean had materialized beside him. The thin man scooted back from the girl, holding his hands up to show compliance.

"Kay," he said in a drunken voice. "Juss won a little taste of that Mex meat." One of the other men who had inspected the girl helped him up from the floor.

The prune-faced little auctioneer started the bidding at $15,000. It went up in fast thousand-dollar increments to $26,000 and then turned into a $500-a-pop haggle between the thin man and a moon-faced Chinese businessman in a blue pinstriped suit. The drunk started to falter at $30,000 and the Chinese got her for $31,500. He stayed seated while a younger Chinese man went to the front, fastened the girl's hands in front of her with plastic handcuffs and led her toward the back of the room. McFadden came through the door from the kitchen as they crossed the room. He was wearing his boating clothes and looked drunk. As Carla passed by, he slapped her hard on the back of the head, causing her to cry out and stumble forward. The Chinese man caught her by the arm to keep her from falling, snarling something unintelligible at McFadden. McFadden laughed. In the front of the room, the Darrin look-alike was drowning his disappointment, flask straight up, throat bobbing. Running along the back of the house, I looked through the kitchen window and saw the weeping cashier going up the stairs ahead of her escort.

Boulder Belly came into the hall a minute later. When the escort came back downstairs, he had a skinny white girl with large, pendulous breasts and a coal black bush. The two men exchanged a few words and a laugh. The girl looked at the floor. She had tattoos on her breasts and thighs. One of Melonhead's bitches. When the escort took her into the great room, the guard lumbered toward the back door. I scrambled across the patio, staying low, and ducked into the garage. Crouched in the darkness in front of the Continental, I heard the storm door open and close. Shortly, the guard strolled by, cigarette glowing in his face.

# CHAPTER FORTY

As soon as he rounded the corner, I poked my head out of the garage. There was no one in sight. I slipped along the edge of the patio, eased the storm door open and tried the doorknob. It was unlocked. A second later, I was inside, .38 in hand. The gun felt different than it ever had before, heavier, like it might kill someone that night. Going in alone was reckless. But the world of the crime is a fluid, intuitive place and I was going with the flow, doing what came next. If they were in the house, which seemed more and more likely, I wanted to get Song and Melanie out as fast as possible.

As I passed the door to the great room, I heard the auctioneer speaking: ". . . nineteen year olds and not disease . . ." With a drawn weapon and the element of surprise, I felt powerful and invisible. A sex slave auction was the greatest diversion in the world. I would be in and out before they settled on a price for Melonhead's blow-job baby.

The stairs and upper hall were carpeted with thick beige. I moved soundlessly down the hall, checking two dark bedrooms before I heard a cackle of laughter behind a third door. It sounded like a woman. I hoped there was only one guard but I didn't really care. Excitatory neurotransmitters were in charge. I was surfing the white foam of the adrenaline flow, silver and brave. I burst through the door silently.

There was no furniture in the room. A skeletal Asian woman in her fifties stood by the wall opposite the door with a short steel whip in her hand. A green-embroidered gown clung to her wizened form. The yellow skin on her face had been refitted, pulled taut and thin across the front of her skull, and her black hair was pulled back into a tight bun. A row of women and girls wearing white terry-cloth robes sat on the carpet in front of her with their backs against the right side wall: Song, Melanie, Carla, a white girl who looked like Melonhead material, several young Asians and a blond girl—Russian, maybe—twelve or thirteen years old. A second blond child, ten or eleven, was standing in front of the madam crying. She was nude and the woman was tickling her in a sensitive spot with the tip of her three-foot whip. Nine heads jerked toward me as I came in the door. The old woman's laughter died in her throat. Two faces flashed hope and excitement. One turned furious and gathered itself to scream.

Before I could reach her or a sound could come out of her bright red lips, Song sprang on the madam, looping something white around her throat. The older blond girl was on her ankles in a flash. Her face turned into a dragon and she slashed behind her with the whip, striking Song twice before I swung the pistol as hard as I could into the side of her head. I caught her as she fell, laid her bony body on the floor.

"Thank God, Robby," Melanie sobbed.

"Who are *you*, man?" the biker girl asked in a thick voice.

Song was clinging to me. I pulled the robe off her shoulders. There were angry welts but no blood. I gave her a quick, hard hug, kissed her ear and pushed her away. The older blond girl was comforting her sister, wrapping her in a robe. The other women were frozen with surprise and fear.

"Tie your robe," I said to Song, handing her the cloth belt she had used to choke the old woman.

"Where's Switch?" Melanie said.

"He's outside with plenty of firepower. The Caddie's around the corner. We have to get out fast, before they come up for another girl."

"I was going to be next," she said, her voice quavering. "They were going to take me next."

"They're not taking you anywhere. Are you ready?"

"Yes."

"Grab that whip. We're going down the stairs, through the kitchen and out the back door. Be as quiet as you can. Anybody tries to stop you, use that on their face."

I took Song's hand and started toward the door.

"What about them?" Melanie was halfway to the door, looking back at the blond children.

"There's no way we can take them all without a gunfight," I said.

"Tay us with you," one of the Asian women pleaded. She had a black eye and a swollen lip. Her thin wrists were fastened together with plastic handcuffs.

"Please take us," Carla said.

"No! You are safer here. We'll send the cops to get you. They'll be here soon."

"But the little girls . . ." Melanie said.

"Move, Mel." I shoved her hard toward the door.

"Who *are* you?" the biker girl asked in the same stoned tone. Carla and two of the Asians were on their feet.

"Stay put," I said, raking them with my eyes. "Wait for the police. You'll be okay." Carla's face was the last thing I saw as I closed the door. It was the second time I'd left her with terror in her eyes, but I couldn't take her. She knew my voice if not my face, might connect it to the restaurant robbery. I couldn't take the chance.

I looked at my watch as we padded down the hallway, Melanie first, then Song, then me. We had two minutes to get outside and hide in the garage before the guard came around the corner by the air conditioner. Even if he put it in second gear and rounded the house a little quicker, I thought we could count on a minute, and a minute would be enough.

So it was a surprise when he came through the door from the great room just as Song reached the bottom of the stairs. He must have cut the circuit short and come back into the house through the front door. Luckily, he wasn't the smartest son Korea ever sent to serve the West. Seeing two girls in the hall, he knew something was up, but there was some processing time while he figured out what, and we kept moving toward the door. When his eyes shifted to me, they brightened with malice. I brought the .38 up, stiff-armed, and pointed it at his head from ten feet away.

"Don't move or make a sound," I hissed.

The girls stopped, too.

"Keep going," I said. "Out the back door and over the side wall. Hurry!"

I don't know if he thought I wouldn't shoot, or if he was so devoted to his job that he didn't mind taking a medium-size slug, but he grabbed at Melanie as she edged past him. She lashed his drooping face with the armadillo tail, opening a bloody gash on his cheek and blinding him with pain. I was proud of her for that. While he reeled back with his hands over his face, she and Song dashed by him into the kitchen. I tried to follow, but he had snapped back from the remote region of his pain and was in the hallway again as I went past him. Snake-quick, one of his plump hands shot out and grabbed my shirt. I clubbed him with the gun, but the blow slipped off the blood on his face and he swung me around as easily as if I were a child, slamming me into the wall. I knew that would bring people quick. Out of the corner of my eye, I saw Melanie jerk the back door open. Using my momentum as I bounced off the wall, I brought my right elbow up hard under the Korean's chin, sending an electric shock of solid contact through my skeleton. Big as he was, that staggered him. Grabbing his flowered shirt with both hands, I took a vicious swipe with my left knee. If it had hooked his groin the fight would have been over. But he was recoiling from the first blow and I misjudged the distance, raking his belly and losing my balance, ending up on my butt on the floor.

Melanie was gone, but Song had stopped in the doorway. I saw her white-robed figure, framed by the night as the guard charged back at me, stomping. One of his size fourteens came down with crushing force on my right shin and calf, sending blue bolts of pain through my body. A barnyard-size kick to the shoulder knocked me flat. I heard people shouting and running in the next room, saw Song on the Korean's back, choking him with her belt. I tried to sweep-kick his legs out from underneath him but it was like kicking the stone legs of a statue. Then someone kicked me in the head from behind. I saw a dense galaxy of four-pointed white stars. They were different sizes, ranging from half an inch to three or four inches across. Each one was perfectly shaped. The rays were thick where they crossed, tapering out to silver tips, pulsing slightly. In the first instant of the flash, the galaxy was the size of a TV screen. The next instant, it was infinite. Then it was dark.

# CHAPTER FORTY-ONE

**I was crammed** into a tight space, lying on my left side with my legs doubled up and my head bent so that my right ear touched my shoulder. It was pitch black. When I tried to move, I couldn't. I was hemmed in on every side. A smothering sense of claustrophobia clogged my chest. I fought off the ruinous urge to thrash and scream, focused on my breathing, trying to take deep breaths to block the panic. But I was wadded like a handkerchief and couldn't expand my lungs. For a horrible moment, I thought I was in the afterlife, trapped forever in a suffocating pocket of eternity, and the impulse to scream surged up again, more powerfully. I clamped my teeth together to keep the shriek inside, focused on my breath again. I could only take in and expel a pint of air with each respiration, but I inhaled and exhaled slowly and steadily and, after a little while, the aura of hell receded.

The lower half of my body—shoulder, arm, hip, leg—was asleep. My hands were cuffed behind my back. The back of my head throbbed with a blade-sharp, lead-dull ache that made me wonder if my skull was fractured.

There was a scent of ammonia in the blackness and it acted like smelling salts. Memory gathered and clarified. I remembered the sequence of raids and counterraids. I'd fought the big guard and lost. Song had come back for me. They had her again. Melanie had gotten away.

I wondered how long I'd been out, and where I was, and where Switch was.

There were voices coming from somewhere in the darkness, from behind me through a door.

"Which one would you take if you had your pick?"

"Brown womans. Her fat butts is fine." A baritone.

"How would you do her?"

"In her dirty butts!"

"Her asshole?"

"Yeh!"

"Why would you want to stick it in that stinky hole when you got a fresh pink pussy right there, ready and waiting?"

"More excitements for me."

The voices were muffled by the door and distorted by my awkward position, coming into my ear upside down or sideways, but I recognized one of them. While I groped around in my damaged head, struggling to put a name and face to the sound, more people came into the room behind me. I heard a door slam, some mumbled greetings.

"You find 'em?" the familiar voice asked. It was Reggie.

"We'll get them. We know where they live." That was the busboy.

"Si, conosco donde viven. Ustedes son muertos."

"Tell your buddy to speak English. Me and Tiny don't dig that taco talk. Right, Tiny?"

"Don't dig!" the deep voice rumbled.

"If he can't understand you, he thinks you're talking about him," Reggie said. "That makes him mad. You don't want that."

"Speak English," the busboy said.

"No pralum."

"What are you going to do with the jack-off in the closet?"

"Kill him," the busboy said. "Whadya think?" He laughed.

"Have some fun furse," the greaser voice said in a cruel tone.

"Have a whole lot of fun," Snuff said. "You guys can get in on it if you want. We're gonna make hamburger out of this motherfucker, a little bit at a time."

"Why not just off him and be done with it?" Reggie said.

"It's personal," the busboy said. "Mr. McFadden wants him to howl. He said we could do whatever we want with him as long as he ends up on the bottom of the bay tonight."

"How you getting him out there?"

"My boss's boat."

"That big Sabreline down at the dock?"

"Yeah."

"Your boss must be doing okay."

"You could say that," Snuff said. "Get him out of the closet."

The door behind me opened and light exploded in my dilated eyes. Someone grabbed me by the hair and dragged me out. The pain was excruciating, needles jabbed into soreness. I stiffened, expecting to be kicked, but the busboy stood above me grinning. He wanted to stretch it out. We were in the stainless steel kitchen.

"Hi, tough guy," he said. "Help him up, Manny." The Latino I'd seen in McFadden's car on the island the night before jerked me to my feet and shoved me into the middle of the room. My numb leg gave way and I fell on my numb side. Manny kicked me in the spine with the point of his cowboy boot and dragged me to my feet again. I hopped to catch my balance. Manny was a thirty-something greaser with a potbelly and a little two-part mustache above his cruel lips. He was wearing blue jeans tucked into brown boots and a brown plaid shirt. He had a big automatic stuck in his belt. Snuff was wearing chinos, sneakers and a white polo shirt with a bulge under it. I was handcuffed and hurt and they both had guns.

Sitting across from each other at a white Formica table, Reggie and the big guard were playing blackjack silently, currency scattered around them. Both of them glanced over at me. Reggie's face was expressionless. The cut on the guard's face had been repaired with three butterfly bandages.

"What happened to the party?" I said.

"You broke it up," Snuff said. "Everybody took their pussy and split in case the cops showed up." He put his face close to mine. "You made a lot of people mad, you know that? Because of you, we're gonna have to find a new location and do the auction over next week."

"But you whone be here to see it," Manny said.

"Did McFadden take Song?"

"That little gook slit you stole from us? Yeah, he took her—with a leash around her neck. He's probably fucking her with a crowbar right now to teach her a lesson. What do you think about that, huh? Why do you want her so bad? You like little girls, tough guy? You some kind of pedo or something?"

"He's a perv," Manny said. "Juss like his amigo Don."

"You hear what we did to your pal Donny boy?" the busboy asked softly, breathing his putrid breath in my face.

"I heard."

"You didn't hear what we did to him before we killed him, though, did ya?"

"No."

"Tell him what we did, Manny."

"We stuck a big rebar up his queer ass," the Latino said. "All the way up. We thought he like it hard in the asshole, but I guess he din. You should uh heard that faggot scream. He beg us to kill him."

"You forgot to tell tough guy the best part."

"Oh, yeah!" Manny nodded, excited, reliving the moment. "We build a campfire in the arroyo and heat the rebar red hot before we fucked him with it. You should have heard that motherfucka scream!"

"Manny used to work for Noriega," Snuff said. "He knows lots of things to do to people, don't you, Manny?"

"Oh, yeah. I work for Pizzaface, man. We kill lots of people real horrible."

"You're gonna be begging to die," Snuff said. His glittering eyes were six inches from mine. Bright needles were shooting through my arm and leg as they woke up. My head was throbbing and whirling. I was nauseous.

"Did you two grab the girls in Long Beach?"

"Fucken right—who you think grabbed them?"

Reggie stirred in his seat, adjusted his money a little bit.

"How did you find the house?"

"You awful curious for a dead guy," Manny said.

"I followed the faggot to Second Street when he met you," Snuff said. "When you split up after your sneaky little trip to Mr. McFadden's office, I followed you back to your fat friend's house."

"I wait for the fag at his house," Manny butted in. "When he showed up I grab him and call *mi amigo*. He came over and we took him out to the hills."

"It worked out great," the busboy said. "I was in the middle of something . . ." He smiled at me maliciously. "I was in the middle of something sweet—but I'll have plenty of time to go back and finish that after we ruin you."

# CHAPTER FORTY-TWO

A **cold fear was spreading** through my body, turning my muscle to water, but I squirmed out from under it with a sudden stiffening of my will. Their masturbatory recitation of Don's murder infuriated me. The busboy's deformed ears infuriated me. I wanted a pair of tin snips to cut them off. If they left my legs untied, I'd give at least one of them a serious injury. Shoulder-butt one of the murdering bastards over the cliff or kick one of them in the face hard enough to fracture nose and cheekbone.

"Where we gone do him?" Manny asked.

"You guys want in on this?" the busboy asked the card players.

"Nah, I gotta get going," Reggie said.

The Korean shook his huge head disapprovingly.

"Suit yourself," the busboy said. "We'll take him out on the boat where no one can hear him scream. Go tell Blockman and Lan get ready to cast off."

Manny sucker-punched me in the side of the head as he went past, shaking loose a few of the silver stars, making my ears ring. He went out the door chuckling.

"Look what I got," the busboy said in his soft voice. The blow had staggered me sideways. When I turned my head back toward him, I was looking down the barrel of my own .38. The busboy was smiling, showing food-caked teeth, reservoirs of bacteria and stink. Lunging at me, he cocked the gun, banging the muzzle against my forehead. "How you like that?" he said. "Remember that?" I didn't see any point in answering. Every muscle in my body was frozen steel. He laughed and lowered the gun, letting the hammer down and starting to turn away. As the tension began to drain out of me, he spun back toward me, cocking the gun in my face again, making me clench from anus to forehead.

"Mr. Park's guys saw your fat friend outside. He got away with the Mex. Where would they go besides his house?"

"I don't know," I said. I looked up at a clock on the kitchen wall. It was three in the morning. I had been out for hours. Snuff saw me look at the clock.

"He's not coming back for you," he snarled. "Your sweet ass is mine. Now, where else would he go?" He cracked me on top of the head with the cylinder of the pistol, sending a blinding spear of pain down through my skull and spine. It felt like a cherry bomb had gone off between my scalp and skull.

"Don't make blood in here," the Korean said.

"Sure. We'll get it out of him on the boat."

"So you going to run me into town?" Reggie asked the big guard, pushing his chair back from the table.

"Okay, Reggie. Soon as they are go."

I couldn't believe he was going to let them take me. I tried to catch his eye but he was gathering up his money and didn't look toward me.

"Reggie . . ." I said. He looked over and shook his head.

"If you play you've got to pay," he said.

"You two know each other?" the busboy asked sharply, stepping back so that he could watch both of us, holding the .38 low, close to his waist.

"Used to," Reggie said.

"From where?"

"We did some jobs together in the old days. Don't point that pistol at me. Tiny might get nervous and shoot you a couple of times with his machine gun."

"You're not giving the orders around here," Snuff said. "He works for Mr. Park, not you."

"Yeah, but we're friends. Right, Tiny?"

Tiny answered with a banana-size smile and a heavy nod.

"Relax," Reggie said. "You're welcome to this prick. He don't mean shit to me." He looked over at me. "I'm in Melonhead's crew now, palsy walsy. Have to be loyal. I'm gonna do some jobs for Mr. Park, too. He says he'll give me all the work and free pussy I can stand. This is my big, bright California life, bro. My big chance. You wouldn't want me to fuck this up like I fuck everything else up, would you?"

Every warning I'd ever heard about not trusting Reggie came back to me with the force and clarity of prophecy. The fear started creeping up again, along with a powerful sadness. The world was slipping away from me—human history, my own detailed life, everyone I'd ever known. The thought of losing Song hurt the most. The love I felt for her may have been just the silly infatuation of a small-time crook pushing forty who was tired of being alone. But it felt more real than God. And I was never going to see her again.

"Bet you wish you'd hired old Reggie when you had the chance, don't you?" my mentor said with a mean smirk.

The busboy relaxed, letting the .38 hang down. "No one's going to help you, tough guy," he said. "You're gonna get the full treatment snitches get in the joint. I'm gonna break your teeth out, pop your eyeballs, take a hammer to your fingers and toes. How's that sound? Before you get too weak to scream, I'm gonna get Mr. McFadden on the phone so he can listen to the silly shit you're gonna say."

Reggie and the Korean had their money counted and put away, the cards back in the blue-checked box.

"You guys got any beer around here?" Reggie asked the guard.

"In refrigerators."

Reggie pushed his chair back and came around the table. He moved slowly, limping, favoring his bad leg. His hands were hanging down beside him. As he went behind the busboy, he brought one hand up casually, as if to pat my tormentor on the back. I saw a silver glint in his paw. There was a loud crack, like a yardstick being slapped on a tabletop, a flash one inch from the busboy's ear. Snuff's head jerked sideways, lying down on his opposite shoulder. Continuing the same smooth motion, Reggie swung his toy pistol toward the Korean and fired three times into his right shoulder. The busboy hit the floor like a sack of cement, blood puddling by his ear. The guard fell backward off his chair. His automatic weapon clattered away from him on the tile while he floundered on the floor, making a strange whistling sound.

"Sorry, Tiny," Reggie said, looking down at him. "Nothing personal."

Sticking his girl's gun in his belt, he went through the busboy's pockets quickly, coming up with a handcuff key.

"Grab a heater and cover Tiny while I cuff him," he said after he unshackled me. I picked my .38 up off the floor by Snuff's hand. I had been wrong about his career trajectory. He had made it past busboy to become a rapist, murderer and corpse.

Reggie had a hard time fitting the cuffs around the Korean's thick wrists. The guard looked at him resentfully while he tried, still making the whistling sound, breathing in and out through a pencil-size opening in his puckered lips.

"You not plays fair," he hissed.

"Show me the rules," Reggie said, hooking the big boy's tentacles together. Crawling a few feet on his hands and knees, he took possession of the machine gun and pulled himself up, holding on to the counter. "Here," he said, tossing me a set of keys. I saw the gold Cadillac insignia while they were in the air, but it took a disoriented moment to realize they were mine.

"They found your car down the street," Reggie said. "Your buddy must have hoofed it. Let's get the fuck out of here before that beaner comes running and we have to kill him, too."

## CHAPTER FORTY-THREE

I walked into a cloud of vertigo as we hurried out the back door, the world going whirligig in echo of the busboy's last, skull-chipping blow. I gave the keys back to Reggie, concentrating to make overlapping images of him merge into a single figure. The Caddie was parked in the garage, next to the Continental. The tires barked as we backed out, the sound of using all the engine's power for maximum movement without any high-school-boy spin. We serpentined around the end of the house and down the curving driveway with our lights off. The gate was locked. Reggie edged the front bumper up against it, pushing until there was firm resistance, then hit the gas, bursting the lock with a loud crack, sending the gates flying. They flapped back as we went through, banging the sides of the Cadillac.

"Hey! Easy on the car," I said.

Reggie made a sour face.

We were sideways across the Paseo del Mar. He cut the lights on and wheeled a quarter turn in reverse, pointing the Caddie toward San Pedro. As he shifted into drive, Manny came charging up the steps from a dock below. He ran into the road ahead of us with his .45 in his hand. Reggie stomped the pedal to the metal. The tires screamed on the asphalt for a fraction of a second, then bit. My head snapped back as the big car leapt forward. Manny fired once as he dove, grazing the roof of the car. The front bumper smacked his feet as we shot past, spinning him in an ugly tumble down the embankment.

"I get him?" Reggie said.

"You got a piece of him."

"Good," he grunted. "Where to, bro?"

"McFadden's office. Take this road into town. I'll tell you where to turn."

Reggie drove fast, squealing around the curves as we followed the shoreline into town. The car hugged the road beautifully, taut suspension smoothing out the imperfections of the pavement, but the shifts in centrifugal force were making me nauseous.

"Slow down," I said.

"They'll be after us in that Lincoln."

"I don't think so. They got one dead guy and two injured. They'll probably take off in the boat for Balboa. Meanwhile, we don't want to get stopped by the cops in the middle of the night with a machine gun in the car."

Reggie put his flat foot on the brake, slowing us down to forty-five. "I wish you'd been this safety conscious back at the ranch," he said.

I looked at him.

"You almost got us both killed."

"What are you talking about?" I said.

"Saying my name wasn't real bright. Lucky Tiny was there, or that punk woulda thrown down on both of us. Why'd you tip your hand you knew me?"

When I didn't answer, Reggie glanced over, reiterating his question with raised eyebrows.

"I was scared," I said. "I thought you were leaving."

"What?"

"I didn't know—the way you were acting—I'm sorry."

"Well, that takes the fucking cake," he said, shaking his head. "You thought I was going to leave you with those fruitcakes? Why? 'Cause we had an argument over a susie-floozie? I know I ain't exactly been a choirboy since I got here, but I'd have gone down swinging against that whole crew before I let 'em do you, Robby. How could you think that?" His Adam's apple bobbed and he blinked his eyes rapidly. "After everything we've . . . you must not think much of me." There was a tremor in his voice.

"I think the world of you, partner," I said, my vision blurring, warm and salty. "The whole wide world."

As we drove on through the silent, starry night, I heard a rattling under the car. Reggie noticed it, too.

"Whud you do to your muffler?" he asked in a cranky voice that reminded me of his mother when she used to complain about us smoking dope in the basement.

"I hit a high spot turning around down by the docks."

He shook his head. "How many times I told you, Rob—you get a cherry ride like this, you gotta take care of it. Otherwise, you're gonna end up with nothing but a piece of junk."

He was right. Besides the muffler, the front and sides of the car had been damaged by the wrought iron gates, and there was a bullet crease in the roof. My vehicle was being destroyed, bit by bit, as the night progressed.

Back in town, we drove past McFadden's place twice before stopping. There was no one in sight. We parked in the same place Switch and I had parked earlier. The door was unlocked. Upstairs, I flipped a light on briefly. Open drawers and cabinet doors everywhere. The safe open and empty.

"He's clearing out," I said, feeling my heart go gray. "He knows we're after him. He knows Switch got away. He's going to take the girl and what he can grab and disappear."

"Where you think he'll go?"

"He could go anywhere. He's got money and connections and a seagoing boat. He'll have to go by his place in Newport before he splits, though. Maybe we can catch him there."

"Let's ride."

We took Gaffey Street to the bridge, sailed up and over the entrance to the busiest harbor in the world. The sparkle of dock and crane lights stretched for miles in both directions, illuminating cargo ships from the ends of the earth carrying every conceivable product, including steel containers full of refugees, living and dead.

"Where did you go when you left the house?" I asked.

"Melonhead's, but he wasn't home."

"What did you do then?"

"You writing a book or something?"

"Just curious."

Finding Melonhead gone, Reggie had holed up at the bar on Fourth Street, drinking for several hours. When he was half numb, he decided to go down to Corona del Mar and get his clothes and his trike.

"Fucking raghead driving the cab couldn't find the place. We drove around for a fucking hour. Then when I got there I found—" He cut himself off in midsentence.

"Found what?"

"Nothing—I found out you weren't there, that's all. I couldn't find my shit in that mess upstairs. So I hopped on my scooter and split."

"Did you see Mrs. Pilly?"

"Naw—I told you, I didn't see anybody."

"Did you go back to Switch's later on?"

"Twice. First time, the girls were home but they wouldn't let me in— like you told 'em, probably." He scowled at me. "When I went back, the place had been broke into and no one was around. Melonhead was back by then, and I couldn't find you and I didn't know what the fuck was going on at your buddy's house, so I decided to ride with him and make five hundred dollars. We drank some beer at a bar Melon goes to, picked up his skanks and drove out to San Peedrow in his van. A shriveled-up little slope was auctioning off puss to a bunch of fat cats when a fight broke out in the kitchen. Next thing I know, they're stuffing you in the pantry. Everybody was grabbing girls and taking off but I stuck around to save your ungrateful ass. Won one hundred eighty dollars from that big Ko-rean while I was waitin'."

I saw a bank clock that showed 4 A.M. as we rolled into Long Beach on Ocean Boulevard. Just past the art museum, we turned inland a couple of blocks and drove along 3rd Street to Switch's house.

"His car's gone," I said as we passed.

"Did he drive it to San Peedrow?"

"No. We rode together."

We parked around the corner on Orizaba and snuck up to the dark house, peeking in the windows and listening at the side door before bursting in. There was no one inside. A couple of Switch's best suits and some of Melanie's clothes were gone. Empty hangers were scattered around the bedroom. Their luggage was missing. The hidden compartment in the garage was open and empty. The jewels from McFadden's were gone. It was just Reggie and me now.

"You think he made it down here somehow and cleared out with his stuff?" Reggie asked.

"Looks like it."

"I wonder how Tiny is doing."

"What?"

"I'm worried about Tiny."

"I don't think those little twenty-five-caliber slugs hurt him very much. That's like a bee sting to a guy his size."

"They put him down," he said.

"They've probably worn off by now."

"He was bleeding pretty bad. I'm calling someone for him in case those other guys take off in the boat and leave him."

While Reggie made an anonymous 911 call to send an ambulance out to the auction house, I grabbed two bottles of water from the refrigerator, drained one and took the other into the dining room.

"Message light's blinking," Reggie said when I handed him the water.

I pressed the play button.

"Hello?" a woman's voice said. "Hello?" There was a long pause. I recognized the voice but couldn't place it. "This here is a message for Mr. Rivers or Mr. Jackson . . . what?" There was a murmur of consultation in the background. "I'm calling to warn you that there's a maniac on the loose . . . what?" Sounding exasperated. "Oh, all right—there's a *sick* maniac on the loose and he may be aheading your way. So batten down your hatches or clear out, one or t'other. Ring 555-6844 just as quick as you get this message . . . and be mighty careful."

I recognized the number, too—the voice and the number. They came together with a magnetic click in my mind. It was Laura McFadden. When I recognized her voice I also realized who it was she had reminded me of when I spoke to her two days before: my landlady, Mrs. Pilly. They made a likely pair, two vintage Southern California ladies with country accents left over from the time when Orange County was a rural paradise with a population that would have fit into a large football stadium.

Her calling Switch's house to warn us—about McFadden, I assumed—made me think there might be a deeper connection between the two women than their accents and ages. I glimpsed a blurry image of it out of the corner of my mind's eye but couldn't bring it into focus.

Hearing from Laura was as strange as hearing from Don after the stickup, scary strange, but hopeful, too, somehow. Had McFadden run there and done something crazy? I punched in the number. No answer and no answering machine hooked up to the old rotary phone, resting in its cradle.

"Who was that?" Reggie asked.

"McFadden's aunt."

"The fuck she calling us for?"

"I don't know. Let's go. If we don't find the girl in Newport we'll try the aunt's place in Orange."

# CHAPTER FORTY-FOUR

**We drove down** Temple and turned left on Ocean, heading south toward Newport Beach. It was the fourth time I'd followed this route in four days. San Pedro Bay was just as beautiful at night as during the day, colored lights on the oil-pumping platforms shining like fairy works out on the black water, harbor lights off to the right, and the tiny lights of ships heading out to, or coming in from, the open sea. The orange segment of moon had dropped low in the sky and the stars were beginning to dim.

We took a deserted 2nd Street through Belmont Shores and Naples to the Coast Highway. It was empty, too, and we rolled toward the equator at a smooth sixty-five miles an hour listening to the surf rumble on the long, unbroken stretch of beach between Bolsa Chica and the Santa Ana River.

As we passed the Arches, Reggie squirmed in his seat. "Why don't we let that motherfucker go?"

I shook my head. "I can't. But you can pass if you want to."

Reggie heaved a melodramatic sigh. "You know how to operate that spray gun?" he asked.

"I don't guess it's too complicated," I said. "But no, I've never used one before."

"I have."

I waited for more information. After a quarter of a mile, I gave in and asked, "When?"

"Fagey stole a couple of them from a dope peddler one time. We took them out in the woods and fucked around with them before we sold them. Exact same gun. Wicked. I cut a little tree down with one clip. We got five thousand dollars for the duce." I waited again. "I'll carry the spray gun," he said. "You take the pistols. If you have to shoot mine, aim for the guy's head. It don't have much body wallop."

"Thanks, Reggie."

"Gotta die sometime."

The light at the intersection by the bridge was red. We stopped directly across from where we had been sitting Monday night when the cop car went past on its way to the old man's accident.

"You can turn right on red," I said.

"No shit?"

Reggie made a reluctant turn onto the bridge. As we went over the concrete arch, I saw the Sabreline tied up at McFadden's dock, people carrying boxes and bundles down from the house.

"They're still here," I said.

"Great," Reggie said. "What's the plan?"

"Try and get the girl without killing anybody else."

"Then what?"

"I haven't thought that far ahead."

"Better start," he said in an irritated tone.

The shops and restaurants along Marine were all closed, the summer strollers all sleeping. Peaceful and picturesque beneath the golden globes of the streetlights, the deserted lane looked like a movie set or a just-constructed street scene in Disneyland: the Balboa Island Adventure.

At Park Street we turned left, crept across the toy bridge onto Little Balboa Island with our lights off, took another left on Abalone. Reggie parked the same place we had on Tuesday night when we hit McFadden's house the first time. He turned off the engine and sat staring out the windshield. I waited for him to say whatever he was going to say.

"You ever kill anybody?" he asked.

"No."

"Ever shoot anybody?"

I hesitated. It seemed to me I might have lied to him years before, told him I'd shot a guy on an out-of-state job. "No," I said. "I've never shot anyone."

His big knuckles bunched up as he clenched the steering wheel.

"It ain't nothing," he said. "You think it's going to be, but it ain't. There is a bang and they fall down. You don't feel nothing. It's just like watching someone get shot in a James Bond movie. That S and Wesson is a good gun. Aim for the guy's middle button and squeeze the trigger. If you hit him anyplace in his gut or chest, he'll go down. Don't worry about whether he's dead. As long as he ain't moving is all that matters. Don't look at the blood." He stopped talking and we both sucked the atmosphere, inflating our chests like swimmers getting ready to dive, held the air in for a few moments and then let it out with a single, audible exhalation. He looked over at me. "Can you handle it?"

"I'll kill everyone in there if I have to," I said.

"That's all I want to know. You can't stop to think about it once lead's in the air. What's the plan?"

"They're busy out front. We'll go in from the back and get the drop on them. If we take them by surprise, maybe no one will get hurt."

"What about afterward?"

"Depends on what happens. If there's a shoot-out, we'll be on the run from the cops. Even if we get the girl without gunplay, we'll have to get out of town for a while. If there's time, we'll make a quick stop at my place to pick up some clothes and gear. If not, we'll head straight for San Diego. I've got money there."

"Old Mexico?"

"Yeah."

"You're willing to give up everything you've got here for that girl?"

"I guess I am."

Reggie shook his head. "You're lucky, Robby. I haven't felt that way 'bout anyone since me and Teresa split up. She's the last one I woulda took on the world for. I didn't know people could still feel that way."

"What happened between you two?"

"Same thing that always happens. I fucked it up."

"She still around?"

"Yeah. She still looks good, too."

"Maybe she'll come out for a visit when this is over."

Reggie made a sour face. "Sure," he said, "when donkeys fly." Then his face got serious. "I'm sorry I fucked Song, man. I wouldn't have if I knew how you felt."

"Yeah," I said, "I know. You ready?"

"Ready as I'm gonna be."

We got out of the car with our guns. Reggie put a full clip in his pistol, handed it to me along with the half-empty clip that had been in it. I put the two chunks of metal in my back pocket, stuck the .38 in my belt. He looked at the machine gun beneath a streetlight, made sure the long, curved clip was full and that there was one in the chamber.

"Showtime," he said.

# CHAPTER FORTY-FIVE

**Salt water sloshed** and sucked at the seawall, making sounds like children urinating and buckets being emptied as we walked through the damp darkness. The clatter of metal tackle and the creak of docks and hulls emphasized the stillness of the summer night. Dawn was coming but the island was still sunk Atlantis-like in the depths of sleep.

The back of McFadden's compound looked the same as it had two nights before: wide, ghost white garage door closed tight against the concrete, dark gangway to the right. Reggie went into the passageway first, his shoulders rocking up and down with the action of his shortened leg. He grunted as he boosted me up so that I could look into the backyard. There was a lightning bolt of pain in my kicked shoulder as I pulled myself up. My stomped calf ached. Light from the front of the house showed through the sliding glass doors that opened into the breakfast room. The upstairs windows of McFadden's office glowed. There was no one in the backyard or kitchen. A piece of unpainted plywood covered the hole in the back wall.

We scrambled over the wall and crouched in the shadows. Back in the world of the crime, I felt rejuvenated. The throb in my head shrank to a mild pulsation, and the sick fear of disaster left me. It was the brain chemistry cocktail, sure, but something more. The pungent scent of crushed mint surrounded us. I hadn't noticed on our first excursion, but McFadden had an herb garden and we were in it. A quote from a botany book floated to the surface of my mind: "The smell of mint makes glad the heart of man." I smiled. Tearing a handful of tough, leafy stems out of the ground, I rolled them between my hands, then held the juicy pulp to my face and breathed deeply.

"What are you doing?" Reggie hissed.

"Smell this." I held the mint out toward him. He snuffed twice.

"Smells like peppermint schnapps," he said.

"McFadden's not expecting us," I said. "Either Manny lied about what happened or they think they scared us off."

"We gonna bust in the back door?"

"Let's try the plywood first. Cover me from here."

"You're covered," he said, shifting his crouch to aim the machine gun at the patio doors, holding it loosely at his side. When I pulled on the bottom of the plywood, it came away from the foundation. McFadden's gunmen hadn't paid attention in prison carpentry class. They had missed the studs, sinking their nails in soft sheathing. I wiggled the wood gently, working it free from the wall.

I poked my head inside and looked around. The spare bedroom was dark and undisturbed. A shadow flashed across the bright crack beneath the door as someone walked past, pounding the floor with quick steps. Pulling out, I waved Reggie over. He kept his eyes on the patio door as he strolled across the lawn. Handing me the machine gun, he lowered himself to his knees in front of the hole and pushed his shoulders between the two-by-fours.

"They need to put these fuckers wider apart," he said.

"You'll fit."

A minute later, I was standing in the darkness beside him listening at the hall door. He held the machine gun in a classic gangster pose he probably learned from watching Robert Stack on television, chest high with his trigger hand against his body. It was pointed at the door. The house was quiet. Then the front door slammed and someone came into the hall and jogged up the stairs. A few moments later, the front door slammed again and someone else took longer coming into the hall and going up the steps.

"How many of them are there?" Reggie said.

"McFadden, the captain, Manny and a couple more," I said, mentally counting the men I'd seen on the dock. "Five guys, tops."

"Wonderful."

Almost immediately, the two who had gone upstairs came back down.

"What's wrong with your leg?" an Asian accent asked.

"Cocksuckers try run me over. Clip my foot."

"Who tried to run you over?"

"Who the fuck you thin'?" Manny said. "Hole up."

They stopped in the hall.

"I thin' it's broken," Manny said. "I ever get my hands on those cock-suckers I'm gonna chop their *cojones* off and shove 'em down their troats."

Reggie nudged me.

"What were Mr. McFadden and the captain arguing about?"

"*No se.* Fuck! That hurts."

"Where are we going? Why are we taking all this stuff?"

"Shut up and quit asking so many questions. Juss do what your toll. Carry these boxes out to the boat."

"You shouldn't talk so tough with your hurt foot."

"Oh yeah? Is this tough 'nough for you?"

"Hey—I'm sorry, Manny. Just kidding you. I'm going."

"You going, all right. Ask Mr. McFadden what else he one us to bring. Then get your ass back here and get the ress of this stuff."

The front door opened and closed. We waited.

"My poor fucking foot," Manny whined. "I'll keel those fuckers." He went into the bathroom next to the room we were in and closed the door. Shortly, the copper pipes in the walls rattled and there was a rush of water.

"Is he taking a bath?" Reggie said, mystified.

"Maybe he's soaking his poor foot. I'm going to see if I can find Song. Stay out of sight unless I run into a problem."

I eased the door open. The hall was empty. Leaving the door open so Reggie could see and hear, I searched the downstairs rooms quickly. They were deserted.

"No one down here," I whispered to Reggie as I headed for the stairs. The upstairs rooms were empty, too. McFadden's wall safe was standing open. I went to the front of the house and peeked out the window. No one on the dock. Back downstairs, I motioned Reggie out of the bedroom.

"Let's take Manny now. We'll grab the others as they come back in. Go up the steps a little way where you can get the drop on anyone who comes into the hall."

"Check."

I didn't want to put Manny on guard by trying the doorknob and finding it locked, and there was no one in the house to hear the noise, so I kicked the bathroom door open, lunging to get my weight into it, stomping the wood beside the knob. The flimsy panel gave way so easily that the momentum of my kick carried me into the bathroom. I caught the vanity top with my left hand to keep from falling, swinging the bullet path of the .38 down to focus on Manny's plaid-shirted back. He was sitting on the edge of the tub with his feet in the rising water, shoes and pistol on the floor behind him. Twisting to look back over his shoulder, he flashed a shocked face at me and reached for his .45. One step carried me across the bathroom, and I stomped on his hand as he grabbed the gun, crushing his fingers between metal and tile. He got out half a yelp of agony before I brought the cylinder of my gun down on the top of his head with a smack that was simultaneously sickening and satisfying. The blow turned his nerves off like a switch. His muscles went slack and he fell backward off the ledge of the tub, feet flipping up in the air with a spray of water, head cracking into the tile. There hadn't been time to exchange a word. His eyes had poured out anger, fear and hatred in an intense beam. I'd never seen anyone look so alive. I don't know what he saw in my eyes.

I turned the water off, grabbed him by his wrists and dragged him from the bathroom into the adjacent bedroom. Leaving him in the middle of the floor with his head bleeding and his feet dripping, I ran across the hall into the front bedroom and looked out the window.

"Nice work," Reggie growled from up in the stairwell when I came back into the hall.

"The captain and a deckhand are coming up the gangway," I said. "The captain has a shotgun."

Reggie's face went flat.

"Get out of sight at the top of the steps," I said.

I opened the damaged bathroom door all the way and stood with my back against it, holding the .38 barrel-up beside my head. If they came around the corner into the hall and went straight up the stairs, they wouldn't notice the door jamb. If they did notice, I'd throw down before they could retreat.

# CHAPTER FORTY-SIX

They came into the house talking.

"I don't like it either, Lan. Not one damn bit. But I'm captain of his boat. I have to take him where he wants to go. That's the way it works. This is it, though. He'll have to find a new captain in Ensenada. I'll get a boat without all this bullshit. You can come with me as mate if you want to."

"Okay, Captain. I'll go along if it's like that. I just want to get away from them. They scare me. Manny pulled his gun on me just now and looked like he might use it."

"Where is he?"

"I don't know. He was in the hall."

"Manny!" The captain's sea voice boomed through the house with a threat in it.

"He must have gone upstairs."

"He needs to get back downstairs, then. Manny!"

They started up the steps. In a second, I was behind them.

"Hold it," I said. When their heads jerked around they were looking down the barrel of the .38. I could see the captain being conscious of the shotgun in his right hand.

"Drop the scattergun, Cap, or I'll cut you in half," Reggie's menacing voice came from the top of the stairwell.

"Don't shoot," the captain said. He lowered the shotgun to the carpeted steps and let go of it. It slid past Lan to the base of the steps. I kicked it down the hallway.

"Put your hands behind your heads and walk up," I said. "Do what you're told and you might not get hurt."

I ducked into the front bedroom where Snuff had lived his final days and looked out at the boat. No one. Upstairs, Reggie had them backed into a corner with the force field created by the machine gun. The captain looked grim. Lan was crying.

"We don't have anything to do with McFadden's bullshit," Blowman said, looking me in the eye. "We're just sailors."

"Where's the girl?" I asked.

"She's on the boat."

"Where?"

"Tied up in McFadden's cabin."

"Where is he?"

Blowman's clear blue eyes clouded over, shifted to look at the empty space beside my head. "He's with her," he said.

Wild horses took off inside me in a dozen directions. My hand clenched the pistol. The captain tried to back through the plaster wall. Lan cried louder. I put the muzzle of the .38 against the crisp, white cloth of Blowman's uniform, pushing it into his hard gut.

"Please don't shoot," he said. "I got a wife and five kids."

"What's his plan?"

"We're leaving for Mexico as soon as the boat is loaded. Ensenada, then on to Mazatlán. I don't know after that."

"Who else is on the boat?"

"Just him and the girl."

"Let's go."

"Where are we going?" Blowman asked.

"To the boat."

"We'll do whatever you say. Just don't hurt us."

"What'll I do with this crybaby?" Reggie asked, jerking his head in Lan's direction.

"Bring him down to the living room."

We went down the staircase—Blowman first, then me, then Lan, with Reggie bringing up the rear. The stocky captain was two steps into the living room when I heard a smack and groan behind me. Whirling, I saw Manny, face and hands bloody, swinging the barrel of the shotgun he'd clubbed Reggie with back toward me, murder in his eyes. Reggie was face-down on the floor, trying to crawl. As hard as I'd hit him with that thirty-two-ounce revolver, as hard as his head had cracked into the tile floor, I'd never have believed Manny could be back up and fighting if I hadn't seen it. His head must have been solid bone, three inches thick on all sides around a walnut-size brain.

I drew a bead on his middle button at the same time as he got the gaping muzzle of the 12-gauge trained on me. Lan dived from between us, crashing into an antique cherry stand, splintering it and sending picture frames flying, glass shattering. As I squeezed the trigger, Blowman grabbed me from behind, deflecting my aim up and to the right. There was an ear-splitting bang and an explosion of plaster dust on the wall beside Manny's head.

"Don't shoot!" Blowman shouted as Manny clicked the trigger on the shotgun. At point-blank range, the 12-gauge would have ripped a hole in my chest that no one could have repaired and probably massacred Blowman in the process. But nothing happened. The captain hadn't pumped a shell into the chamber when he took the gun from the boat's arms locker.

Manny charged with the shotgun at quarter arms. I stomped on Blowman's instep and tried to wrench free, but his arms were like steel bands. So I shoved backward against him just as Manny brought the butt of the gun up at my face in a jaw-destroying swipe. The walnut stock grazed my cheek as the captain and I fell backward. Blowman used my own force against me, adding his strength to it, turning as he went back and flinging me against the wall hard enough to break bones. My head banged against the plaster and the .38 flew out of my hand. As I slid down the wall, Blowman grabbed the shotgun from Manny, shoving him back toward the breakfast room.

"You stupid son of a bitch," he roared. "You could have killed me!"

Reggie was up on his elbows, reaching for the machine gun. Blowman kicked it away and racked the shotgun. I had the .25 halfway out of my pocket when he turned the gun on me.

"Toss it!" he said.

I tossed it. My head was spinning again, vision going in and out of focus. Manny was leaning against the wall, throwing up. Blowman backed a few steps into the living room where he was out of reach and covered Reggie and me with the shotgun.

"Lan!" he shouted. "Get McFadden!" Lan crawled out from behind a sofa and scrambled, wild-eyed, toward the door. Before he got there, McFadden burst into the room, nearly tearing the heavy wooden door from its hinges.

"What the fuck is going on in here?" he screamed, face wadded with rage, big fists clenched.

"These two jumped us," Blowman said, panting, red-faced. "Manny clubbed that one and that one tried to shoot Manny. I don't know what happened to him. They must have jumped him. Manny! How did you get hurt?"

Manny made a loud retching sound. McFadden's eyes slashed around the room, taking in the broken antique and the blood on his immaculate walls and floor.

"You're Rivers, aren't you?" he said. "You're the guy who's been causing all these problems." His voice was low and furious, rumbling in his chest like the growl of a lion.

It may have been my blurred vision, but his face looked more distorted than before. His out-of-place eye had floated higher up on his forehead and his jaw was wrenched to the side like the slipped jaw of a robot. His clothes were as elegant as ever, his fingers sparkling with jewels.

"Where's my mommy's necklace?" he said. That meant that Switch had definitely gotten away. I was glad of that. But the baby word in McFadden's deformed mouth sent chills up my spine. "You shitcup sharkbait, where's my mommy's necklace? I'll shove a butcher knife up that little bitch's pussy and make you eat it. I'll burn your guts in front of your face. Where is it?" Spittle bubbled around his lips as he spoke. He was losing it. Syphilis reaching a new stage, or mental illness blossoming under the stress of seeing his rotten lifestyle collapse. Blowman had a horrified look on his face.

"I'll give it back," I said, with a bargaining smile. "I'll give everything back. The money, the jewels, the disks. Just let me take the girl."

"You'll get her back in a sausage grinder. I'll grind you both up together." He bent over to retrieve the .38 and .25, straightening up with

Reggie's gun tiny in his left hand and mine, more proportionate, in his right. He looked crazy. "You'll give everything back when you're dead! I'll break a bloodwood in your gutcup sharkbait shit! Drink shitblood fuck-mommy in the fuck, fuck, fuck gook bitch ratfuck . . ." He caught himself raving and shook his head violently, slinging off the look of insanity that clung like a reptile to his face. "You'll give everything back, all right."

"Leh me at 'em, Mr. McFadden," Manny whispered through a vomit-sore throat. "I'll make 'em talk."

"You'll help. Get cleaned up first. Get that bloodcup off of you. I hate the smell of brown blood. Chink!" He turned to Lan, who was crouched in a corner. "Help him."

He turned back to me as Manny left the room, leaning on Lan. "Dusky skin shows the presence of animal blood," he said in a friendly tone, as if we were discussing sports over a drink at the Balboa Club. Then his face spasmed again. A fish hook sunk in his cheek was jerked back and to the side. He showed his teeth in a rigor mortis–like grin and clenched his eyes shut. When he opened them again, I noticed they were netted with red veins. There was a patch of blood by his right pupil where a tiny vessel had ruptured.

"People always try to stop me from getting what I want," he said. "I know how to take care of people like that." He took a step toward me and drew back his size-thirteen suede shoe and tried to kick me in the stomach. I caught most of the sickening force with my elbow, arm folded and tucked in tight. "People tried to stop me from getting what I wanted in high school and college, but I got what I wanted. Daddy's partner tried to stop me from getting what I wanted after Daddy died. Do you know where he is?" The friendly tone again. I shook my head. "In a coma in the state hospital in Fresno. No one knows who he is. Just a nameless vegetable blood sleeping in his own shit because the niggers are too animal to clean him. I visit him sometimes and make cuts on his body with a razor so his blood comes out." He laughed harshly. "I got what I wanted. From dirty brown bitches, too, their stinking fuckholes. They say no, but I hurt them and take their stink. I always take care of people who try and stop me. You have been trying to stop me. I'm taking care of you."

Reggie was sitting on the floor with his back against the wall. He had a grim look on his bloodhound face. It didn't look good for our side. Manny and Lan came back into the living room from the hall. Manny was cleaned up but still looked sick. He had reclaimed his .45.

"Blowman, you and Manny take this sharkbait out to the boat and tie them up. We'll dump them in the ocean. The chink and I will get the rest of the stuff that goes to Mexico. Be ready to cast off when we come out."

"Listen here, McFadden," the captain said, trying to sound brave. "Running illegals is one thing, but I won't be party to murder." He'd faced years of storms at sea, waves as tall as five-story buildings, but he couldn't keep a tremor our of his voice.

"You'll do what I tell you to do unless you want to go to prison," McFadden said, regaining his hardass businessman's tone and demeanor. "You are in this up to your thick neck, Blowman. Neither of us is safe if we leave them here. We'll have some fun with him." His voice took on a coaxing tone. "We'll cut them so they bleed and drag them on a short line behind the boat to attract blood sharks. No one will ever know what happened to them. Sharks will solve our problem. They are better than lawyers. They are always hungry for blood. Do you ever dream of blood, Blowman? Busted red oceans of sweet black blood—"

"No!" Blowman cut off the maniac's tirade, shouting to override the quake in his own voice. "I won't do it!"

"Yes, you will," McFadden said. "Don't forget about the pictures, tree trunk. You don't want me to send them to the police and the maritime union, do you? You don't want the world to know about the little-boy stink in your pants, do you?"

Blowman's face turned white. "You said you destroyed them! You said we were square after the last trip to San Francisco. You bastard!"

"Don't ever call me that," McFadden screamed. "I still have them and you'll mind your fucking manners if you want to keep your freedom and reputation. People see those pictures and the land sharks will eat you alive. They're worse than salt sharks, Captain. I'll give you the pictures in Ensenada and we will go our separate ways, but until then you do what I say. Is that clear?"

"Yes, sir." Blowman had shrunk at the mention of the pictures. He looked older and weaker, as if his thick body had been hollowed out and was collapsing under the atmospheric pressure at sea level.

McFadden and Lan disappeared into the hallway. I caught Reggie's eye, trying to communicate not a plan, exactly, but a state of mind. We looked into each other's eyes. It seemed to me that we were on the same wavelength.

# CHAPTER FORTY-SEVEN

"`All right, you two.` Get up." Blowman sounded broken. He would do what he was told. We got to our feet, slowly and painfully, standing about ten feet apart with our backs to the wall that separated the living room from the staircase. The front door was to our right. Blowman was in front of us in the middle of the living room. Manny was in front and to our left, at the edge of the breakfast room. He stuck the .45 in his belt and picked up the machine gun, checked the clip and safety. He'd learned his lesson with the shotgun.

"Less go, sharkbait," he said, pointing the weapon at me. I turned and started toward the door. Reggie came behind me, Manny behind him. Blowman was still off to the side, out of reach. There was no way I was going to let them tie me up and take me out to sea. If they were going to kill me, they'd have to do it on Balboa Island, and there was going to be a fight.

The sun wasn't up but the faint light of dawn was materializing in the air, photon by photon, evoking the mystery and promise of a new day in the world. I took a deep breath of the cold, luminous air, smelling the sea and the flowers in the front garden, rose and mimosa. My head and vision cleared as fresh oxygen brightened my blood and bathed my brain. The water in the channel was still black. It would be easy to dive from the dock as we walked out to the boat and swim underwater to the far shore, surfacing for quick gulps of air. They might not be good shots. Even if they were, my head would be a difficult target, appearing and disappearing in the half-light. But I couldn't do it. I couldn't abandon Song. Or Reggie.

Off to our right as we walked toward the front gate, two women came around the curve of the island, walking toward us, arm in arm, on the wide sidewalk. They wore long cloth coats, one gray and one tan. Their faces were obscured by the half-darkness and the old-fashioned scarves tied around their heads. One of them reminded me of the cameraman's daughter, but I wasn't sure if it was her.

Blowman saw them, too. "Hold up," he said as I reached the iron gate in the low stone wall around McFadden's front yard. "Let them go by." His voice was threatening. He was more dangerous since his dressing-down. We knew his shameful secret. Both he and Manny would be quick to shoot. I glanced back over Reggie's shoulder. Blowman had lowered the shotgun along his leg. Manny was hiding behind a yew.

The women were coming on, steady and slow, out for an early stroll. Despite their old-lady clothes, something about them reminded me of little girls running away from home. They were about a hundred feet away when McFadden came out the front door. "I told you to get to the boat," he said to Blowman, instantly furious.

"Some people coming," Blowman said. McFadden pushed past the captain and looked at the women, eighty feet away, walking with their heads slightly bowed.

"Fuck them," he said. He had a briefcase in one hand, my .38 in the other. "We'll be on the dock before they get down here. Get this gutcup shit on my boat."

"Go on," Blowman said to us in a choked voice. McFadden slammed the front door and herded Manny and Lan, who carried a large cardboard box, toward the sidewalk with his big body. The women were fifty feet away. Glancing back to see where the weapons were, I saw someone coming fast and silent around the canal corner of the island. With their attention focused on the ladies approaching from the opposite direction, the bad guys didn't see the figure bearing down on them like vengeance in human form.

I jerked my eyes back so as not to tip McFadden, counted two beats and stopped in my tracks. Reggie bumped into me and I felt the impact as Blowman bumped into him. Taking a wide sidestep to my right, I pivoted to my left, shoving Reggie aside and flinging myself on Blowman before he had time to bring the shotgun up from beside his leg. As I crashed into him, I saw Switch swinging the Glock into the back of McFadden's square skull. Blowman absorbed the impact of my lunge without going down. We grappled over the shotgun and he shoved me back over the stone wall into McFadden's yard. Switch had crashed full tilt into McFadden, sending him stumbling forward into Manny, who was still shaky from the blows to his head. The two of them went down in a tangle, taking Reggie with them. The machine gun flew over the seawall and splashed into the channel. The .38 slid along the sidewalk. As I landed hard on my back in the grass, the captain took off in a bowlegged run, brushing past the women. Lan dropped the cardboard box and took off after him.

"I've got you now, you son of a bitch," Switch said, pointing the Glock at McFadden as the big man got to his feet.

"Yes, deed, but I have gots *you*." The miniature Korean who ran the auction had stepped out of the passageway between the two houses, holding a large automatic in his hand. To this day, I have no idea where he came from. He may have come down on the boat from Palos Verdes or driven down to take Song back for the postponed auction. His seventh-grade body was sheltered by the gray trunk of a magnolia tree, giving him an advantage over Switch, who was standing in the open. There was a shrunken-head smile on his wrinkled face.

"And I've got you, little man," said the gray-coated lady. She and her companion had come up beside the Korean, still walking with their heads down, seemingly oblivious to the scene around them. Now, suddenly, she had a Luger in her hand. Pulling myself up on the stone wall, I saw that it was Mrs. Pilly with her husband's prize pistol. I didn't recognize the other lady, but McFadden was looking at her like someone seeing a ghost or monster.

"Drop it or die, little man," Mrs. Pilly said. The ringmaster, still wearing his formal clothing, simpered and dropped the automatic. It thudded to the ground.

"Sometimes there's been making mistakes here," he started in soothingly. "Not good so many guns because police is been coming sometimes."

The other lady walked past Mrs. Pilly, stretching out her arms to McFadden. "It's okay, Lewis," she said to his stricken face. "It's not your fault. Give the little girl back and we'll make the best of it. You've been sick in your head for a long time. You need doctoring. I'll stand by you, Lewis—you're family and I'll stick with you till the end."

"How did you find me?" he said.

"It don't matter, Lewis. I'm here to help."

"No, you're not. You always said things about me. You tried to stop me from doing what I wanted."

"Only when you was a-doing wrong. For your own good, Lewis."

Mrs. Pilly was watching the reunion between Laura McFadden and her nephew, a fact noted by a darting glance out of the corner of the ringmaster's eye. He struck the Luger from her hand and dodged back down the passageway, agile as a schoolboy. In that moment of distraction, McFadden swung a gorilla arm and backfisted Switch, knocking him to the ground, and grabbed his aunt, jerking her body in front of his.

Mrs. Pilly went for her Luger and I scrambled down the walk toward my .38. By the time we came up with the guns, McFadden had pulled the .25 and was holding it to Laura's head as he dragged her toward the dock, using her body as a shield. Reggie had subdued Manny and was sitting on him, panting, with his back against the seawall. He grabbed at McFadden's leg but the big businessman sidekicked him in the face.

"Don't try and stop me from doing what I want," he shouted as he backed rapidly down the dock with his aunt in front of him. "I'll let this bitch's blood out." Laura was a good-size woman and she struggled hard as he dragged her down the dock, but his grip was too powerful for her to escape. I leaned against the magnolia to steady my aim and drew a bead on McFadden's big block of a head.

"Don't, Robby." Mrs. Pilly pushed my gun down. "You might hit Laura."

"I can't let him go," I said. "The girl is on the boat."

McFadden had reached his trawler. Holding on to his aunt with one hand around her throat, he jerked the lines free. Laura was wearing old-fashioned nylons held up with clips and her white thighs and girdle were exposed as he yanked her onto the boat. I started down the dock after him. Looking back, he fired the .25, hitting me in the left shoulder, then flung

Laura over the stern into the black water. The bullet hit me with the force of a hard punch and I slipped and fell on the wet boards, banging my head one more time for good measure, shaking loose a spray of four-pointed stars. The diesel engines coughed and growled. Laura was floundering in the water, calling for help as the trawler churned the brine around her. Blood ran down my arm as I crawled toward my gun. The boat was clear of the dock and the engines roared as McFadden started down the channel toward the mouth of the harbor.

"Help!" Laura cried, weighed down by her coat and clothing, choking on the salty water.

"I'm a-coming," Mrs. Pilly yelled. She had stripped off her coat, scarf and shoes and was climbing over the seawall. Reggie was watching from his seat on top of Manny, looking over his shoulder with saucer eyes. Switch was trying to stop the blood streaming from his nose with a white handkerchief.

I came off the dock in a staggering run.

"Where you going?" Reggie called after me as I went into the passageway between the houses, which led to the street where my car was parked. He sounded curious and not too concerned, as if he might ask me to pick up a six-pack for him if I were going by a store.

## CHAPTER **FORTY-EIGHT**

The only way to save Song would be to cut McFadden off at the mouth of the harbor and, at the rate he was going, there wasn't enough time. He would be small at sea by the time I got to the north jetty, unless . . . The coast guard station was between him and the jetties. That might make him think twice about racing out of the harbor. If he played it safe and slowed down to the posted speed limit of five miles an hour, I might be able to intercept him.

The banged-up driver's door wouldn't latch, and I peeled out with my right hand on the steering wheel and my left on the inside door handle, holding it shut. My shoulder ached and burned. Across the little arched bridge over the canal, I floored it, flooding the 4.5-liter V-8 with high-octane gasoline, crossing the island in thirty seconds, squealing into the ferry lane with no consideration for cops or sleeping citizens.

The car ferry bobbed sluggishly at the base of the ramp in the foggy dawn. The kid with the absent father was sitting on the railing of the ferry, puffing on a joint. He jumped to his feet looking shocked and scared and flicked the joint into the bay as I clattered down the ramp.

"Take me across," I yelled from the car. Peering out of a blended cloud of mist, car exhaust and marijuana smoke, the kid recognized me. His look of panic changed to one of confusion and concern.

"What happened to your car, man? What happened to you?" My shirt was bloody and I had enough lumps on my head to start a franchise.

"There's been some trouble," I said. "Here." I held out two twenties in my bloody left hand. "Take me across as fast as you can and don't tell anyone you saw me or this car."

"You don't have to give me any money. I won't say anything. I never saw you."

He ran to the little pilothouse and revved up the old diesel engine. We backed out of the slip and started across the narrow stretch of water between the island and the peninsula. When we bumped into the slip on the far shore, the boy hurried to the car.

"Are you going to be all right?" Stoned and emotional, he looked like he was about to cry.

"I'll be fine. Be more careful with that weed or you'll end up in trouble."

"I'm sorry about your car, man," he yelled as I went up the ramp.

I sped toward the tip of the peninsula on Balboa Avenue, made a quick right and then a quick left onto Oceanfront, and raced for the jetty. I hit seventy on the narrow, residential lane and, on slick pavement in the fog, ran out of road before I could slow down. Oceanfront ends at Channel Road across from the little park at the base of the jetty. The Cadillac shot across Channel, took out a park bench and plowed into the rocks.

I crawled out of the wreck and continued toward the channel, climbing over the boulders that form the base of the north jetty. McFadden's trawler was fifty yards to my left, still coming out of the harbor as I leaned on a rock and took aim. I could see him at the wheel as the boat came nearer. My first shot shattered the glass on the side of the pilothouse. McFadden disappeared but I didn't know if he was hit or had just ducked. The boat continued straight toward the harbor entrance.

I emptied the gun into the boat, firing five more slugs, trying to disable the engines. The last bullet hit the gas tank or a fuel line and there was a small explosion. A moment later, there was another, larger explosion and the boat burst into flames and began to sink. I pulled off my shoes and shirt, but before I got to the water's edge, the trawler disappeared beneath the turbulent surface, taking McFadden and Song with it.

I thought about trying to escape before the police and coast guard arrived, but my getaway car was destroyed, like McFadden's yacht, and I didn't have the strength or will to flee on foot, weighed down by a sudden and overpowering sadness. Everything seemed to share in a common ruin. So many people were dead, I had lost track of the exact number, and for the living, life would never be as good again. It was, as someone once wrote, a fine setting for a fit of despair.

Then I saw a slender arm rise out of the water, followed by a dark-haired head. Light was coming up in the eastern sky beyond the San Joaquin Hills and the fog had dissipated somewhat. Jumping to my feet, I saw that it was Song, alive and swimming toward the far shore, which was nearer to where the boat sank. My eyes blurred for the second time that morning and energy flooded through me.

I shouted, waving both arms above my head. Song paused in the water and turned, searching the north shore. When she saw me, I waved her on toward the other side, where there was a small beach at the base of the rocky promontory where Reggie and I had stood two nights before and seen McFadden heading out to sea to meet the freighter that carried her across the Pacific.

I wrapped my shoes, my gun and a fist-size rock in my bloody shirt, and threw the bundle out into the channel. Then, without a glance back at what was left of my car or my life, I dove into the cold, choppy water.

We got away.

# EPILOGUE

S●ng was waiting for me on the beach, shivering in a white T-shirt that hung to her knees and was plastered to her slim body. I hugged her so hard that she cried out, then hurried her up the stone steps that led to the street above the cove. Flashing lights were coming down the peninsula behind us and a red patrol boat was roaring toward the harbor entrance, but we made it back to Mrs. Pilly's house without being spotted.

We changed clothes, cleaned out the stash and packed a bag. The bullet had only grazed my arm and Song washed and bandaged the wound. I knew where Mrs. Pilly kept her spare keys, and we made our getaway in her Impala, Song dressed like a Vietnamese hip-hop girl in an oversize shirt and pair of shorts, her eyes still dilated with adrenaline.

By 8 A.M. we were getting off the I-5 at 1st Street in downtown San Diego. When the bank opened, I got $10,000 from my safe deposit box to go with the $17,000 I was carrying. I bought Song some traveling clothes at Horton Plaza and, after half a dozen phone calls, a California driver's license and citizenship certificate with the name Nguyet Rivers.

I left Mrs. Pilly's car in the parking garage at Horton Plaza and paid cash for a nondescript blue Taurus at a used car lot. Late that afternoon, we entered Mexico at Tecate, a sleepy little town thirty miles east of San Diego where few tourists cross and record-keeping is lax. While the Newport Beach police ran around Balboa Island like Keystone Kops, licking the tips of their pencils and scratching their heads, we vanished into the Guadalupe Valley, winding south on Highway 3 toward the Tropic of Cancer, vineyard-covered hills rising above us in the golden light, sweet Spanish love songs playing on the radio.

It wasn't until later, when I talked to my partner and Mrs. Pilly, that I understood how she had hooked up with Laura McFadden and Switch and showed up at dawn on Balboa Island like the U.S. Calvary to save Reggie, Song and me.

When Reggie and I had passed Snuff and Manny on Marine Avenue the night we rescued Song, they were on their way to my apartment. When they got there, they forced their way into Mrs. Pilly's house and tied her up before ransacking my place. They left her bound when they took off.

The next day, McFadden had them stake out Don's house to see if he was up to something. When Don came out and climbed into his car, the Cavalier we borrowed after we robbed Cow Town, Snuff followed him to Hof's Hut, leaving Manny to watch the house. As he told me shortly before he died, Snuff followed Don and me to San Pedro and back, then followed me to Switch's house.

During all that driving around, he must have got to thinking about the woman he had left, tied up and helpless, in Corona del Mar. After tailing me to Switch's, he returned to Mrs. Pilly's house and let himself in the back door. He was salivating on her and cutting her clothes off when Manny called him on his cell phone and told him that Don was home. The busboy made some vicious promises to my landlady about what was in store for her when he got back, then went and murdered Don.

While he had prepared to rape her, the busboy had talked freely about what he was going to do to me and Song, and about McFadden's power and plans. Snuff intended to kill Mrs. Pilly after assaulting her and giving McFadden the opportunity to assault her, so he wasn't shy about bragging.

Mrs. Pilly didn't know who Song was, but a picture of the situation emerged from the things Snuff said. She told me later that it was while she lay tied up and terrified on her bedroom floor after Snuff left the second time that she realized McFadden, the busboy's boss, might be someone she knew from her own past, her mind drawn back to the quarrel that had divided her family decades before.

It had started at a Fourth of July picnic at her cousin Laura's house in Orange. It was 1965 and Mrs. Pilly's husband had shipped out for Indochina a few months before, a colonel at the head of one of the first marine battalions to land in Da Nang at the start of the war. On that long-ago day, she was thirty-two years old, attractive, lonely and drinking more than she was used to in the hot Southern California sun. She and her husband lived in Oceanside then, near Camp Pendleton, and she had driven up for the family gathering, planning to spend the night.

Late in the afternoon, she was sitting at a picnic bench next to an overgrown high school sophomore whom she had never liked. He was her cousin's nephew by marriage and had spent a good deal of his childhood at Laura's house because of problems in his own home. Mrs. Pilly was sure the boy had stolen money from her purse on more than one occasion. On her last visit, he had walked into the bathroom without knocking when she was in there.

On that sad patriotic holiday, though, she felt sorry for the boy and spoke kindly to him. His mother had died the same week her husband had arrived in Vietnam, going ashore in a landing craft filled with frightened boys not much older than the kid sitting beside her at the backyard picnic.

When she went upstairs to take a bath before dinner, the boy followed her. She was able to fight him off, but was bruised and badly frightened. The boy said she had invited him upstairs. One old lady at the picnic said her sundress was too skimpy for a married woman and unbuttoned too far down. Some people took her side, some took the side of the boy and his powerful father, and a family feud was born.

The busboy had talked about his boss coming from an old, rich Orange County family. Mrs. Pilly knew that Laura's husband, Elmore McFadden, had come from a family like that, too. Snuff had said that his boss had boats and restaurants and sex slaves. Mrs. Pilly remembered that Lew, the boy who attacked her, was the son of Elmore's brother, Marshall, who was known to frequent prostitutes and who owned a shipping business. Lew later began a restaurant supply company. By the time she was able to free herself from the non–Boy Scout knots tied by the busboy, my landlady was sure that the slobbering sophomore who had tried to rape her at the picnic must be the same McFadden who was after me.

She was too humiliated by the things Snuff had said and done to her to call the police but she knew she had to get out of the house before he came back. It was then that she got the idea to go to her cousin's house. She told me later that she really wasn't sure why she went there, except that she needed to be comforted by someone and had no other family member to turn to. She remembered how close she and Laura had been when they were girls together in the 1930s and 1940s. They had been bridesmaids at each other's weddings. She also hoped that Laura could help her stop McFadden from hurting me or her or the girl that Snuff had talked about.

It was at that point that Reggie's taxicab pulled up in front. When he came back down from my wrecked apartment and climbed onto his trike, Mrs. Pilly called him in and asked him to take her to Orange. She was too shaken to drive. He agreed, and she packed her husband's pistol and some overnight things and climbed into his sidecar. Fearful of pursuit by the busboy and embarrassed by what had been done to her, she made Reggie swear not to tell anyone what had happened or where she had gone.

Laura was astonished to see her when she arrived in Orange, but welcomed her with tears and hugs. The years of hard feelings fell away. When Mrs. Pilly told Laura what had happened, and what she suspected about her nephew, Laura agreed that he had to be stopped. That's when they called Switch's house. He and Melanie were packing their bags when the message I later heard came through on the answering machine. Switch kept packing and cleared out, then called Laura's number from the road. After talking to Mrs. Pilly, he changed his mind about going to Mexico. He took Melanie to her aunt's house in Lakewood instead, then rendezvoused with Mrs. Pilly and Laura in Orange. The three of them drove to Balboa, saw activity at McFadden's dock, and closed in from two sides, arriving just in time.

After the shoot-out, Reggie and Switch got Mrs. Pilly and Laura off Balboa Island before the cops arrived and had Mrs. Pilly call my car in stolen early that same morning. When a uniform came to take the report, she told him I was out of town on business for an indefinite period of time and that she had noticed the car gone when she went out to get the paper. Reggie convinced Laura to keep quiet about everything that had happened in order to avoid scandal and possible legal complications with McFadden's estate, which she stood to inherit.

The cops were frantic. Because of the gunplay at McFadden's house and the bulletholes in his boat, they knew some gangster shit had gone down in their postcard town, but they couldn't find anybody to question. Dazed and injured, Manny drowned trying to swim across the channel to the mainland. McFadden was dead. Everyone else got away. Because of the stolen plate on the Cadillac, it took them a couple of days to trace the car to me. By the time a detective came by my apartment, the stolen car report had been in for two days and Reggie and Mrs. Pilly had their stories down pat.

They picked Blowman up at his sister's house in Pasadena a couple of weeks later. He was registered as the captain of McFadden's boat and the police were very curious about where he was the morning the boat sank and why no one had heard from him since. Apparently, he gave the police an accurate description of me and Reggie. Because the Cadillac was registered in my name, they showed him my DMV mug shot in a photo array and he was able to identify me.

After that, the detective, a short, slovenly, Columbo type named Burros, started coming by Mrs. Pilly's every few days, asking the kind of questions they ask in a murder and racketeering investigation. He found out I'd done time in Florida and asked Mrs. Pilly about that. He wanted to know exactly when she noticed my car missing, exactly where I was, when I would be back and how to contact me. For some reason or combination of reasons — the rebellious streak a lot of conventional people have, fear that she would get in trouble, affection for me, the pleasure of being in on a big secret — she stonewalled like a pro, using her matronly charms to dissuade and mislead Burros.

The cops picked Reggie up twice for questioning and got nothing but saucer eyes and shrugs. He had been asleep in my apartment that night, house-sitting while I was away, didn't know anything was up until the police came by. After the second grilling, Reggie hired a slippery little Armenian lawyer to run interference for him, using some of the money he got when Switch fenced the loot from McFadden's. That backed Burros off.

———

Mexico was pretty good. Song and I spent our first night together in a little hotel overlooking Ensenada harbor. The next day, I called Switch and found out some of what had happened and told him where Mrs. Pilly's car was. We continued south to the old French copper-mining town, Santa Rosalia, on the Gulf of California, and took the ferry over to Guaymas. From there we drove in easy stages to Mazatlán, Puerto Vallarta, Manzanillo and, finally, Acapulco, where we checked into the El Mirador, the famous old hotel that overlooks the cove where the cliff divers plunge into the sea with torches at night.

We went to the beach early each morning before it got too hot, walked hand in hand at the edge of the lacy water, swam, sunbathed, met lots of friendly Mexicans. We bought silver jewelry and stylish resort wear at bargain prices, went to nice restaurants and nightclubs with our Mexican friends, watched movies, went for drives along the coast.

I heard a song on AM radio one time with the refrain, "When you are in love, it's a young world," and that's the way I felt that summer in Acapulco. I woke to days filled with a sense of magical possibility. Mexican culture seemed mysterious and meaningful and I made rapid progress improving my Spanish. I noticed the fine details of plants, people and architecture, as if I were looking at the world through new prescription lenses after being unknowingly nearsighted for many blurry years. The future brimmed with promise.

Song gave me all of herself, over and over, each day and night. Her affection and gratitude never flagged. She was always exactly what I wanted her to be, soft or wild, animal or angel, more beautiful all the time in my eyes, gentle face lit by the setting sun, dark hair ruffled by the sea breeze.

As the weeks went by, though, it gradually dawned on me that the deep, dreamy love was all on my side. Song was always responsive to my feelings, and she genuinely liked me because I had saved her and was very nice to her and we had fun together, in bed and on the beach. But sometimes I saw her attention wander and realized she was just going through the romantic motions to please me.

I didn't care, though. Not very much. As long as I had her with me, at my side, in my arms, in my bed, I was happy.

After a while, when it seemed like things had cooled down, we went back to Orange County, tanned and colorful in Mexican outfits. It was September and the kids were back in school, waiting early in the morning at suburban crosswalks with lunchboxes and laughter for tottering old-timers to risk their lives escorting them across empty streets.

I drove her to the church in Little Saigon and the ladies there took her in like a long-lost daughter. For a while, she divided her time between my apartment in Corona del Mar and their houses and restaurants and shops in Little Saigon. Gradually, her life shifted away from me into the Vietnamese community, where the people shared her memories of the green countryside and war's terrible losses.

They took her to a Vietnamese surgeon who decided he could fix her voice. It seemed that her nerve had not been completely cut and, with some herbal potions and poultices and skillful surgery, the young doctor gave her back the ability to speak.

Naturally, he fell in love with her, and she fell in love with him, too, or at least decided under the tutelage of the church ladies that he was the right one for her to start a new life with.

It took a while for her to recover from the operation. The last time I saw her, her throat was still bandaged and she wasn't supposed to try to talk. But she kissed me and spoke to me, a single word—the only one I ever heard her say.

## About the Author

STEVEN M. THOMAS is a Southern California crime fiction writer. He was born in Ohio, grew up in St. Louis and lives in Orange County. He is a graduate of the writing program at the University of California, Irvine.

MAR 0 3 2008

Madeline Olewine Memorial Library
2410 N. 3rd Street
Harrisburg, PA 17110